Praise for the novels of Sheila Roberts

"If, like me, your idea of a good time on a cold December night is to curl up with a cozy blanket, a steaming cup of hot chocolate, and a feel-good, Hallmark holiday movie, then you are going to love this book."
—*The Romance Dish* on *A Little Christmas Spirit*

"With this neatly wrapped, sweetly charming treat, Roberts once again proves her mastery of uplifting, heartwarming love stories." —*Booklist* on *A Little Christmas Spirit*

"Christmas wouldn't be Christmas without a Sheila Roberts story. This can't-miss author has a singular talent for touching the heart *and* the funnybone." —Susan Wiggs

"A tender story guaranteed to warm your heart this holiday season. When I read anything from Sheila Roberts, I know I will laugh, cry and close the book with a happy sigh."
—RaeAnne Thayne on *A Little Christmas Spirit*

"(Roberts) creates characters with flaws and challenges, characters like us, human and imperfect. But also, characters who grow, evolve, and learn from life's lessons."
—*The Romance Dish* on *One Charmed Christmas*

SHEILA ROBERTS

The ROAD *to* CHRISTMAS

mira

mira™

Recycling programs for this product may not exist in your area.

ISBN-13: 978-0-7783-0525-5

The Road to Christmas

First published in 2022. This edition published in 2023.

For questions and comments about the quality of this book, please contact us at CustomerService@Harlequin.com.

Mira
22 Adelaide St. West, 41st Floor
Toronto, Ontario M5H 4E3, Canada
www.Harlequin.com

Printed in U.S.A.

For Robert, my favorite road trip companion

1

Michelle Turnbull would have two turkeys in her house for Thanksgiving. One would be on the table, the other would be sitting at it.

"I can't believe he's still there," said Ginny, her long-time clerk at the Hallmark store she managed. "You two are splitting, so why not rip the bandage off and be done with it?"

Rip the bandage off. There was an interesting metaphor. That implied that a wound was healing. The wound that was her marriage wasn't healing, it was fatal.

She tucked a strand of hair behind her ear and went to unlock the door. "Because I don't want to ruin the holidays for the girls."

"You think they aren't going to figure out what's going on with you two sleeping in separate bedrooms? Don't be naive."

Ginny may have been her subordinate, but that didn't stop her from acting like Michelle's mother. A ten-year age difference and a long friendship probably contributed to that. And with her mother gone, she doubly appreciated Ginny's friendship and concern.

Michelle turned the sign on the door to Open. "I'll tell them he snores."

"All of a sudden, out of the blue?"

"Sleep apnea. He's gained some weight."

Ginny gave a snort. "Not that much. Max may have an inch hanging over the belt line but he's still in pretty good shape."

"You don't have to be overweight to have sleep apnea."

"I guess," Ginny said dubiously. "But, Michelle, you guys have been having problems on and off for the last five years. Your girls have to know this is coming so I doubt your sleep-apnea excuse is going to fool anyone."

Probably not. Much as she and Max had tried to keep their troubles from their daughters, bits of bitterness and reproach had leaked out over time in the form of sarcasm and a lack of what Shyla would have referred to as *PDA*. Michelle couldn't remember the last time they'd held hands or kissed in front of any of their daughters. In fact, it was hard to remember the last time they'd kissed. Period.

"You have my permission to kick him to the curb as of yesterday," Ginny went on. "If you really want your holidays to be happy, get him gone."

"Oh, yeah, that would make for happy holidays," Michelle said. "Audrey and Shyla would love coming home to find their father moved out just in time for Thanksgiving dinner and their grandparents absent."

"If you're getting divorced, that's what they'll find next year," Ginny pointed out.

"But at least they'll have a year to adjust," Michelle

said. "And this is Julia's first Christmas in her new home and with a baby. I don't want to take the shine away from that."

The coming year would put enough stress on them all. She certainly wasn't going to kick it all off on Thanksgiving. That wouldn't make for happy holidays.

Happy holidays. Who was she kidding? The upcoming holidays weren't going to be happy no matter what.

"Well, I see your point," said Ginny. "But good luck pulling off the old sleep-apnea deception."

Their first customer of the day came in, and that ended all talk of Michelle's marriage miseries. Which was fine with her. Focusing on her miserable relationship didn't exactly put a smile on her face, and wearing a perpetual frown was no way to greet shoppers.

After work, she stopped at the grocery store and picked up the last of what she needed for Thanksgiving: the whipped cream for the fruit salad and to top the pumpkin and pecan pies, the extra eggnog for Shyla, her eggnog addict, Dove dark chocolates for Audrey, and Constant Comment tea, which was Hazel's favorite.

Hazel. World's best mother-in-law. When Michelle and Max divorced he'd take Hazel and Warren, her second parents, with him. The thought made it hard to force a smile for the checkout clerk. She stepped out of line. She needed one more thing.

She hurried back to the candy aisle and picked up more dark chocolate, this time for her personal stash.

Hazel and Warren were the first to arrive, coming in the day before Thanksgiving, Hazel bringing pecan pie and the makings for her famous Kahlua yams.

"Hello, darling," Hazel said, greeting her with a hug.

"You look lovely as always. I do wish I had your slender figure," she added as they stepped inside.

"You look fine just the way you are," Michelle assured her.

"I swear, the older I get the harder the pounds cling to my hips," Hazel said.

"You look fine, hon," said Warren as he gave Michelle one of his big bear hugs. "She's still as pretty as the day I met her," he told Michelle.

"Yes, all twenty new wrinkles and five new pounds. On top of the others," Hazel said with a shake of her head.

"Who notices pounds when they're looking at your smile?" Michelle said to her. "Here, let me take your coats."

Hazel set down the shopping bag full of goodies and shrugged out of her coat with the help of her husband. "Where's our boy?"

Who knew? Who cared?

"Out running errands," she said. "I'll text him that you're here. First, let's get you settled."

"I'm ready for that," Hazel said. "The drive from Oregon gets longer every time."

"It's not that far," Warren said and followed her up the stairs.

Half an hour later Max had returned, and he and his father were in the living room, the sports channel keeping them company, and the two women were in the kitchen, enjoying a cup of tea. The yams were ready and stored in the fridge, and the pecan pie was in its container, resting on the counter next to the pumpkin pie Michelle had taken out of the oven. A large pot of vegetable soup was bubbling on the stove, and French bread was warming. It would be a light evening meal to save everyone's tummy room for the next day's feast.

"I'm looking forward to seeing the girls," Hazel said.

"So am I," said Michelle.

She hated that all her girls had moved so far away. Not that she minded hopping a plane to see either Audrey or Shyla. It wasn't a long flight from SeaTac International to either San Francisco International or LAX, but it also wasn't the same as having them living nearby. Julia wasn't as easily accessible, which made her absence harder to take. She'd been the final baby bird to leave the nest, and dealing with her departure had been a challenge. Perhaps because she was the last. Perhaps because it seemed she grew up and left all in one quick motherly blink: college, the boyfriend, the pregnancy, marriage, then moving. It had been painful to let go of her baby. And even more so with that baby taking the first grandchild with her.

Maybe in some ways, though, it wasn't a bad thing that her daughters were living in different states because they hadn't been around to see the final deterioration of their parents' marriage.

Michelle hoped they still wouldn't see it. She consulted her phone. It was almost time for Audrey's flight to land. Shyla's was getting in not long after.

"Audrey's going to text when they're here," she said.

"It will be lovely to all be together again," said Hazel. "Family is so important."

Was that some sort of message, a subtle judgment? "How about some more tea?" Michelle suggested. *And more chocolate for me.*

Another fifteen minutes and the text came in with Max and Warren on their way to pick up the girls, and forty minutes after that they were coming through the door, Shyla's laugh echoing all the way out to the kitchen. "We're here!" she called.

"Let the fun begin," said Hazel, and the two women exchanged smiles and left the kitchen.

They got to the front hall in time to see Max heading up the stairs with the girls' suitcases and Warren relieving them of their coats.

"Hi, Mom," said Audrey and hurried to hug her mother.

Shyla was right behind her.

"Welcome home," Michelle said to her girls, hugging first one, then the other. "It's so good to have you home."

"It's not like we've been in a foreign country," Shyla teased.

"You may as well be," Michelle said. "And before you remind me how much we text and talk on the phone, it's much better having you here in person where I can hug you."

"Hugs are good," Audrey agreed.

"We brought you chocolate," Shyla said, handing over a gift bag.

Michelle knew what it was even before she looked inside. Yep, Ghirardelli straight from San Francisco.

"I know you can get it anywhere, but this is right from the source," said Shyla.

More important, it was right from the heart.

"And you don't have to share," Audrey said. "We brought Dad some, too."

Sharing with Dad. There was little enough she and Max shared anymore. "That was sweet of you."

"We figured you might need it," Audrey said.

Was she referring to Michelle's troubled relationship with their father? No, couldn't be.

"After last Thanksgiving," Shyla added.

Michelle breathed a sigh of relief. Of course, they were talking about the power outage, which had ruined both the turkey and the pie she'd had in the oven.

The girls had loved it, settling in to play cards by candlelight. Michelle had been frustrated. And far from happy with her husband who'd said, "Chill, Chelle. It's no big deal."

It had been to her, but she'd eventually adjusted, lit the candles on the table and served peanut butter and jelly sandwiches along with olives and pickles and the fruit salad she'd made, along with the pie Hazel had brought. Hazel had declared the meal a success.

Max had said nothing encouraging. Of course.

"Oh, and this." Shyla dug in the bag she was still carrying and pulled out a jar of peanut butter. "Just in case we have to eat peanut butter sandwiches again."

Hazel chuckled. "You girls think of everything."

"Yes, we do," Audrey said, and from her capacious purse pulled out a box of crackers. "In case we run out of bread."

"Now we're set," said Michelle and smiled. It was the first genuine smile she'd worn since the last time she'd been with the girls. It felt good.

"Oh, and I have something special for you, Gram," Shyla said to Hazel. "It's in my suitcase. Come on upstairs."

Michelle started. She didn't need Hazel seeing where the girls were staying and wondering why they were stuffed in the sewing room and not the other guest room. "Why don't you bring it down here?" Michelle suggested.

"I should stir my stumps," Hazel said and followed her granddaughter up the stairs.

Audrey fell in behind, and Michelle trailed after, her stomach starting to squirm. Suddenly she wasn't so sure about that excuse she'd invented for changing her husband's sleeping arrangements. But the excuse was going to have to do because she didn't have time to think of anything better.

They passed the first bedroom at the top of the stairs, which had once been Audrey's and had been serving as a guest room ever since she'd graduated from college and got her first apartment. It was where Warren and Hazel slept when they came to visit. Then came the second room, which had been Julia's but was serving as Max's new bedroom. The door was shut, hiding the evidence. Shyla reached for the doorknob.

"Not that room," Michelle said quickly. "I have you girls together," she said, leading to Shyla's old room, which was serving as the sewing room. It still had a pullout bed in it for overflow sleeping when Michelle's brother's family came to stay. Bracing herself, she opened it, revealing the girls' luggage sitting on the floor.

Audrey looked at Michelle, her brows pulled together. "We're in the sewing room?"

"You girls don't mind sharing a room, right?" Michelle said lightly.

"What happened to Julia's old room?" Shyla asked.

"We're not using that room for now," Michelle hedged.

"More storage?" Shyla moved back down the hall and opened the door. "What the…"

"Your father's sleeping there," Michelle said. Hazel looked at her in surprise, igniting a fire in her cheeks.

"Dad?" Audrey repeated.

"He snores," said Michelle. "Sleep apnea."

"Sleep apnea," Hazel repeated, trying out a foreign and unwanted word.

"Has he done a sleep test?" Audrey asked.

"Not yet," said Michelle. She kept her gaze averted from her daughter's eyes.

"Gosh, Mom, that's a serious sleep disorder."

"How come you didn't tell us?" Shyla wanted to know.

"Is he getting a CPAP machine?" Audrey sounded ready to panic.

"Don't worry. Everything's under control," Michelle lied. Audrey looked ready to keep probing so Michelle hustled to change the subject. "Shyla, what did your bring Gram?"

"Wait till you see it. It's so cute," Shyla said, hurrying to unzip her suitcase. "I found it in a thrift shop."

"Still shopping smart. I'm proud of you," Hazel said.

"I learned from the best—you and Mom." She pulled out a little green stuffed felt cactus inserted in a miniature terra-cotta pot and surrounded by beach glass. "It's a pin cushion," she said as she presented it.

"That is darling," said Hazel.

From where she stood by the doorway, Michelle let out a breath, then took another. Like a good magician performing sleight of hand, she had diverted attention to something else and pulled off her trick. *Now you see trouble, now you don't.*

How long could she keep up the act?

2

The next day started with cinnamon rolls and coffee, as always, with everyone squeezed around the kitchen table since the dining table was already set with the good china.

"So when are you going to get a sleep test?" Audrey asked her father.

That again. The girl was tenacious. Michelle and Max exchanged looks, his accusing—*Told you that was a stupid excuse*—and hers defensive—*Want me to tell everyone the truth right now and ruin Thanksgiving?* Michelle could feel her mother-in-law's concerned gaze. Hazel wasn't buying the snoring excuse. The stomach squirming started again.

"Don't worry, honey. I'm okay, and it's no big deal," Max said to Audrey, giving her nose a playful tweak. "So, Dad, want to see the changes I've made at the store?"

"Sure," Warren said, and the two men exited the room.

Hazel, bless her, moved the conversation into new territory. "Catch me up on what you girls have been up to."

Audrey shrugged. "Just working. Nothing very exciting."

Only a broken heart, still mending. It grieved Michelle to see her daughter so unhappy. "Come back to Washington," she'd urged after the breakup. *Come back to the nest.* "You can always find work up here."

But Audrey had been adamant. "I like my job, and I'm not going to quit after only being there a year."

That was the bottom line. Pride. After moving to be with the man she'd thought was The One only to break up, her daughter was determined not to come home looking like a failure. As if she ever could. Audrey was brilliant.

Except when it came to picking the right man.

"This new year will be better," Hazel said, patting her arm, and Audrey lifted her chin a little and nodded.

"And how about our Shyla?" Hazel asked. "I saw your latest offering on Etsy. So darling."

At least all was well with Michelle's middle child. In addition to her side business, creating fanciful children's costumes, she was happily working designing costumes for a small theater company in San Francisco. And she appeared to have sorted out her love life. Michelle and Max hadn't met the man in person yet, but they had on Zoom. He seemed nice, and it was obvious he was smitten with Shyla. Who wouldn't be?

"The business is going great," Shyla said. "Thank you, big sis, for kicking me in the butt to start it," she added.

Audrey smiled. "I know stuff."

Shyla rolled her eyes. "Don't remind me."

The conversation floated happily along, easing them through the morning. Then it was time to get going on their holiday feast, with everyone busy in the kitchen, cutting up fruit for the salad, whipping cream and peeling potatoes.

The power stayed on, and the turkey got carved, and

the family settled at the table. "Gram's Kahlua yams, yay!" said Shyla, dishing up a small spoonful.

"Take more than that, dear," Hazel urged.

"I have to pace myself," Shyla said. "Maybe if I eat slower, the pounds will find some other butt to pack onto. Where's the wishbone? Maybe I can wish 'em away."

Michelle looked to the other end of the dining-room table where her husband of too long sat smiling at their middle daughter.

He happened to look Michelle's way, and the smile disappeared. She lost her smile, too, turning them into stony-faced human bookends. Table ends. Whatever. Suddenly, the Kahlua yams didn't taste that good.

Neither did the pumpkin pie.

"It's time to Zoom with Julia," Audrey announced, taking charge. The girl was twenty-seven now and had been in charge since she was six.

Everyone followed her into the living room where she set up her laptop on the coffee table and plopped on the couch in front of it. She summoned Hazel and Warren to sit on either side of her. Shyla took her place behind the couch and Michelle and Max stood next to the parents, one on each side, using them as a buffer.

"Isn't modern technology amazing," declared Hazel as Audrey logged in to the meeting. "There's our girl." She waved at her granddaughter's on-screen face and said, "Hi, darling," even though Julia couldn't hear her yet.

Julia was seated on a sofa with six-month-old baby Caroline in her lap. She waved back as her husband got their sound up and running. Such a sweet face, all smiles and freckles. Her reddish hair was now a rich maroon, and she'd added a small gold nose ring to her collection of piercings. She looked so happy in her new home with her new husband seated next to her, his family gathered around them.

Too far away, though. Once she was on her own, Michelle was going to move closer to her daughter and first grandchild. Maybe she'd find someplace geographically equidistant from all her girls.

"Happy Thanksgiving, everybody," Julia said as soon as her sound was on.

"Happy Thanksgiving," Michelle and company chorused back.

"It looks like you're all settled in the new house now," Hazel said.

"Yep. We love it here. You guys all need to move to St. Maries."

"Yes, I should," Michelle said. Oops. There was a slip. Had anybody heard?

"There's no beaches in Idaho," said Shyla. "And too much snow," she added, wrinkling her nose.

"Since when don't you like snow?" Julia argued.

"I like snow. On Snoqualmie or Big Bear," Shyla said. "Not up to my neck on the sidewalk."

"It's not that bad," Julia said. "And there's lots of lakes...with beaches. You'd all love it here. Really."

Michelle knew she would. She hadn't held the baby since August, and that was too long to go without holding your grandbaby.

"We'll take your word for it," said Audrey.

"I don't want you to take my word. I want you to come see for yourselves. Come for Christmas. You can stay at the new house, and we can all be together. It's plenty big enough. We have two guest rooms, one for Mom and Dad, and one for Gram and Grandpa, and we've got a sofa bed in the living room."

Michelle could almost feel Hazel's questioning gaze on her. *How would you and my son get out of sharing a bed there?*

"We have a guest room, too, so there's no need for anyone to sleep on the sofa," put in Julia's new mother-in-law, Lina, who was getting to be with the kids for Thanksgiving and Christmas. Both holidays. How was that fair?

Michelle was having a hard time adjusting to this whole sharing kids with the other parents thing, and it had been hard to be gracious when Julia had said she and Gino didn't want to do long trips with the baby yet and were spending Thanksgiving with his family. Of course, it had been the sensible thing to do, but hard to accept. This sounded like a great alternative, and she loved the idea of being with all her girls for that most special holiday. But was it practical? Was it even possible?

"Honey, you know how iffy it can be getting over the pass in December," she said.

The Cascade mountain range was gorgeous to travel in the summer and a feast for the eyes in the fall when the leaves were turning, but winter was another matter. Too much snow and both the North Cascade Highway and the I-90, the interstate over the pass that they would use, got closed. Even when it was open the trip could still be a white-knuckle one.

Driving anywhere in the snow was that kind of experience for Michelle. All it had taken was one slide across the street into a car to wipe away her love of the white stuff, and she no longer went near the slightest incline when so much as an inch of it fell, let alone a mountain pass. Picturing herself in a car on a slippery mountain road made her antsy.

It had been different when she and Max were younger. Michelle had loved driving up into the mountains with the kids to spend a weekend in Leavenworth, the charming Bavarian town in the heart of the Cascades, enjoying their holiday festivities and the beautiful setting. But it had been ages since they'd made that trip. Not for the first time, she wished Julia and her husband had chosen to stay in Washington state.

"We'll make it," said Warren.

"It's a long drive for you coming from Oregon, Dad," Max said to his father.

It wasn't exactly a short skip to come to Maple Valley, Washington, either, but Warren and Hazel never let that stop them. Although, now that they were getting older, maybe it should.

"Perhaps we could fly partway," Hazel said thoughtfully.

"We can make the drive," Warren said.

"It's a long one, Dad," said Max.

"I'm not ready for the rest home yet," Warren replied with a frown. "And seventy is the new…" He turned to Hazel. "What is it?"

"Fifty," she said. "But whoever said that hasn't had bursitis."

"And you're not seventy anymore," added Max.

"A couple years, give or take. Big deal," Warren said.

"Don't worry, Grandpa. We love you even if you are old," Shyla teased him.

"Who said anything about being old? Just because there's snow on the roof, it don't mean there ain't fire in the fireplace."

"Speaking of snow," Michelle said, "you're bound to encounter some."

She could envision the parents' car careening off the road, the two of them stuck freezing in a snowbank somewhere between Oregon and Idaho. What if a passing car went out of control or a tree fell? She wasn't sure her seventy-four-year-old father-in-law's reflexes were what they once were.

"I grew up in North Dakota, remember? I got no problem driving in the snow," Warren insisted. "And that Charger of mine is the best car they make for snow. Plus we got snow tires. Piece of cake."

He'd said the same thing about driving up from Oregon, and Michelle had worried all through the day on Wednesday until they'd arrived.

"Well, I'm in," said Max.

No *we*, just *I*. Like her.

Even though Michelle didn't want to be with Max, the idea of spending time with all her daughters sent visions of special shared moments dancing in her head like sugarplums. If they went over a day or two early she'd have extra time to play with the baby. She could help Julia with the cooking. She'd bake the red velvet cake for Christmas Day like she always had. They could make it work.

Unless the weather failed to cooperate. She could wind up snowed in halfway to Christmas with Max. "Halfway to Christmas." That sounded like a title for a country song. One she didn't want to sing.

"We'll let you know." Even as Michelle said it she could feel Max's disapproving frown burning into her. She quickly changed the subject to something safe, asking how Julia's first Thanksgiving meal had turned out.

"Amazing," Julia replied, smiling at her husband. "Gino deep-fried the turkey."

Everything Gino did was amazing. *Give it time*, Michelle thought cynically, then hoped she was wrong. Just because the fire between her and Max had died, it didn't mean that would happen for her daughter.

"Looks like we're going to be on the road this Christmas," Warren said after the chat had ended.

"I was thinking you'd all want to come stay with us again this year," said Hazel. She had a gift for hospitality and loved having company.

"They don't always have to come to us," said Warren, who wasn't as into entertaining as his wife.

"I just thought that way we wouldn't have to drive," she said.

The folks really needed to move closer.

To Max. Once they split, Michelle would no longer be part of the picture. Parents hung on to their offspring, not the import. There would be no more special times with her mother-in-law, no lunches out, no garage sales, no long weekends keeping the folks company and playing pinochle. The thought saddened her. With her own parents gone, she'd be an orphan.

But with Max gone...she'd be relieved. Wouldn't she?

"It's not that far," Warren said to his wife. "And you want to see Julia's place, don't you?"

"Of course I do," she replied. "I certainly don't want to miss out on being with all of you."

"It might be better to wait and see it in the summer," Michelle suggested. Like her, her mother-in-law wasn't a fan of driving in the snow, and the last two Christmases they had all gone to Warren and Hazel's place so the folks wouldn't have to be on the road.

"Oh, no. If you're all going, so are we," Hazel said with a determined nod.

"Speaking of going, we'd better get moving. Got a long drive ahead of us," Warren said.

"You should spend the night here, Dad," Max said to him. "Get an early start in the morning."

"Nah, we'll be fine," Warren told him. "We'll stop at Best Western for the night if we get tired. Come on, hon. Let's get the rubber on the road."

Ten minutes later they were gone, and Max had settled in to watch a rom-com with the girls, who weren't leaving until Friday. He preferred action movies and gory mysteries, but he always humored them and watched whatever they wanted. He was a good dad. He also never liked to say no to them, hated being the bad guy. He'd always preferred to leave the disciplining to Michelle.

So, of course, the girls adored him. How disappointed would they be once he and Michelle split? Would they blame her? Resent her?

"It is kind of a long way to come," Gino said to Julia after they ended their call with her family.

"Not that far," she insisted. "It's not like we're on the other side of the country."

"Maybe we should go see them," he said.

She shook her head. "I don't want to travel with the baby. Anyway, I really want everyone to see the new house."

Gino pursed his lips and shook his head. "I don't know. It's asking a lot of your family."

"Family is important," she said.

"We have family here," he pointed out.

"Yeah, yours. What about mine?"

"They're important, too," he was quick to say. "But maybe we should wait and have them come in the summer."

Julia frowned at him. "It's not Christmas in July."

"It can be."

"Not to Mom. The holidays have always been a big deal to her. Even though things haven't been going good with her and Daddy, she's always made it special for us. Remember last Christmas?"

Gino patted his stomach. "Between everything her and your grandma made I couldn't eat until New Year's. And she bought enough presents for two of me."

"She will again this year. And she's not going to want to miss being with us for Caroline's first Christmas."

Caroline had Gino's big, brown eyes, and her little curls were dark as a raven's wing. She was the most gorgeous baby ever. Julia already had her Christmas dress ready and waiting for the big day.

"We can Zoom again," Gino suggested.

"It's not the same. Mom can't reach through the computer and hold Caroline." The baby was still on her lap, and Julia turned Caroline around to look at her. "What do you think, baby girl? Do you want to see your grammy?"

Caroline gave her a drooly smile and patted the air with her plump little hands.

"There, you see? Caroline wants everyone to come see us for Christmas," Julia said to Gino.

She could already envision it. Staying up late drinking eggnog with her sisters and yakking. Putting silly gifts in each other's Christmas stockings. The three of them serenading Gram with "Grandma Got Run Over by a Reindeer." She had great in-laws, and she was looking forward to enjoying some of their Christmas traditions, but those couldn't take the place of the ones she had with her own family. Families should all be together during the holidays.

"Hey, if they want to come it's fine with me. But do they really? Can you see your parents staying here? We don't have enough bedrooms for them to each have their own."

The separate-bed thing. Shyla had texted Julia about that. It had been unnerving. Her parents had been having trouble for the last few years, but this was a new development, and not a good one. Not one Julia liked to think about.

"Maybe it would be good for them to be stuck together," she said.

"And maybe they'd both kill each other," he said. "I still think you should wait on this."

"Easy for you to say. We're here with *your* family."

"Hey, you said you were cool with moving here," he protested.

"I was. I am. But I'm not cool with not getting to be together for Christmas. I don't care how many buñuelos your mom makes."

Gino held up his hand in surrender. "Fine, fine. Whatever you want."

That was better. "Thank you," she said sweetly. "And my family thanks you."

"You better hope they'll thank *you*," he retorted.

Michelle was still wrestling with the same question from the night before as she sat with her daughters at the kitchen table the next morning, discussing Julia's invitation. Were the girls going to be okay when she and Max split?

They'd be fine, she assured herself. They were busy with their own lives.

Shyla adored her job, and Michelle suspected she'd

be the next daughter to get married. Audrey did like working as a copywriter for a large insurance company. She was smart and capable and was bound to eventually find someone who appreciated her. As for Julia, she was absorbed with her new home and family. Yes, they'd all be fine.

"It's not like there are any direct flights to St. Maries," said Audrey. "So typical. She's going to turn everyone's lives upside down, including Gram and Grandpa's, just so she can get her way."

"She misses us," Michelle said, coming to Julia's defense. It was what you did for the baby of the family.

"Then, she could come up here for Christmas instead of making everyone go there," Audrey argued.

"It's not that easy traveling with a baby," Michelle told her. "I wouldn't want them risking it."

"It would suck not to be all together," Audrey admitted. "But what a pain in the butt. The closest airport to her is in Pullman. Then, we'd have to rent a car and drive for another couple of hours."

"Forget flying, and forget renting a car. Let's just do a road trip," Shyla said, pouring more pumpkin spice creamer into her coffee. "That would be fun."

"Yeah, it would," agreed Audrey.

"You can fly to San Fran, and we can take my car from there," Shyla said to her.

"Oh, no," Audrey said. "Look up *undependable* on Wikipedia and there will be a picture of your car. Plus I know how you drive."

"I drive just as good as you," Shyla retorted.

"Just as well," Audrey corrected, making her sister frown. "And I'll drive," she said firmly.

"Feed me, Seymour," taunted Shyla, who loved to

tease that when it came to naming Audrey, Michelle had been thinking of the infamous plant from *Little Shop of Horrors* instead of Audrey Hepburn, the glamorous actress Michelle had always admired. Shyla had worked on the costumes and set for the play in high school.

"You are obnoxious," Audrey informed her.

"And being controlling isn't obnoxious at all, right?" snapped Shyla.

Michelle tuned out the blooming squabble. Those two had done their share of it growing up, and even as adults they still had their moments. In spite of that they loved each other dearly. They'd enjoy a road trip together. As long as Audrey was in charge.

She wasn't so sure about her in-laws. Max was their only child, and they adored their granddaughters. They'd stayed rooted in Oregon all their lives, content to come up for frequent visits and host family vacations at their riverfront home. When Warren had helped Max finance his new business, they'd resisted the offer to move to Maple Valley. But they'd never missed a special occasion.

Still, with them getting older Michelle didn't think this was a good idea for them, especially in possibly inclement weather, and it wasn't right of Warren to insist they make the trip.

Hazel would go anyway, though, because those two were welded at the heart. It was more than Michelle could say about herself and Max.

Audrey's phone dinged. "We need to leave for the airport," she announced and drained the last of her coffee.

"Yes, ma'am," Shyla said, saluting her, and Audrey made a face.

"I'll get the car keys," Michelle said.

She stood up just as her husband came into the room. "I can take the girls to the airport," he said.

No way was Michelle missing out on that last half hour of time with her daughters. "I can take them." It sounded more like a shutout than an offer.

"I said I would." His words weren't exactly sugary, and Michelle was aware of Audrey and Shyla exchanging the same worried glances she'd seen on their faces more than once over the holiday weekend.

Yes, Mommy and Daddy weren't happy these days. Mommy and Daddy hadn't been happy for quite some time.

They'll adjust. We all will.

"Fine. I'm coming with," Michelle insisted.

The girls' chitchat on the way to the airport floated above the undercurrent of their parents' discontent like a life raft Michelle couldn't reach. It was all she could do when they hugged goodbye at the passenger drop-off to let go of them.

"Let me know when you get back home," she told them.

"We know, Mom," Audrey said, bearing the burden of motherly concern and hugged her.

"Love you both," Shyla said as she turned from Michelle to hug Max.

Was that some kind of a hidden message? *Please stay together.*

Of course, she was imagining things. Guilt could do that to you. Except she had nothing to feel guilty about. This wasn't all her fault.

The girls disappeared inside the building, and Michelle and Max got back in the car. Neither said a word as they merged into the flow of cars with people dropping off and picking up loved ones.

"I don't know about driving to Idaho in December," she finally said once they were back on the freeway. "If the pass closes..."

"Nobody's twisting your arm to go," he said. "I'll just tell Julia her mother didn't want to see her that bad."

"Cute," she snapped.

He shrugged.

"I do want to see Julia," Michelle insisted. "I just think December is not the time to make that trip."

"I can do it."

Another sentence with no *we* in it. Hardly surprising since they weren't a *we* anymore—only two *I*s talking about the big D.

"And I don't think it's a good idea for your parents," she added.

"They're adults. They don't need you making their decisions for them."

"I wasn't," she said, irritated. "Honestly, Max."

"Look. It's your call if you want to stay behind, but Julia wants us there, and I'm going."

"Sweet, noble Daddy, who can do no wrong. Keep the facade in place," she muttered. Except, his behavior toward the girls was no facade, and that had been a snotty thing to say.

She was about to retract the remark until he shot back, "It's shit like that the counselor said undermines a relationship."

"You're quoting the counselor you only went to with me twice? Seriously?"

"The only reason you wanted to go was so you could dump on me." Now he was the one muttering. "A waste of time."

It sure had been.

It was too late for counselors. He'd been sleeping in Julia's old room for the past two months.

"You are such a jerk," she said, frowning at him.

He clamped his lips together.

Yep, a perfect match, the jerk and the bitch. What a pair. But they wouldn't be a pair much longer.

It had been a long trek to reach this fork in the road, with many stops along the way, most of them for small issues and petty disagreements, each one piling on top of the other like bricks in a wall.

The first brick had been far from petty, though.

One of the last conversations Michelle had had with her mother before she died was about her rocky marriage. "You have to forgive him, darling," her mother had said.

"I have." It was a lie. The resentment was like mortar, always looking for a new brick.

"You haven't. I can see the gulf widening between you two. If you don't close it soon, you won't be able to."

"Maybe I don't want to," Michelle had said.

"Then, maybe you need to rethink what you want out of life."

What Michelle wanted she couldn't seem to reach. She wanted the happy marriage she'd enjoyed when the girls were small, but she couldn't get over the wall. In spite of the occasional moments of truce when it looked like maybe they were going to be okay, in spite of stubbornly continuing to live in the same house, the wall kept getting higher.

Max was right. The counselor had been a waste of time.

A final argument over Max's Harley, a crazy, costly midlife purchase, had brought things to a head, with her accusing him of being selfish and wasting their money and trying to kill himself, and him pointing out that she wouldn't care if he did. The angry words had rolled on downhill from there, and when he finally tried to make up in time for the holidays, she realized she didn't want to. She'd had enough.

He was already checking online for a place to live come the new year, and she was postponing her Christmas letter. *By the way, Max and I are splitting. Here's his new address.*

A road trip to see their daughter for Christmas— what a way that would be to finish things off. She'd have liked to suggest taking separate vehicles, but that wouldn't be practical. Of course, they'd have to take the SUV with its all-wheel drive rather than her little compact, which she drove to work. He obviously couldn't take the bike or the car he was restoring, which had parts scattered all over half the garage. So they would be stuck in the same small space for hours. It felt like a sick present from the Grinch.

Michelle's cell phone pinged, and she read the text from Julia. You guys coming to visit is all I want for Christmas.

We're coming, she texted back. Julia had no idea how much this little present was going to cost her parents.

"That guy is looking at you," Shyla said to Audrey as they stood together in line at Starbucks before heading for their separate gates.

Audrey cast a quick glance in the direction her sister was looking. Said guy was standing not far from the pickup counter, obviously waiting for his order. He was dressed in jeans and a crisp white shirt and light gray sports jacket, a laptop messenger bag slung over his shoulder and a small carry-on in his hand. He looked like a model. He did seem to be smiling in their direction, but if he was, it wasn't at her.

"He's looking at *you*, goof," she said.

"Nuh-uh. His eyeballs are wandering your direction. A meet-cute at the airport. Except to qualify for that you might have to go over there and spill coffee on him."

Audrey shook her head. Her sister, the romance addict. "Burning someone with coffee, good idea. Anyway, you're the cute one." And Audrey was the smart one. That was the way it was. That was the way it had always been.

"Not every man likes blondes, you know."

Blondes with boobs, Audrey added mentally. Unlike her sister, who had gotten an extra dose of boobage, Audrey was slender. *Willowy*, Mom liked to call it. *Deprived*, Audrey had called it when she was a self-conscious teen. Now that she was a mature twenty-seven-year-old, she called it…*deprived*.

Even with her current fantasy-color mix of pastels that her hairstylist had convinced her to try, she couldn't compete with her sister's cute overload. That was how it had worked out in her end of the gene pool. She'd been happy to place in science-fair awards finals—even went to State twice—and to get a small college scholarship. Okay, so maybe it hadn't been so smart to major in English lit instead of business or communications, but she'd landed okay on her size-nine feet and liked being a technical writer.

"You could have been a model," Shyla insisted.

"Yeah, I'm the Heather of the family. And you're

so full of gas you could be a hot-air balloon," Audrey retorted.

"I am not. And I'll never understand why you don't see how hot you are. Do you look in the mirror with your eyes closed?"

"Stop already."

"You know, it is possible to be smart and pretty at the same time," Shyla pointed out. "And he *is* looking at you."

"So what if he is? Who ever finds true love in the airport? Who ever finds true love anywhere?"

Okay, how cynical did that sound? Was she in danger of becoming a modern-day Miss Havisham?

No, that woman hated men. Audrey didn't hate men. Only Cupid.

"Don't give up. Not every man is a douchebag."

"The ones who aren't are hiding," said Audrey.

"Or you're not looking that hard. Why not try airport speed dating? It can't be any worse than meeting men online. At least when you meet someone in the airport you know he's not lying about what he looks like."

The crack made Audrey smile. Her little sister should have opted for doing stand-up instead of working behind the scenes in theater and taking the occasional small part. She was a big enough ham. She'd always loved getting attention. The three-year difference between her and Audrey had given her baby of the family status for a nice four years before Julia arrived on the scene, and she'd never quite let go of it.

The smile was short-lived. "Will you stop already?" Audrey said in disgust as Shyla cast one of her own along with a wave at their handsome fellow traveler.

"I'm only being friendly. Which is more than I can say for you, Ice Queen."

SHEILA ROBERTS   35

"I don't have time to be friendly. I have a flight to catch."

"Yeah, you're so rushed after making us get here two frickin' hours early."

"That's how early you're supposed to arrive at the airport. You do remember that Thanksgiving weekend is the busiest travel time, right?" Audrey retorted, pointing to the long line of people in front of them, all waiting for their caffeine fix.

"It didn't take that long to get through security," said Shyla, who never liked to lose an argument. Although it seemed she should have been used to it by this point in their lives.

The traveler who had supposedly been fascinated by them was joined by a preppy-looking man. A name was called, and they both picked up two large to-go cups and two small bags with pastries in them.

"So much for your airport speed dating," Audrey said as the sisters watched the two men exchange intimate smiles as they walked off.

"Okay, so I was wrong. And don't say *as usual*, or I'll whack you with my backpack."

"I wouldn't dream of it," said Audrey.

"No, you'd just do it."

They inched up in line, and Shyla fell quiet. And suddenly looked very serious.

"What?" prompted Audrey.

"The separate-bedrooms thing. Do you think Dad really has sleep apnea, or are things getting worse between them?"

The topic of their parents was one the two of them had been returning to on a regular basis for the last year. Like two love nurses, constantly taking the temperature of their patients.

Audrey shook her head. "The way they kept dodging the subject, I don't know. I hope not. Twenty-nine years together down the drain."

Except the last five of those had not been happy. Her parents had always seemed so strong, but losing that baby had undone them. Instead of growing closer they'd fallen apart. They were a great inspiration for staying single.

Them and the last man Audrey had fallen for. She was quickly coming to the conclusion that love was a four-letter word.

"How can they give up after so many years together?" Shyla lamented.

"People give up all the time."

"I don't want them to. It doesn't seem right."

Audrey sighed. "I know."

"When we were growing up I used to think how lucky we were compared to our friends whose parents had split and had to go back and forth between houses, their holidays all screwed up. Now it looks like they're about to screw ours up. There has to be a way to get them back together."

"If there is, they have to find it," Audrey said. She couldn't get her own love life together. No way could she fix her parents'.

They finally reached the order desk, and each put in an order for her favorite latte.

"They seemed fine when we were kids," Shyla said after they'd paid and moved away to wait for their drinks. "Maybe it was all an act. You know, stay together until the kids are grown."

"No," Audrey said, "I think it started with the baby." The little brother who never made it.

"What were they thinking, anyway?" Shyla said.

"They were thinking they'd try one more time."

Shyla wrinkled her nose. "I sure wouldn't want to have a baby in my forties."

"Lots of people do," said Audrey, "and they were excited about it. Especially Dad. Losing the baby broke them."

"All those years together, then one bad thing, and it's over? That's depressing. I hope they don't split."

So did Audrey. Her parents had been the bedrock of their young lives. Even though she was grown, she found it terribly disconcerting to see that foundation turning to sand.

"You don't think one of them has met someone else?" Shyla ventured.

Audrey had asked herself the same question, but she couldn't picture either one of her parents sneaking around on the other. They were too ethical for that.

"No. I think they're just…done."

"There's a depressing thought," said Shyla. "I guess we can always hope for a miracle."

"You can hope," Audrey said, "but don't hold your breath."

Shyla dug out her phone and started texting.

"Who are you texting? Santa?"

"Julia. I'm telling her to stock up on mistletoe. It can't hurt to give Mom and Dad a nudge."

"Well, then, here's to mistletoe," Audrey said as she picked up her order. But she was afraid it was too late for that.

3

"How did you survive Thanksgiving?" asked Michelle's sister-in-law Ellie.

"We got through it," Michelle said. "Now on to the next holiday adventure."

Max had already left for his usual Saturday workday, and Michelle was grabbing a quick breakfast before heading out the door herself. She put her phone on speaker and set it on the counter so she could butter her toast.

"Speaking of, Jay and I were wondering if you'd like to fly down for Christmas. We thought you might want to get away. Bring the girls."

"That's sweet of you guys, but it looks like we're all going to Julia's."

"All? As in…all?"

"Yep."

"I can't believe you and Max are sticking it out."

"Only until after Christmas."

"I'm sorry everything went sideways for you guys," Ellie said. "I always thought you were the perfect couple."

Michelle had thought that, too, once upon a fantasy. "There is no such thing." There was a nice depressing thought. And why was she saying that to her sister-in-law, who was happy in her marriage? "Sorry," she said. "Pay no attention to me, the Grinch's holiday helper."

"Things are bound to get better," said Ellie.

No, they weren't. "I appreciate the encouragement. And I hate to run, but I've got to get to work," Michelle said. "Thanks for checking on me and for the offer. Give Jay a hug."

"I will. And you hang in there," Ellie said.

"I will." It was what she'd been doing for the last five years.

She'd finished her toast and was grabbing her car keys when a text came in from Hazel.

Just checking in, darling. I'm worried about you two.

Poor Hazel. She'd been worried for a long time. She wasn't the kind of mother-in-law to interfere, but she was kindhearted enough to try and be supportive, sending little *Thinking of You* greeting cards, texting an *I love you* every week. When Michelle had lost the baby, she'd offered to come stay with her and Max and help out. Michelle had thanked her but turned down the offer. The last thing she'd wanted in her angry state was her mother-in-law in the house, seeing what was happening with Michelle and her son.

She thumbed a quick response that she knew would be both unsatisfying and discouraging. But it was honest. She sighed, then put her phone to sleep.

Hazel reread her daughter-in-law's response to her text for the tenth time as she sat in her favorite chair in the sunroom the Saturday after Thanksgiving. Ever since getting home she'd debated saying anything, but worry had finally gotten the better of her, and she'd had to call Michelle on the sleep apnea and ask if everything was okay. Of course, it wasn't.

Going through a rough patch, the text said.

What did that mean? Hazel knew what it meant for the short term. But what about the long term? The reply was so…evasive.

I'm not trying to be nosy, she texted back. Just concerned.

I know, came the short reply much later, followed by a heart.

That was all she was going to get. How could she help if Michelle wouldn't confide in her? She'd been concerned long before they arrived at the house the day before Thanksgiving, but seeing her son and his wife using separate bedrooms had set off the alarm bells. She hadn't bought the nonsense about Max snoring, not for a minute. Her son and his wife had had their ups and downs, but now, separate bedrooms. They were way too young for that.

"They're going to break up, I know it," she said to Warren after she'd read him the text.

"Not much you can do about it," he told her.

"After almost thirty years," Hazel said miserably. "I still remember how crazy in love those two were when they first got together."

"Now they're just crazy," he said, returning his attention to his morning paper.

"That's not funny," Hazel informed him.

"Hon, you're gonna have to let the kids work out their problems themselves."

"But what if they don't?" she fretted.

"Then, they don't. You'll still see the girls. We'll still see Max."

But would they see Michelle? "Michelle's been like a daughter."

Hazel and Michelle had enjoyed a great relationship, with never a cross word between them. She'd been the daughter Hazel had always wanted. They'd done so much together over the years: visiting their local nursery every spring for annuals, hitting garage sales, checking out that adorable tearoom in Seattle's University District. Michelle had been the one to get Hazel hooked on Pinterest. She never failed to do something special for Hazel for Mother's Day, and Hazel had loved lavishing her with gifts at Christmas and on her birthday. Michelle was so much a part of their family, if she and Max divorced it would be as if they'd lost a child.

"I'm sure no matter what happens, you'll still get to see her, too," said Warren, reading the question behind the remark.

How would that go over with Max? Would he expect them to take sides? From what she'd observed over the years, divorce separated not only the couple but the relatives on both sides, as well.

"I wish I could do something to help them," she said.

"If a counselor couldn't help them, you can't."

She knew the counselor visits had been short-lived. Not because Michelle had told her. Max had confided in Warren. Michelle's mother had a friend with a practice, and they'd mostly gone to humor her mom. He'd reported that it hadn't worked and left it at that. Michelle had skated past concerned questions and said very little about their troubles, especially the last couple of years.

Hazel had always had an excellent relationship with

her daughter-in-law, but as things cooled between Michelle and Max, Hazel could feel a shift in her relationship with Michelle, as well. There had been a time when Michelle could talk openly about her life. She'd been open enough about her frustration with Max for wanting to try for one more child. Those days were gone. Michelle still chatted with Hazel about what the girls were doing or shared her latest garage-sale find, but all mention of Max stopped. Unless Hazel asked what was new with her and her son. Then she got a vague "Same old, same old." If she pressed, Michelle suddenly had something she had to go do.

The last thing Michelle had shared with her had been four months after her miscarriage. "We've lost more than the baby."

Hazel had been so sure they could put it behind them and move forward. They hadn't.

"Oh, Warren," she said miserably.

Seeing the tears in her eyes, he set aside his paper and beckoned her to join him on the love seat. She came and snuggled in next to him. Warren was a hefty man, a former football star, strong both physically and emotionally. When it came to offering comfort, he was pro.

He wrapped his big arms around her and kissed the top of her head. "It'll be okay, no matter what. We'll get through this."

"We will," she said. But she didn't want it to be another sad marker in their life.

They'd already gotten through a lot in the last few years: the loss of the last one of their parents, followed by the deaths of both Warren's brothers and Hazel's sister, as well as a brush with prostate cancer for him. And then there was Warren's heart issue.

But they were still standing strong. Hard times either brought you together or pulled you apart. They'd chosen to stay together.

She'd tried to encourage Michelle not to let what had happened to them pull her and Max apart. She, herself, had lost a baby early on in her marriage. She knew the pain of it. But at some point you had to let it go. Michelle hadn't, and Hazel was convinced it had soured her daughter-in-law's relationship with Max. Holding grudges—it was the girl's one flaw. If only Michelle could see that a grudge was a burden no one could afford to carry.

But it took two people to make a problem. Much as she loved her son, close to perfect as she thought he was, she couldn't hold him blameless. Max tended to internalize his hurts. Bridging emotional gaps was a long process, and she feared he'd given up too quickly.

"Why don't you do some baking, hon?" Warren advised. "You'll feel better if you're doing something."

"That's a good idea," she said.

Doing something positive always helped swat away worry. Hazel went to the kitchen. It was time to make gumdrop cookies for the neighbors. And Warren would appreciate some also. He loved them almost as much as the little girls next door did.

Baking didn't solve your problems, but it could at least distract you from them.

Hazel did a lot of distracting that day, and she kept right on distracting herself clear up until December 21, the day before they were to begin their road trip to Julia's house. With all the distracting she'd been doing, even her stretchy winter pants were starting to feel snug. If they had a flat tire, Warren could use her for a spare.

Oh, well, it was the season to…gain weight, and self-medicating with sugar had helped her keep a positive attitude. So far, there had been no serious phone calls prefaced with *Mom, Dad, we have to talk*. No news was good news. Maybe she could find time to talk to Michelle when they were at Julia's. Surely seeing her whole family gathered together around the tree, Michelle would remember what was important. Maybe, just maybe, the holidays could work their magic.

Something had awakened Michelle. A sound. There it was again, coming from downstairs. It wasn't the creak of the house settling. It was more…human. It said that something wasn't right. Her bedside clock showed almost one in the morning. Max had to be up by seven to go to work and went to bed every night promptly at eleven, so she knew it wasn't him making that noise. It could only be a burglar.

Max always locked up the house at night. He patrolled the place like it was Fort Knox, checking to make sure every window was closed and the wooden rod was in place in the bottom of the door to the kitchen to block anyone from opening the sliding glass.

But locks and wooden rods couldn't keep out a pro. They had tools for picking locks. And they liked nice, cozy neighborhoods like Michelle and Max's, homes filled with treasures collected over a lifetime, and two-car garages with nice cars. Never mind that most of the homes were mortgaged, and their residents lived paycheck to paycheck. They spent those paychecks on computers and left wallets filled with credit cards lying around.

If only they'd gotten another dog. Dogs made good

burglar deterrents. Buffy, their little terrier, would have alerted the entire neighborhood and probably raced to the phone to dial 9-1-1 with her paws. She'd been that smart.

But Tasers worked well, too. Michelle grabbed her pink combo flashlight/stun gun from her nightstand drawer and slipped out of bed, her heart running around her rib cage in terror. She wished she could just hide under the bed. Except it was never a good idea to hide there, where bad guys always looked. She'd seen the movie *Taken*. She knew.

She swallowed hard and edged toward the bedroom door, then cracked it open. There was no light on in the hallway, and the door to Max's room was shut. She should go wake him up. Did she have time? Where was the burglar?

Probably stealing her laptop at that very moment. Or her purse. Or her phone, which she'd left on the kitchen counter. That would be a worse loss than her purse. It had pictures she'd taken of the baby in it.

The lyrics from the song "Bad Girls" by one of Shyla's favorite bands began playing in her head. No housebreaker was going to steal her stuff. Yeah, she was bad, she was buff. She had a Fitbit.

She was a middle-aged cream puff. What the heck was she doing?

There went the sound again. Footsteps. In the kitchen. The burglar had, indeed, come in through the sliding door. He must have cut the glass. Burglars these days were so efficient.

She picked up her pace, going stealthily down the stairs. Then down the hallway. Into the kitchen.

Where she saw the silhouette. Her heart did a leap

clear up to her throat, but she managed to scream "Freeze!", aim her pink Taser, pull back her head in case of, well, she didn't know what, half shut her eyes and squeeze the trigger.

"Wha—" yelped the burglar.

The Taser took out the kitchen table with a zap, and Michelle dropped it, let out a screech, turned and ran for the stairs crying, "Max!" *Everyone under the bed. Now!*

"I'm here," called the burglar.

"Max!"

"Michelle!"

Michelle already had a foot on the bottom stair when she realized she knew that voice coming from the kitchen. The hall light flipped on, and she turned to see Max coming toward her, his brows dipped into an angry V.

"What the hell, Michelle? Are you trying to kill me?"

She collapsed onto the stairs. "I thought you were a burglar."

"So you were going to protect us with your little pink Taser?"

"Don't you make fun of me," she snapped. "It scared you plenty. It would have scared a burglar."

He sighed and came and plopped down next to her. "You could have electrocuted me."

"I heard a noise," she said in her own defense.

"So did I," he admitted. "I think it was that idiot Bobby next door, drunk and mistaking our front door for his."

"I heard someone down here."

"Me."

"Oh."

"I told you not to buy that thing," Max added with a frown. "You could hurt someone with it."

"A woman needs to be able to protect herself," Michelle insisted.

"I'm still here. I'll protect you."

"I don't need you to protect me," she snapped again. Because she had such good aim. The kitchen table would never try and take her down again.

"Yeah, I know. You don't need me for anything," he said, his words bitter.

I sure don't need you to make my life miserable, she thought. But, in all fairness, he hadn't been trying to make her life miserable just then. He'd been trying to be noble.

She suddenly remembered a time when they were dating. They'd been on a bike ride, and a dog had rushed out at them, growling and barking. Back then she'd been afraid of dogs, and knowing that, Max had kept his bike between her and the angry animal until they were safely away. She'd been hugely impressed. And grateful.

Was she so small that she couldn't dig up some gratitude and acknowledge his effort to keep her safe? "I'm sorry," she said. The words came out stiffly. "Thanks for coming down to check out the noise," she added.

"All you have to do is come get me," he said.

A rare moment of communication and kindness. If she wasn't so done with him, it might have given her hope.

But they were beyond hope, just two people occupying two different parts of the house. They communicated as needed, but since the last big fight, they hadn't exchanged so much as one smile. They'd stopped accepting invitations to parties at friends' houses, and the

invitations had finally dried up with everyone probably waiting for them to split so they could decide who
would be kept in the phone contacts and who would be
deleted, who would be invited to parties and who would
be removed from the guest list.

In the evenings he'd stay in the den, eating whatever
she might have left for him on the stove—still cooking for him: old habits died hard—the sports channel
keeping him company, and she'd watch TV up in the
bedroom, binging *Downton Abbey* or *Bridgerton*, leaving him to clean up.

"Thanks," she said again.

"Go on up to bed. I'll check on everything," he offered.

For one crazy moment she was tempted to suggest
he come to bed with her. Nothing like a near-burglar
experience to make a woman want a nice hard body in
bed next to her.

But that would be a stupid idea. In only a couple
of days they'd be spending the whole day together in
the SUV, and that was more than enough togetherness.
They'd both agreed that they were through, and they
needed to stick with the plan. It was for the best.

She returned to the bedroom, climbed under the covers and told herself for probably the hundredth time how
nice it was to be able to stretch out and have the whole
bed to herself. She didn't need Max in her bed, and she
didn't want him in her life. He was selfish and unfeel-
ing, and she couldn't remember the last time they'd
shared a smile, and...

Oh, what had happened to them? It was a rhetorical
question. She knew.

She didn't want to be with him anymore, and he, ob-

viously, felt the same. Otherwise, he'd have tried harder
to save their marriage, fought her over breaking up.

When she finally fell asleep, she dreamed about the
two of them. They were on some kind of cruise ship,
standing at the ship's railing, looking for all the world
like a couple in a travel ad. She wore a white dress that
showed off a beautiful tan (something she was incapable
of ever getting on her hopelessly white skin in real life).
Her hair was naturally blond again with no gray hairs
lurking beneath the color job and blowing in a gentle,
tropical breeze. He wore fancy dress pants and a crisp,
white shirt. His stomach was flat and hard, and his dark
hair glinted like coal in the moonlight.

He draped an arm over her shoulder as they looked
out at the endless sea. "Just you and me, babe," he said
softly. "That's how it should be."

From far off somewhere in the ship, music began
to play.

"Dance with me," he said, and she turned and moved
into his arms.

Next thing she knew they were dancing down the
deck of the ship, gazing into each other's eyes. Everything was so beautiful, so perfect.

Until the dream scene shifted. The turquoise tropical water disappeared, eaten by a gray and choppy sea,
and they were suddenly much farther north. They hit
an iceberg, and the ship began to sink. Still in her sum-
mery dress, she grabbed a blanket from a deck chair and
rushed to the railing. She looked down and saw a life raft
bobbing in icy waters. It was filled with other women,
who were also wrapped in blankets, all of them crying.

"How did I get here?" one of them wailed. "I thought
we'd be together forever."

"Get in," another woman called up to Michelle. "Save yourself while you can."

Max was still on the boat. Now he stood farther down the deck. He wore the same dressy black pants and white shirt he'd been wearing. He had no blanket, and he was shivering and his lips were turning blue and he was looking at her with pleading eyes.

The same woman who'd urged Michelle to get in the life raft called to her again. "Jump, you idiot. Get out while you can."

Michelle looked to where Max stood. "We'll make it to land," she said to the woman.

"No, you won't. Look what you're on!" The woman held up a life preserver. On it was stamped the name *Titanic*.

Michelle's eyes flew open, getting her off the boat and out of the dream. All the bed covers had slid onto the floor. She pulled them back over herself with a sigh. If that wasn't a message, she didn't know what was. Only a fool would stay on a sinking ship.

4

"Thanks for holding down the fort yesterday," Michelle said to Ginny when she got to the store.

A couple dozen customers milled around, some searching for Thanksgiving-weekend bargains, others snapping up collectible Christmas ornaments. Probably everyone in there had happy families and was looking forward to a cozy Christmas. Michelle sighed inwardly. She knew hers would be bittersweet.

"Amber and James and I had it all under control. Although, let me tell you, it was busy."

"We like busy," Michelle said.

"And we like the extra dollars that went in our pockets," Ginny said with a smile. "A win-win for everyone."

"Yes, it was," said Michelle just as a woman with several Disney-princess ornaments came up to the cash register.

"My granddaughters are going to love these," she said.

Ah, yes. Who didn't love princesses? Too bad nobody warned you that life in the castle didn't always end well.

"How was your Thanksgiving?" Ginny asked when they had a lull between customers.

"Too short," said Michelle. "I wish the girls could have stayed for the whole weekend."

"I hear you," Ginny said. "That's the frustrating thing about kids growing up. They spend all those years driving you nuts, and just when you get them to the point where you can enjoy them, they go and get lives of their own."

"At least we got them for Thanksgiving. And we'll get to see them all at Christmas."

"Oh. Is Julia coming out?"

"No, we're all going there."

"You and Max?"

Michelle nodded.

"Together?"

Michelle frowned and nodded again.

"Now, that should be interesting."

"We'll manage," Michelle said, then sighed. "What am I doing?"

"Biting the bullet so you can see your girl. May as well get used to it. Getting divorced doesn't mean getting him completely out of your life. You know that."

"I know." There was a time when the idea of not being with Max had seemed unthinkable. Now the idea of staying together was unthinkable.

"Well, you'll manage. Take plenty of chocolate. If you've got enough of that you can get through anything."

That made Michelle chuckle.

"And who knows? Maybe somewhere along the way you two will fall in love again."

"Right," Michelle said with a sneer. It was way too late for that.

* * *

By the time she and Warren were ready to leave for St. Maries, Idaho, Hazel had pretty much put the entire neighborhood into a sugar coma, distributing everything from frosted sugar cookies to gingerbread boys and girls. She'd also baked up a batch of her granddaughters' favorite cookies to take: spritz, dyed green and shaped like little trees and decorated with candy sprinkles. She and Julia had texted back and forth several times—Hazel loved texting—deciding what treats they wanted to bake together when Hazel got there. They'd settled on Hazel's special fruitcake cupcakes with rum frosting as well as almond puff pastry for breakfast on Christmas Day. Michelle would be in charge of baking the red velvet cake when she arrived. Julia's mother-in-law enjoyed baking, too, and was also planning on contributing to the festivities, and Hazel was looking forward to trying her specialties.

"You'd think we were leaving home for a month," Warren complained as he wedged the last bags with presents in the trunk. "You know, there's nothing wrong with gift cards, hon."

"Gift cards are great, but not for Christmas," she said. "They're so impersonal, and there's nothing to unwrap. Be careful, that one's breakable."

"You know, all the granddaughters didn't need quilts for Christmas," he said as he jockeyed a suitcase around a huge box.

"I couldn't give Julia one and not the other girls."

"Sure you could. She's the one who bought a house."

"It wouldn't look right. Audrey and Shyla would feel left out. You can make it all fit," she said blithely, and he groaned.

She left him to wrestle with the suitcase and the various boxes and bags and went back to the front hall for the last load of things: the small shopping bag with the extra ingredients for the baking she wanted to do with Julia, her tote bag containing her toiletries and the bag with her latest RaeAnne Thayne book, her journal and her Bible. Then there was the bag with her supply of chocolate (snow was predicted along their route, and she'd need that chocolate to soothe her nerves) as well as protein bars to keep them going and Cheetos for Warren. And the cookies in the vintage black tin with the tole painting that had been her mother's. She set those on the roof along with her mug of coffee and got busy arranging things in the back seat. Now, did she pack extra batteries for her hearing aids in her purse?

And were her glasses in there?

She was still double-checking when Warren slid in behind the wheel. "We ready?" he asked.

"I feel like I'm forgetting something," she said, making one last rummage through her purse.

"Yeah, the kitchen sink. Come on, buckle up. We're burning daylight."

"Honestly, Warren, you have no idea how much goes into getting ready for a trip like this," she said irritably. "All you have to do is pack your medicine, toothbrush and electric shaver and grab the car keys."

"Okay, okay. I stand corrected."

"And it rattles me when you get in a hurry," she added. She checked her purse again. Yes, her acid-reflux pills were in there.

"Sorry," he said. Probably more to placate her than because he really was.

Oh, well. They were good to go. She shut the door and buckled up and off they went.

They'd gotten about three blocks when she reached for the eggnog latte she'd made herself and realized it wasn't in the cup holder. "My drink."

"Did you forget it back at the house?"

"With all the rushing around we were doing to get out the door," she began. And then she remembered. "Oh, no! My cookies."

"Your cookies?" he repeated, not making the connection.

"I set my latte and the cookies on the top of the car. Warren, pull over."

"They're not going to be there now," he protested, but he pulled over.

She got out and looked down the street. Nothing in that block. Maybe the cookies had just fallen out onto the parking strip.

"We have to go back," she said.

Warren hated turning back home for forgotten items. Once they started a road trip, that was it. But, smart man that he was, he knew better than to argue this time.

They were a half a block away from the house when she saw the cute vintage cookie tin that had been her mother's lying on the sidewalk where it had obviously rolled. She'd thought she'd secured the lid but in her haste she must not have. It had popped off and a family of crows were feasting on her cookies.

"No," she wailed.

Warren parked the car, then got out and flapped his arms and sent the crows flying off, one of them with half a cookie in its greedy beak. She hopped out, stepped over her spilled to-go cup and rushed to the scene of the cookie crime. A few crumbs were all that was left of the previous day's labor of love. Hazel swore.

Warren picked up the tin. It had a small dent.

Hazel swore again.

"This is what comes of rushing me," she informed him.

Then Warren swore. But under his breath. He handed her the tin, walked back to the car, got in behind the wheel and waited.

She got back in the car, dropped the tin onto the floor, set her empty mug in the cup holder and slammed the door shut.

"Sorry," he said again as she buckled up, and this time she could tell he meant it. "Are you going to be okay?"

"Yes, I'm going to be okay," she said, still irritable.

"It could be worse," he offered.

She sighed. "Yes, I guess if losing my cookies is the worst that happens to us, we can be glad." With all the bad things happening in the world, the loss of a few cookies was nothing.

Thankfully, they made it to their first stop, Biggs Junction, where they'd planned to stay the night, without further mishap. Although, on seeing their motel, Hazel wasn't so sure about the choice they'd made.

"This doesn't look quite like the pictures online," she said. The Family Hideaway looked like it needed to be hidden away. Far away.

The alluded-to family hadn't painted the two-story motel in a long time, and the paint was chipping. If the scraggly bushes around the outside could talk, would they tattle that the gardener had gone on strike for higher wages? Or any wages at all?

"I don't know about this," she said.

"It'll be fine," Warren assured her.

"We should have stayed at Best Western."

"This was a bargain."

Fifty years of marriage, and she and Warren still hadn't been able to come to an agreement on the definition of a bargain. Warren looked for price. She looked for quality. And this place was definitely lacking quality. If it looked this forlorn on the outside, what did it look like on the inside?

She walked with him into the reception area where a woman in a skirt and blouse and a smart red blazer stood at a computer behind the desk. She looked okay, but the reception area was dowdy, with a fake leather couch that had a small tear in one corner and a glass coffee table with a centerpiece of dusty plastic flowers. Some of the tiles on the floor were cracked. What kind of family was this?

"Welcome to the Family Hideaway," the receptionist greeted them. No smile.

Hazel couldn't fault her. If she had to work in a dump like this, she wouldn't be smiling, either.

"We have a reservation," Warren said.

Hazel had a whole heap of reservations. She should never have let her husband talk her into going for one of his *bargains*.

The room didn't match up to the pictures on the website any better than the outside of the place. Hazel stared at the bedspread on their king-size bed. Little tufts of fabric stood up all over it, like tiny mountains waiting for mice to climb them. For all she knew the mice had never summited but had had mousy heart attacks and were dead under there.

"It smells," she said, wrinkling her nose.

"It's a little musty is all. If we turn on the heat…" He walked to an ancient metal box under the window and turned the dial on it. It came to life with a rattle.

That was where the mice had gone to die. "Oh, no," Hazel said, stepping back. "I am not staying here."

"It's fine," Warren insisted.

"If we sleep in that bed we will get bitten by something," she said.

He made a face. "Come on, Hazel. It's not that bad."

Warren's eyesight was obviously going. She started for the bathroom to see what awaited her there but stopped short. At the edge of the ancient dresser where a TV was parked, two tiny mushrooms poked up from the carpet.

She didn't say a word. Just pointed to them.

"Okay, let's go," he said.

But before he left he took a picture of the mushrooms. "Good for laughs at Christmas dinner."

"Good for spoiling everyone's appetite," she said. "It's almost enough to spoil mine."

Half an hour later they were in a motel with a clean lobby and a room with smooth bedspreads on a king-sized bed and a 'shroom-free carpet. Warren agreed that, yes, this was a much better choice.

"Have you got your appetite back?" he teased as he set their suitcase on the luggage stand.

"I definitely do. Let's go check out the diner next door."

"Good idea," he said.

"Oh, grab your medicine," she reminded him. "I put your toiletries bag in the bathroom."

A moment later Warren called from the bathroom, "Hon, have you seen my Eliquis?"

He'd come away without his blood thinner?

She hurried to the bathroom where he was pawing through his toiletries bag. "You didn't pack it?"

Warren's only reply to that was a frown.

Oh, dear. "Honey, you can't be running around without your blood thinners." If his A-fib acted up, he'd be in trouble.

"I must have forgotten to pack 'em," he said with a shrug.

After a certain age it didn't matter if you forgot to pack some things. No more need for condoms, and they could easily replace toothpaste or a toothbrush. It was the same with deodorant. A comb.

But medications were a different animal altogether. A scary animal, especially in Warren's case as they never knew when his heart would start acting up. The blood thinner helped fight against potential clots, a terrifying possible side effect of a misbehaving heart.

"We need to call your doctor and get him to call in a prescription. Where's the nearest drugstore?" *Don't panic, don't panic.*

Oh, yes. Panic.

"It's only for a few days. I'll be fine. I'll pick up some baby aspirin," he said.

"Oh, no, you won't," she said in her best bossy-wife voice. "You get Dr. Phillips on the phone right now." She hurried to her purse, pulled out her own phone and began a search for the nearest drugstore.

"All I'm getting is a recording," he called from the bathroom a moment later.

"Well, then, leave a message, and tell them it's an emergency," she called back. "The receptionist is probably busy with a patient."

"It ain't an emergency," he insisted. "I'll be fine."

She came and stood in the bathroom doorway. "Warren. Please."

"Okay, okay." He turned his attention back to the phone. "Uh, this is Warren Turnbull. My wife and I are on a trip, and I came away without my blood thinner. I need the doc to call in a prescription for me. Can you have him call me?"

Good, she thought as she walked away. That would be taken care of.

"From now on we can't be in such a hurry," she said to Warren when he came back out. "We're getting sloppy in our old age."

He nodded. "Yeah, I guess we are."

"I'm glad you discovered it was missing when you did."

"I'd have probably been okay."

She wasn't so sure about that. Warren loved to minimize things. He was supposed to take the medication twice a day. Not that blood thinners were a total solution. There was really only one real cure for his problem, and so far she hadn't been able to convince him to take it.

"Let's go get something to eat and relax."

"Relax? After the day we've had?"

"Everything's gonna be fine now," he said. "And you can't take a road trip without a little adventure. Otherwise, what have you got to talk about later?"

"How about all the things that went right?" she suggested.

He chuckled. "That's boring."

"I've reached the point in life where I'm perfectly happy to be boring," she informed him. "And I have enough gray hairs now." A whole head full to be exact.

Unlike her husband, who barely had any. Ha! That was because he preferred to give them to her.

At least the problem is solved, she told herself, threading her arms through one of his as they walked into the diner. And after that moment of stress, she was going to reward herself. "I'm going to have a hamburger. And pie for dessert." The diet damage had already been done thanks to her baking spree, so why not live it up until January 1?

"I think I will, too," he said cheerfully. "Then, after dinner, we can go back and see what there is to watch on TV."

"That sounds good to me," said Hazel.

"Smooth sailing from here on," Warren said.

Yes, smooth sailing.

Except by the time the doctor called it was too late for them to pick up the prescription. "Well, never mind calling it in for here," Warren told him. "We'll be on the road."

Spending the holidays without his blood thinners? Oh, no. "Wait," Hazel said, grabbing Warren's arm. "Don't let him go. Ask him if he can call it in to a drugstore in St. Maries."

She searched her phone for drugstores at their destination, then passed it on to Warren, who passed it on to the doctor. The doctor assured them that the prescription would be called in and waiting for them when they arrived.

On the way back to the motel, they picked up some baby aspirin. A poor substitute, if you asked Hazel.

"We could have waited for the drugstore to open and gotten your blood thinner in the morning," she said.

She really should have insisted on that. What had she been thinking?

"I'll be fine. We'll be there in another day. Nothing's gonna happen between now and then," he said. Warren the psychic. "You worry too much."

Maybe she did. He was probably right. There was no sense borrowing trouble.

Their nice, clean room was a welcome sight. "I am looking forward to stretching out on that bed and relaxing," she said to Warren.

"Same here," he agreed.

She'd gone into the bathroom to brush her teeth and Warren was plopped on the bed with the remote control, searching for something for them to watch on TV, when she heard the commotion. What on earth had he found?

"What are you watching?" she asked as she came out of the bathroom.

"Nothing yet." He frowned at the wall behind the TV and dresser.

"Oh, my gosh, that was coming from the room next door?"

There it was again. A man's voice, muffled. "Urr-grr-ga-grr," it hollered.

This was followed by a female voice. "Eee-shee-shee! Shee-shee-shee!"

Something thudded against the wall. Was it a person?

"Warren, we need to do something," Hazel said. "Our neighbors are trying to kill each other."

"I'll call the front desk," he said, reaching for the phone.

She rushed for the door. "There might not be time."

He got there before her and stopped her. "You can't

go running over to that room. If it's a domestic distur-
bance, you could get hurt."

"Someone's already getting hurt," Hazel protested.

Then, as if to prove her wrong, they heard a high-
pitched giggle. What on earth?

This was followed by a rumbling male voice. "Urr
grrr-grrr-oom."

"What are they saying?" Hazel wondered.

"It sounded like, 'Go to your room,'" Warren said.

Music invaded from next door—rocking, loud, party
music.

"I guess nobody's getting killed," Warren concluded.

"My gosh, they're going to turn us deaf," Hazel complained.

"You already are," Warren said.

"I only have a little hearing loss. And you're not
funny," she added, pointing a finger at him.

Maybe their neighbors thought he was, because fresh
laughter, both male and female, accompanied by the
music, drifted over to them.

"Are they high on something?" Hazel wondered.

"Who knows? At least they're not trying to kill each
other. Come on. I found an old *Law and Order: Crimi-
nal Intent* we can watch."

She got into her jammies, then plopped down on the
bed and tried to concentrate on the show, but between
the loud music and the bursts of crazy voices coming
at them from their neighbors, it was impossible to track
what was going on.

"What did Detective Goren say?" she asked Warren at one point.

"Miss Scarlett did it in the kitchen with the candle-
stick? Who knows?" Warren replied with a scowl. "If

those two don't knock it off, I'm going to do it with the lead pipe."

He turned up the sound on the TV and was rewarded by an angry banging on the wall and more muffled words delivered by the male voice.

Warren kept the sound where it was and the music in the room next door got louder.

"Oh, good grief," Hazel said. "Turn the TV off. We may as well read."

Their neighbors didn't participate in the truce by bringing down their noise level.

"They've got to settle down eventually," Hazel said.

Maybe not. Two hours later the revelers were still reveling, and the wads of toilet paper Hazel had stuck in her ears weren't doing any good. She could have done with a little more hearing loss.

"We're never going to get any sleep," she said miserably.

"Okay, enough," Warren growled. "We're getting a different room. Get dressed. I'll be right back."

Ten minutes later he was back. "Come on, hon, we're moving."

"Oh, thank heaven," she said and gathered her things.

As they passed the room, Warren shook a fist at the door and said, "Urr-grr-ga-grr to you, too."

The next room was much better. They got into their pajamas, climbed into their nice, comfy king bed, found their program again and settled in for the night. Hazel finally got to hear what Detective Goren was saying, and Warren got to turn his fingers orange eating more of his Cheetos. Yes, much better. They'd get a good night's sleep and be ready for the long drive the next day.

They finally turned off the TV. All was silent, and

Hazel burrowed her head into her pillow, smiled and shut her eyes.

She was drifting off when the sound of a baby crying made her eyes pop back open.

Hazel loved babies. She could hardly wait to hold her adorable first great-grandchild. Seeing sweet little babies in TV commercials made her put a hand to her heart and sigh. Hearing a baby's laugh—music to anyone's ear.

Hearing a baby cry (and this one was CRYING) when it was time to go to sleep, when you were staying in a motel where you had paid for a room so you could sleep, was a different matter. Why weren't those parents home where they belonged?

Probably because, like her and Warren, they were on their way to spend the holidays with loved ones. You could hardly begrudge young parents that.

Although, she wanted to.

She put her pillow over her head. It didn't help. And Warren thought she couldn't hear? She could hear just fine.

He, on the other hand, was starting to snore. The beginning of the "Anvil Chorus." Warren and the baby spent the next hour creating a very interesting duet, and Hazel lay in bed thinking maybe they should go back home and mail the girls their quilts.

5

"You forgot to tell me you had royalty coming," Shyla's boyfriend Milton joked.

"Almost," Shyla replied. "She sure ruled over Julia and me when we were kids. Of course, to be fair, she's also why I got good grades. And if she hadn't helped Julia pass geometry, she'd have probably never graduated from high school on time."

"Oh, so she's a saint. Maybe I need to go home and change into a suit and tie."

Shyla eyed Milton's jeans and T-shirt with the smiling piece of poo wearing a halo. Underneath the graphic it said *Good Shit Happens*.

"No, this look is more you. Shitty," she teased.

He grinned. "Yeah?"

"Yeah."

"Well, you're the best shit that's ever happened to me."

"You know it." She stopped to give him a kiss, then went back to setting the table. Her apartment was a three-hundred-square-foot studio with a small but efficient kitchen, complete with granite countertops, a dishwasher and an eating bar. The walk-in shower in the bathroom made her feel rich, and the elegant Edwardian-style brick building in Lower Nob Hill that it was in made her feel classy. With light rail and bus lines abundant, it was perfect for her. She'd fixed it up with old movie posters she'd scored over the years, including one for *Raiders of the Lost Ark* that her mom had found for her at a garage sale back when she was a teen. That baby was worth about a thousand bucks now. Not that she'd ever sell it.

She'd set up the antique drop-leaf table that her grandma had given her by the window, along with three antique chairs she'd found at a flea market. She'd pulled it out enough so all three of them could sit there for dinner and had spread it with a small, white linen tablecloth (another gift from Gram) and put out the Christmas dishes Mom had given her the year before. She'd made a simple centerpiece, filling a small Mason jar with fairy lights and then adding a couple of silk carnations—red and white. The finishing touches were flatware and the napkins, red damask, also a flea market find. Oh, yeah. Livin' large on a small budget. Mom, the garage-sale queen, had taught her well.

She stepped back to admire her handiwork, and Milton came up behind her and slipped his arms around her waist. "Looks great."

She smiled over her shoulder at him. "You think so?"

"Oh, yeah. And dinner smells amazing."

Vegetarian lasagna, her specialty. She'd bought a baguette to go with it and had olive oil ready for dipping. Dessert was going to be black bean brownies, a recipe she'd gotten from one of her friends at Prestige Presentations, the theater company she worked for. Audrey was kind of a snob when it came to dessert, and Shyla hoped she'd be impressed with the cleverness of this one.

Probably not. Audrey whipped up stuff like croquembouche without batting an eyelash. She made croutons from scratch (who did that?) and knew how to make chocolate truffles. Audrey the overachiever didn't stop with gourmet cooking. She also spoke Spanish and French fluently. When she wasn't busy reading *War and Peace* or working sudoku puzzles, she was picking up facts and statistics to sprinkle into her conversations. Audrey was the family's designated shadow-caster, the brainy big sister who knew everything. Shyla admired the heck out of her, resented her and adored her. And was determined to impress her, both with her cooking skills and her boyfriend. Ha! That was one thing Audrey hadn't gotten right.

Except Shyla wanted her sister to get the man thing right. How could someone so smart be so stupid when it came to men? For all her smarts she didn't seem capable of telling losers from winners.

"So is meeting your sister up there with meeting your parents?" Milton asked as he plopped on the love seat. That and an overstuffed chair were the only furniture in the room besides the table and chairs and her bed and nightstand, which she had hidden behind an ancient screen decorated with peacocks.

"No, but close. And isn't it the guy who's supposed to bring the girl home to meet Mama?"

Which he hadn't yet, although they'd done an online version of the Meet the Parents. In person was more of a challenge, partly because his parents lived in Florida, and she and Milton hadn't been together all that long.

Long enough, though, for her to know she'd found her keeper. Milton was a nerd, who came complete with glasses, and a software programmer. But he was a buff nerd with scruffy hair and a sexy jawline who hit the gym regularly and liked to bike. He also happened to enjoy theater. They'd met at an improv class, and she loved his humor and the way he improvised, especially when it came to thinking of sweet things to do for her, like buying her a gift card to Goodwill, one of her favorite bargain-hunting grounds. She was expecting a ring by Valentine's Day.

"I want that to happen soon," he said. "Speaking of soon, it's almost nine. How close is she? I'm starving."

"She said nine. That means she'll be here any minute." Because Audrey planned everything down to the tiniest detail.

Right on cue, the buzzer rang. "She's here!" Shyla announced and hurried to press the intercom.

"I'm here," came her sister's voice, and Shyla buzzed her in. Let the fun begin!

"This is almost scarier than meeting the parents," Milton said. "I should have brought her flowers."

"Too late now. She'll have to take you as you are, like I do. And you're worth taking."

A moment later Audrey was walking in the door, looking glam in a chunky white faux-fur jacket over a gray cable knit sweater, ripped jeans and half-boots. She hated being tall, but she had no idea how beautifully being tall paired with clothes. No matter what she wore she always managed to look elegant.

"About time you got here," Shyla joked, hugging her.

"I hope you've got the Gewürztraminer ready."

"Of course. Milton brought it."

"Ah, Milton," Audrey said as they edged farther into the apartment.

Shyla caught the glint of male appreciation in his eyes at the sight of her sister and wanted to smack him. But only for a minute because Milton would never cheat. She knew that. And Audrey would never poach. She knew that, too.

Still, she couldn't help giving him a playful whack on the shoulder when he joined them. "Wipe the drool off your chin."

He gave a guilty start, then shrugged and smiled and said, "Sorry. Glad to finally meet you, Audrey."

"Nice to meet you, too."

"I hope so, 'cause I don't think Shyla's gonna keep me unless I pass the Audrey test."

"Not much of a test there," Audrey assured him. "If Shyla's into you, you have to be great."

"He's amazing," Shyla said, and Milton the Amazing puffed up like an exotic bird during birdie mating season.

"Put your stuff in the bedroom," Shyla said, "and I'll get the wine poured."

Audrey pulled her carry-on behind the screen and ditched her coat while Shyla poured the wine. "Lasagna will be ready in another five."

"Good. I'm famished," Audrey said.

And to prove it, after they sat down at the table, she ate two helpings of lasagna and two—*two!*—slices of French bread. "This is really good," she complimented Shyla as she polished off that second piece.

Another advantage of being tall. Audrey claimed height had nothing to do with it, but what did she know? Oh, yeah, everything. Whatever the reason, when it came to eating, Audrey was a metabolic magician. Calories disappeared, and pounds stayed away. Instead, they went looking for Shyla's butt. It was so unfair.

"I guess so. Honestly, I don't know why you can't be like the rest of us and gain weight," Shyla said, eyeing that second piece of bread jealously.

"I wish I could," Audrey said.

"Don't tell me, let me guess. They called you Bean Pole when you were a kid," said Milton.

"Oh, yeah. Or Leaning Tower of Pizza. Stilts Girl."

"Four Eyes," Milton said, pointing to his glasses. "Thank God glasses are cool now 'cause I could never get used to contacts." He looked to Shyla, waiting for a confession.

"They called her cute," Audrey supplied. "Everyone loved Shyla." She sounded half-jealous. "But then, what's not to love?" she added, warming Shyla's heart.

"My brattiness? You sure spent enough time telling me what a brat I was."

Audrey shrugged. "Well, you were. You still are. Loves to get her way," she said to Milton, who smiled and nodded in agreement.

"Hey, I'm right here," Shyla said, scowling at her sister.

Milton laughed and reached over and brought Shyla to him for a kiss. "We love you, babe."

"Yes, we do," Audrey agreed.

And it was great to see two people she loved hitting if off so well. Dinner conversation flowed as smoothly as melted chocolate. He appreciated Audrey's shared interest in history, and he scored points with her for making her laugh.

Once they finished eating, Milton and Shyla cleaned

up, letting Audrey sit at the eating bar and sip wine while they worked. Afterward they wound up playing Wii bowling with Shyla and Milton competing like they were in a tournament, knocking down those virtual pins like crazy. Audrey did a lot of groaning.

"Sports were never my thing," she said when they were done.

"Mine, neither," said Shyla.

"You were good at soccer."

Shyla smiled. Yes, she was. "But mostly I liked partying with my friends."

"And designing," Audrey put in.

Shyla had always enjoyed arts and crafts, and especially sewing, thanks to both grandmas. Gram Turnbull especially, who had been the one to get her addicted to sewing, letting her play with bits of leftover fabric from her many projects, which Shyla had used to design outfits for her Barbie doll. She'd gotten into cosplay and drama in high school. Funny how Dad had worried that she was going to starve if she chose a career in the arts. Maybe she would have simply doing theater, but her side business was going great, and her savings account was slowly growing.

"She's good," Milton said. He pulled up a picture on his phone and turned it so Audrey could see the Halloween costume she'd made for him. As if Audrey hadn't already seen it. "Glow-in-the-dark bluefish, and look who caught me."

Yep, there he was with his fins and tail and fishy face. She was dressed as a fisherman, and he was hooked at the end of her pole. They'd won first prize at their favorite bar.

Time sneaked past as the three of them drank more

wine and talked, and finally Audrey yawned and Milton checked his Apple Watch. "Guess I'd better go," he said. "Sweet sorrow, and all that." Shyla walked him to the door, and he gave her a three-alarm-fire kiss. "See you when you get back. I got something special for you."

Maybe she was going to get that ring earlier than she thought. "I have something for you, too," she said. She'd found a really cool piece of CryptoArt that she knew he'd love.

"It won't be as cool as what I got you," he teased.

"Oh, yeah, it will."

He sobered. "There's nobody else for me, Shyla. You feel the same way, right?"

"You have to ask?"

That made him smile. "Just makin' sure."

He kissed her again and then left her feeling all squishy and warm inside.

"So what do you think?" she asked Audrey when she came back into the living room.

"I think he's adorable."

Not that Shyla needed her big sister's approval, because she knew Milton was one in a zillion. Still, it was nice to have it. "Think Mom and Dad will like him for a son-in-law?"

"Of course they will."

"Good, because I suspect I'm going to get a ring for New Year's," Shyla said. A perfect job, a perfect man—did it get any better than that?

"You guys will be great together," Audrey said. She yawned again. "I'm pooped."

"You're old," Shyla teased.

"You really are a brat," Audrey retorted as she went in search of her toothbrush and makeup remover.

* * *

Shyla had always loved to talk, and once they were stuffed into her vintage double bed, she kept it up. Of course, it was all about Milton and how wonderful he was and how happy they were, and Audrey listened with mixed emotions.

She was glad her sister had found someone so perfect for her. But she was also a little bit jealous. That crack about her being old hadn't been malicious, but it had hit a nerve. Audrey was only three years older than Shyla, but at twenty-seven, with thirty right around the corner, that three-year difference might as well have been ten. She felt ancient and marooned on Loveless Island, a romance-shipwreck victim, aging by the day with no hope of rescue in sight.

She kept insisting that she wasn't in a hurry to find someone. Even to herself. What a liar.

She wanted someone with whom she could share a private joke, a good meal, a play or movie. A life. But she didn't want just anyone. She didn't want to settle. She wanted a man who'd appreciate her for who she was. There had to be someone out there who liked smart, strong women.

She'd thought Dennis was that man. *Looking for someone intelligent with a variety of interests*, he'd written in his Right 4 U profile. Someone who wouldn't be threatened by her intelligence. Great. She'd responded, and they'd met for coffee…at a Barnes & Noble café. Meeting in a bookstore. Oh, this had to be The One.

He'd sure seemed like it. He was smart and friendly and had not only read everything Stephen Hawking had ever written but also had read all the classics. He was the first man she'd ever met who, like her, had read *War and Peace* from beginning to end. And he was looking into taking a French cooking class. Definitely well-rounded.

And not bad-looking, either. Plus he wanted to take her to dinner. He not only took her to dinner the next night, he also brought her Godiva chocolates. How could a man who brought you Godiva not be perfect?

He took her to dinner again, and she took him to bed. Yep. He was perfect.

So, high on chocolate and sex, she set aside her brains and jumped right into love. And it was great. When they weren't watching a foreign film or taking a cooking class together, they were hiking in the Cascades. When he had to travel for business, they texted. Sometimes even sexted. She was way too busy being happy to notice the little red flags that began to wave.

If only she'd seen them before he got that new job and she followed him to California. Alas, she hadn't. The Dennis facade of smarts and charm kept her blinded.

With the twenty-twenty vision that comes with hindsight, she could see the flaws as big and bright as neon signs. Dennis had an overweight ego. He fattened it up by feasting on the flaws of others: his new boss, who never quite measured up, or his brother, who he deemed not half as fabulous as himself. Even Audrey when she disagreed with him. "You haven't thought that through," he liked to say. Or, worse, "You don't really understand."

It irked him no end when she ignored his financial advice. How could she? After all, he knew everything.

Especially when it came to investing. Dennis played the stock market like some people played the horses. He was always following some new stock or other.

And that brought to light another red flag. Dennis had to be right; therefore, anyone who didn't agree with him had to be wrong.

"I don't need your advice," he'd said irritably when she'd suggested he dump one of his pet stocks before its price fell any further. "I know what I'm doing."

He hadn't. The stock tanked. And when he complained about it and she made the mistake of pointing out that she'd tried to warn him, it not only ruined their dinner conversation, it ruined the rest of their evening. His foul mood was a giant buzzkill.

"You always have to be right," he snapped.

He could have been talking to himself.

Obviously, she didn't like admitting when she'd made a mistake, either, because she stuck with him, ignoring his flashes of arrogance, the mansplaining and the times when he proved he wasn't really listening to her by talking right over her.

Because Dennis could still be charming. He could be fun.

And she wanted things to work out. Her pride demanded it. He'd convinced her to move so they could be together, and she had. It was a colossal error to acknowledge.

"You're moving awfully fast," Mom had said.

"I know, but I know what I'm doing," she'd insisted.

She hadn't, and her idyllic new start in LA soon became a disastrous end-of-the-love trail.

The Dead End sign finally lit up at a party.

"Is there anything you don't know?" he'd demanded when she'd had the nerve to point out that the new-car smell he was raving about was composed of over fifty volatile organic compounds.

They'd been talking about cars with two of his work buddies she hadn't met yet, and he'd been bragging about the car he was planning to buy. "Nothing like that new-car smell," he'd said. That was for sure.

She'd thought she was sharing an interesting and rather creepy factoid. They'd thought it was a conversational buzzkill.

"Where'd you hear that?" asked New Friend Number One, frowning.

"I stumbled on it one day when I was reading a page about little-known business facts."

New Friend Number Two had looked at her as if she'd suddenly revealed she had an extra head growing out of her armpit. "Do you surf the net looking for weird stuff?"

"No," she'd said, feeling defensive. So she liked discovering little-known factoids. So shoot her.

Dennis had done worse than that. He'd told her right in front of his new buds that nobody was interested in her useless facts, then cold-shouldered her the rest of the night.

The party had been torture after that, with her trying to cover her embarrassment with smiles and small talk.

He'd finally spoken to her. "You ready to go?" he'd asked, his tone of voice sullen.

"More than ready," she'd replied. Parties were supposed to be fun. That one had been anything but.

Neither of them talked as he drove her home, until she finally said, "I just thought it was interesting." No need to specify what she was talking about. He'd known.

"You were being a know-it-all, as usual," he'd said with a scowl. "What are you, Wikipedia with legs?"

"Sorry," she'd muttered. Although she'd been more offended than sorry.

"Yeah, well, me too. I'm sorry I took you with me."

His words had hit her like a wrecking ball.

"Just because I mentioned something I thought was interesting?"

"You think anybody wanted to hear that?" he demanded, his voice rising.

"I guess not."

"I guess you're right. Shit, Audrey, you're always throwing around facts like you're handing out ecstasy or Special K. It's irritating. And it's embarrassing. And I'm sick of it."

Sick of you.

He hadn't said it. He didn't have to.

"You once thought it was cool that I'm smart." Was that small, sad voice hers?

"I did. But guess what, Einstein Girl. It's not as cool as I thought 'cause you never know when to turn it off."

That had made her mad. "Oh, so I should just keep my mouth shut so you can feel smart?"

"Hey, I don't need you to *make* me feel smart. I already am. You made me look like an idiot," he muttered.

"No, you made yourself look like an idiot," she said.

The rest of the ride to her apartment had been filled with frigid silence, and he hadn't come in. Instead, he'd roared off, leaving behind half the rubber from his tires.

It didn't take an Einstein to see that their relationship was in trouble. Sure enough, a couple of days later he'd dumped her. At least he'd had enough class not to text her, but in a way she would have preferred it. That way he wouldn't have seen the tears in her eyes and her trembling lower lip.

He had texted a warning. We need to talk.

Still, she'd hoped that those words meant they were going to work on their relationship. It had been their first fight, and every couple had a first fight, right? You always patched up first fights with great make-up sex.

She'd been sure they'd make up. He loved her, and she loved him. Which was why she'd let him talk her into moving to LA.

He was a salesman who sold products for a pharmaceutical company, but he could have sold hair color to bald men. He was that good. He'd sure sold her on himself. On them as a couple.

It hadn't been hard. On top of being smart and well-read, he even knew how to dance. Plus he was a whole inch taller than her. It had felt like a match made in heaven. But she hadn't yet found the vein of insecurity lurking at the back of his brain.

When they were first dating, he'd said things like, "It's a relief to be with a woman who I can actually have a conversation with. And beautiful, too. I won the lottery."

He didn't act like a lottery winner that night at her apartment. She'd greeted him at the door with a hopeful smile. He hadn't returned it. And he'd passed on the offer of something to eat. Didn't want anything to drink, either. All bad signs.

"I'm sorry I was an ass Saturday," he'd begun once he'd settled on her couch.

Okay, that was a good sign. "We're all asses once in a while."

"But I can't keep up with you, and I'm tired of trying. I don't want somebody smarter than me."

"Wait a minute. What happened to liking being with

a woman you can have a conversation with?" she'd protested.

His only answer had been to shake his head. She'd felt sick. She'd given up so much for him. He'd led her to believe they were that serious, that they had a future together. And there he was, slamming the door on the future.

"I'm not that smart. I followed you here," she'd said bitterly.

"Yeah, well, I guess that was a bad idea."

"Yeah, it was yours," she'd pointed out.

He'd grunted in disgust. "You really know how to make a guy feel great."

She'd bit her lip, determined not to say anything more. Definitely determined not to cry. She'd failed at both.

"I thought we were in love," she'd said.

He'd sighed. "I thought so, too. I'm sorry, Audrey. It's not going to work. Better to admit it now and move on. I don't need a professor. I want someone—"

"Dumb so you can feel superior," she'd muttered. This was all about his ego. Jerk.

"Yeah, I guess so." At least he'd had the grace to admit it. "It's not that you're not great."

"Just that you're sick of me."

"I never said that."

"You did. In the car."

"I just said I was sick of you always throwing around stupid facts. Nobody cares how much fat there is in a Big Mac meal."

"They should."

"Or how many traffic accidents there are every year on I-5."

"I care when I'm in the car with you and you're tail-gating someone."

"Everyone in California tailgates!" He sighed, shook his head. "Look, it's not working. I'm sorry, but I need to move on."

He'd had the nerve to kiss her cheek before walking out of her apartment and leaving her alone with her cat, the only male who seemed to appreciate her.

"He wasn't good enough for me," she'd said to Tommy as she picked him up.

Better to think that than to think she hadn't measured up. Was she a know-it-all?

It was a question that still haunted her. No one knew everything, so that slur was ridiculous. It seemed to her that there was a cultural prejudice against smart people, one fueled by envy. Being smart was a gift, the same as being beautiful or athletic. Men fell at the feet of beautiful women. Athletes were adored and paid high salaries. Why were people who got straight A's and college scholarships treated like pains in the ass? And if you had your life together, there was another point against you. What was with that?

"I hope you can find somebody as great as Milton," Shyla said sleepily.

"I'm in no hurry," Audrey told both her sister and herself.

"Go confidently in the direction of your dreams. Live the life you've imagined." So said Thoreau.

She'd thought she was doing that when she moved to LA. Instead, she'd been a love prospector, thinking she'd found gold when it was only pyrite. Fool's gold.

That was what happened when you made decisions with your heart instead of your head. You committed to relationships that blew up in your face. The sunniest beaches in the world and the hottest clubs were useless trimmings when a relationship went sour, and Thoreau was full of shit.

"It'll happen. When you least expect it, I bet," mumbled Shyla.

"Like in the movies?" Audrey retorted.

"Maybe. You never know."

"Well, he'd better come with references."

Audrey almost snickered at the thought. From whom? Ex-girlfriends? *The only thing wrong with him was that he didn't like chick flicks.* Ha! Ex-girlfriends were usually exes for a reason much bigger than that.

Or maybe from his mother. *Such a good son.* Yeah, like moms were never prejudiced.

Although Audrey's aunt Ellie had once told her and her sisters to watch how a man treated his mother. "If he treats his mom well, he'll be a good husband."

Come to think of it, Dennis had been known to tease his mom, making fun of her occasional malaprops. And before he'd moved to California, she'd still done his laundry. A twenty-nine-year-old letting his mom do his laundry. *Now, there was a character clue, Sherlock.*

Shyla began to snore lightly, and Audrey lay in bed, listening to her, wishing she could fall asleep. Hard to relax into slumber when you were busy psychoanalyzing yourself.

She pulled out her phone and began to read the latest book on her app. It was a romance novel by one of her favorite authors.

The woman was driving him nuts with her stubborn refusal to cooperate, but he couldn't stay away. She

*was like a drug to him. He didn't care about her faults.
Even diamonds had flaws.*

Gack! Why did she keep reading this stuff when it
left her feeling discontent with her own life? Was she
a masochist?

No, just a hopeless romantic. With an emphasis on
hopeless.

She frowned and abandoned the tale of the besotted
male and his siren and moved instead to *The Future of
Humanity* by Michio Kaku. Fascinating as she found
the book, it wasn't holding her attention any better.
Probably because she couldn't shake thinking about the
future of one particular member of humanity. Herself.

So what if her love life sucked sand? At least her
family loved her. She could be thankful for that. They
would always be there for her.

Even her family was going to look very different if
her parents weren't going to be there for each other. She
sure hoped she was wrong about them.

She gave up on Michio. She needed to sleep. "Things
will look better in the morning," Gram liked to say.
After all the wallowing in the past that Audrey had
been doing, she sure hoped Gram was right.

6

"Come on, Michelle, we need to get going," Max said, and not in his most patient voice.

But, hey, she was the one who wanted to make sure they got over the pass before it possibly closed.

Actually, so did he, and the weather was not cooperating. Heavy snows had hit the mountains. Chains required. Under better conditions the trip would only take about five and a half hours, but if they got stuck they'd be lucky to get to Julia's by New Year's let alone Christmas Eve. The SUV was packed, and they really did need to get moving.

She appeared in the hallway, carrying her purse and travel bag and wearing a black sweater, black boots and jeans that hugged her lovely long legs.

"I'm coming," she snapped and grabbed her winter coat from the hall closet.

Michelle was still a beautiful woman, tall with hazel eyes and hair she kept the same honey color it had been when they first met. She looked more like thirty-nine than forty-nine, and she had a great smile…when she chose to wear it.

She sure never chose to with him anymore, which made him angry with both of them—her for turning sour on him, and him for resenting it. But honestly, how much could a man do? It was just as well they were splitting.

"Don't get bitchy on me," he snapped. "I'm trying to get us over the pass before they shut it down."

"I had a lot to do to get ready," she shot back, upgrading her frown to a glare. "All you have to do is brush your teeth and grab the car keys."

And grub around in a snowstorm once they reached the chain-up area putting chains on the tires. Yeah, soft life.

"I have to wrap presents and pack everything."

Part of the *everything* she used to pack was a lunch for them to eat along the way when they took a road trip. In nice weather, they'd find someplace nice to stop and have a picnic. When the girls were little, those stops usually involved playing Frisbee or looking for rocks at a river's edge. When it was just the two of them, they often found a secluded spot and played a much more grown-up game.

Those days were gone, and there was no bringing them back.

He sighed. "Let's just go. Okay?"

She said nothing in return and marched out the front door.

He frowned as he followed her out. Yeah, this was going to be a fun trip. He should have used his common sense and told Julia it wasn't a good idea for him and her mother to try and make the trek over there in December.

Michelle was no longer a fan of driving in the snow.

She was already wound tight, a sure sign that she was worried about a possible accident.

Still, Julia had wanted them all to come to her place for Christmas so badly, and he hadn't wanted to disappoint her, especially knowing this would be the last Christmas they'd all be together. What future Christmases would look like he had no idea.

Anyway, Michelle could have said no, but she'd opted to come along, so she was going to have to trust him to get her there safely. Which he knew he could do.

Of course, she'd been more than happy to insult his driving skills by reminding him about when he'd wiped out on his bike.

The wipeout was something he didn't like to remember, even though it hadn't been his fault. He was lucky he hadn't gotten more than a collection of bruises and a broken arm from trying to avoid the driver who hadn't seen him. Yeah, that had been fun.

It had also been the final straw for Michelle. He regretted both the purchase and the way he'd handled their final big argument.

The bike had been a foolish, selfish splurge, but instead of acknowledging that, he'd held on to his pride. He'd worked hard all his life. He'd gotten Audrey and Shyla through college and Julia married. (Okay, Michelle had been part of all that, too, but still.) He'd tried to be a good husband, and what thanks had he gotten? Nothing. He deserved to have something for himself. So he had bought a Harley.

And he was losing his wife.

The thought returned for the millionth time. If he hadn't pushed for a fourth child, they'd never have reached this point. They'd still be happily together. They had three great girls. Why had he thought he needed a son? Just so he could have someone to play catch with? Michelle had been hesitant when he'd first broached the subject because she didn't think they could afford a fourth kid; then, later, because she'd worried she was getting too old. She'd been right, and in the end she'd held it against him that things had gone wrong.

He cringed at the memory of her grief after losing the baby and the bitterness that rushed in like a flood. She'd been inconsolable. Everything he'd said had been wrong. It had been as if she was the only one to lose something precious. He'd mourned that baby, too.

But damn, bad things happened. You had to move on.

They hadn't moved on, they'd limped along, neither one openly acknowledging out loud for too long that they had a growing problem.

He'd preferred to ignore their own personal climate change—the coldness that crept into her voice, the laughter that dried up. She'd been in choir in high school and college—loved to sing. She sang to the girls when they were little, she sang around the house. Sometimes, they even went out to a neighborhood pub, and she sang karaoke. But that stopped. It was as if she lost her voice when she lost the baby. She didn't look at him the way she once did, either. Her smiles became rare, and the few she managed couldn't seem to reach her eyes. Menopause stepped into the picture and tipped the merry-go-round they'd been on, leaving him more confused and frustrated. She found excuses not to have sex. Then she finally came right out and said she didn't want to. They used to laugh together. The laughter dissolved into sniping. Or, worse, silence. Their anniversaries went from landmarks to jokes, even their twenty-fifth, which should have been a big one. He was married but alone. Empty.

So he bought a bike.

The words of that fool counselor they'd tried still rang in his ears. "What do you think you could do differently, Max?" What was the point of trying to figure it out now?

Still, even though they were splitting, he didn't want Michelle to hate him. He didn't want to lose her that completely.

Who was he kidding? He already had. She resented him, seemed to resent his very existence. Separate lives, separate bedrooms, and now divorce, the final seal on the deal looming.

He hadn't told her yet, but he had an interested buyer coming after Christmas to look at the Harley. Another middle-aged man on a quest for his youth.

Why hadn't he told her? Maybe because he didn't want to hear her say that it was too little, too late.

And she'd be right. They were through. The only thing left was to make it official and tell the kids come January.

Once they were in the car, she immediately turned on the radio to her favorite talk show. There would be no conversation on this trip. He could remember a time when they could fill every minute of a car trip with conversation. If someone had told him when he was twenty-two that this was how it would be when he was fifty-two, he'd have laughed in that person's face.

"Today we're talking about last-minute holiday gifts," said the radio host.

Max sighed inwardly. The only holiday gift he wanted

was his wife. Fat chance of that. She didn't want him, so what was the point of wishing?

He stole a glance at her. She was looking straight ahead, her expression stony. He used to be able to make her smile. There was a time when it had been easy to do.

His mind drifted to the Christmas they got engaged. He'd made her smile then.

"You sure you know when to come in?" Max said yet again to his friend Jack as he handed over the ring box.

"Of course I do," Jack said and twirled his Santa hat. "I'll be there in plenty of time."

"During dessert."

"I know already. Get going. You're gonna be late."

Max got going. He was wearing his best slacks and shirt, looking every bit like the financial success he hoped someday to be. Running Dad's car-supply franchise was just a stepping stone. One day he'd have his own business. He'd make buttloads of money and take Michelle to the kind of romantic places women dreamed about: Paris, Hawaii, London. They'd have it all.

But not because of all the things he planned to give her. They'd have it all because they'd have each other.

He got in his Honda Civic and made his way to her house. He had reservations at the Windjammer. Okay, so it wasn't Canlis, but it was a nice restaurant just the same. They'd have steak and lobster and for dessert, cheesecake, her favorite. Along with dessert would enter Santa, bringing Michelle an early Christmas present, that diamond ring Max had picked out with a lot of help from her best friend.

Inside her front door, he and her dad exchanged

knowing smiles because Max had gone the traditional route, asking Dad's permission to marry his daughter.

"As if I could stop her from being with you," his future father-in-law had joked. "I'm glad she picked a great guy."

A great guy. Max liked the sound of that, and he intended to be a great husband. She appeared, wearing a red dress that made him think of Christmas parties, and he could hardly wait to start their two-person party.

"I'm ready," she announced, smiling at him.

"Good. Then, let's go."

"Okay, now, tell me where we're going," she insisted once they were in the car.

"The Windjammer."

"Ooh, fancy. That's kind of expensive, though, isn't it?"

"You're worth it," he said.

"Yes, I am," she said with a cheeky grin. "But still. What are we celebrating?"

"Us. It's been a year since we met."

"Our one-year anniversary. You remembered."

"Of course I did. Didn't I tell you? I'm putting up a shrine at Balls and Brews," he added, making her giggle.

He loved it when she laughed. He loved everything about her. She was always happy, always smiling. And so tenderhearted. Almost too tenderhearted. It seemed she was easily hurt: a careless word taken the wrong way could pierce her heart. Kind words made her glow.

"You look beautiful tonight," he said as they settled in at their table.

She cocked her head and smiled at him, as if checking the bullshit meter. "Yeah?"

"You know you do."

"I'm not as pretty as you are handsome," she said. "I swear, the woman at that table is staring at you. And she's old enough to be your mother."

"Mrs. Robinson," he cracked.

"Even the waiter was checking you out."

He just shook his head. "You exaggerate."

"Don't pretend you don't see this stuff."

"How could I see anything else when I'm busy looking at you? You know you're the only woman for me."

Their waiter chose that moment to come up for their food orders.

"This is costing a lot. We could have gone without the appetizers," she said after they'd ordered.

"Like I told you, you're worth it."

And it was worth every penny watching her lap up that shrimp cocktail and then the lobster. Once they'd ordered dessert, he sauntered off, pretending to be in search of the men's room. He was relieved to see his friend, padded out in his red suit, approaching the entrance. All right!

"I told you not to worry," Jack said as soon as he was inside. "When have I ever let you down, man?"

It was a rhetorical question so Max didn't bother to answer. Instead, he scurried back to his seat. "So, babe, what do you think Santa's going to bring you for Christmas this year?" he asked casually.

In answer came a hearty "Ho ho ho!" from behind him. Heads turned as Santa entered the dining area.

Jack, his old football teammate, had done several plays in both high school and at the U, and he was in full-ham mode. "Santa is in the building," he announced in a booming voice, throwing his arms wide and making the black cloth bag he was carrying swing back and forth.

This inspired a murmur of voices and a couple of giggles.

"Somebody went all out," Michelle observed.

Somebody sure had.

Her eyes grew wide as Santa approached their table, and she recognized the face behind the fake beard.

"Well, now, here's a nice young lady. Michelle, have you been a good girl? Never mind, don't answer that," he said and chortled.

Michelle looked from him to Max, half laughing, shaking her head, her cheeks turning pink.

"Santa has a little something for you, but it's not from me. It's from this turkey you've been dating." He dug in the bag and pulled out the little black ring box, held it aloft for all to see, which definitely created a stir—with several *ooh*s and much clapping. He set the ring on the table in front of her and said, "My work is done. Now you'll just have to decide if this is what you want for Christmas."

She put a hand to her chest, looked across at Max and smiled bright enough to light every Christmas tree for miles around.

Max picked up the box, did the down-on-one-knee thing and opened it for her to see. "So what do you say, Michelle? Will you marry me?"

"Yes," she cried and threw her arms around him.

"Congratulations, man," said Jack. Then, as everyone was applauding, he waved and left.

She watched as Max slipped the ring on her finger.

"Your mom gave me your ring size. Do you like it?"

She nodded. "Oh, yes."

"'Cause if you don't, we can go pick out something together."

"No. I love it. And I love you."

He'd thought she always would. His dad had helped him into a car-part franchise of his own, and although they'd had some lean years, he'd done well enough. They'd stretched to buy their dream home and built a life in it, filled it with friends and laughter and kids and noisy slumber parties. They'd done backyard barbecues and taken the girls camping and even managed some weekend getaways, just the two of them. For so many years everything had gone fine.

Until their life fell apart, and the laughter stopped. Now, here they were, on the road to the last Christmas they'd spend together. It felt wrong.

There had to be a way to turn back the clock, but he had no idea where to find it.

7

Nothing like staying up too late and drinking too much wine to make a girl oversleep. Which was exactly what Audrey and Shyla did.

Audrey checked the time on her cell phone and was instantly awake. Ack!

"Wake up," she said, giving her sister's shoulder a shake.

"Not now, Milton," Shyla mumbled.

"Wake *up*," Audrey repeated, shaking more vigorously.

"Wha?" Her sister swallowed and half opened an eye.

"We need to get on the road," Audrey said and jumped out of bed.

Shyla pushed her hair out of her face and rose up on one elbow. "What time is it?"

"Time to get up, that's what time it is. Come on."

"Okay, okay. You can shower first, and I'll make the jet fuel."

"Don't go back to sleep," Audrey commanded and started digging out her clothes for the day.

"Wouldn't dream of it," Shyla said and flopped her head back down.

"Oh, no, you don't."

Audrey yanked off all the covers, and her sister sat up and glared at her. "Hey."

"Get. Up."

"Okay, okay. Give me a minute to adjust to morning."

"Adjust standing up," Audrey advised.

"Hey, not all of us are morning people."

"And not all of us are slugs. Come on."

Shyla slid out of bed, still wearing the glare. "I sure hope coffee improves your attitude."

It almost did, along with the bear claws she'd brought for their breakfast. But then her sister the poke took forever getting ready, and that irritated her afresh.

Shyla had just finished drying her hair and was about to spend another half hour transforming an already-pretty face when Audrey put her foot down. "You can do your makeup in the car. We need to get moving if you want to stop in Reno."

"All right already. Sheesh. We'll be fine. Don't be so anal."

"I am not being anal. I'm trying to keep us on schedule."

"And being bossy. Don't forget *bossy*."

"Are you going to be a pain the butt the whole trip?" Audrey demanded.

"I was about to ask you the same thing. Unwind, sissy. It's Christmas."

Yes, it was, and Audrey wanted things to go smoothly. What was Shyla's problem?

The fact that Audrey was being bossy.

Darn, it was a hard habit to break. She'd always been

in charge: translating for Shyla when she was first learning to talk, helping her with homework, doing her best to protect her from jealous mean girls and comfort her when she broke up with her boyfriend of the week. Well, and okay, so she'd acted like Mom 2.0 sometimes. Big sisters were supposed to be in charge.

You're not the boss of me became Shyla's favorite phrase once she hit first grade.

Audrey still remembered the last time she'd said that, right before she trampled through poison ivy taking a shortcut back to their tent on a family camping trip. Audrey had tried to point out the jagged edges and tears that said *Danger, danger!* and told her not to take that shortcut, but Shyla hadn't listened.

They weren't kids anymore, though. And so what if they got out of the city a little later than planned? Was it really that big a deal?

"Okay, fine," she said, forcing herself to chill. "I'm not the boss of you," she added, which made Shyla smile. The smile got bigger when Audrey finished with, "Unless we run into poison ivy."

"Or contaminated drinking water. Let me know about that."

"Or rattlesnakes?"

"Or kidnappers."

"Anyone kidnapping you would end up paying Mom and Dad to take you back," Audrey teased.

"No, that would be you. Me they'd like."

She was probably right. Audrey was the smart one, but Shyla was the one with the social skills. She could speed-read people faster than Audrey could read the title of a book.

Still, Audrey knew how to plan a schedule. "But you

still need to put your makeup on in the car," she said and went to load her suitcase.

Finally on the road, they started to crawl their way out of San Francisco traffic. At one point Audrey had to tap on the brakes, which didn't do Shyla's beautifying any good.

"Hey, will you watch it?" she said. "I almost poked my eye out."

"Don't blame me. Blame this traffic."

"It's no worse than LA."

"It's no better, either. At the rate we're going we'll never make Reno, let alone Winnemucca."

"We'll be fine," said Shyla, totally unconcerned.

Easy for her to say. What did she have to worry about? She hadn't planned the trip or made the motel reservations. She was just along for the ride.

It seemed they'd barely got going before Shyla was ready to make a stop. "I need a Starbucks fix," she announced.

"Seriously? It hasn't been that long since breakfast."

"I don't want to eat. I just want an eggnog latte."

Audrey gave up and gave in. "Okay. What's ten more minutes?"

"Exactly," said Shyla.

"Except I thought you were dieting."

"I am. Those black bean brownies weren't fattening."

Audrey couldn't help cocking an eyebrow at her sister. "Who told you that? There was sugar in them. Plus black beans have a high carbohydrate count."

Shyla frowned. "They do? Well, then, it's a good thing I sent the last of them home with Milton. And I still want a latte."

"Actually, a latte sounds good," Audrey admitted.

"And you have to make fun stops on a sister trip, right?"

"Right. But not too many," Audrey warned. Good grief. If her sister was in charge of this trip, they'd never make it to Julia's in time for Christmas.

"I thought you were in a hurry to get over the pass," Michelle said as Max turned in to her favorite coffee shop. It sounded like a jab instead of gratitude. But really, what was he thinking? They needed to get over the pass.

"I thought you might want a caffeine hit," he said. "If you don't I can pull out before we get in the drive-through."

"No. Since we're here we may as well stop."

Max was doing something nice, and she sounded like an ingrate. But really, was buying a latte supposed to make everything right between them?

Still, there was no need to be a bitch. "Thanks," she added.

He didn't say anything, just nodded.

She didn't have to tell him what she wanted to drink. He knew.

"Thanks," she said again when he handed over the peppermint mocha, trying to inject some civility into her voice.

"You're welcome," he said, his voice frosty, a sure sign he was still miffed over her ingratitude.

Which didn't do much for her own attitude. So what if he was miffed? Let him be.

She thought back to the last car trip they'd taken together. Before things blew up. They'd gone to the Washington coast and rented a house right on the beach. He'd had the radio on, and she'd sung along with Adele all the way down.

"I never get tired of hearing you sing," Max said after Michelle and Adele had finished serenading him. "You could have been a star."

"Making a job out of singing would have taken the fun out of it," she said. "I like to sing because I'm happy."

"Well, you make me happy," he said and reached a hand over to rest on her thigh.

She was going to make him even happier, she knew. Now that she'd agreed to go ahead and try for a fourth child.

The same doubt that had made her balk when he first brought up the subject four years earlier came rushing back at her. She had to be out of her mind to finally agree to this. Yes, they were doing fine financially, so money wasn't a concern anymore. But age was. And unlike money, you couldn't replace the years you'd spent. They were too old to be trying to make another baby. Audrey had finished college and was out of the house. Shyla was finishing up college, living on campus and busy with school and a whirlwind social life. And Julia was in high school. Two girls grown and one nearly there. They were practically empty nesters. What were they thinking? By the time this new child graduated from college they'd be getting senior discounts.

Of course, lots of people had children later in life. One of her regular customers at the Hallmark store had recently had a baby at forty-five and was deliriously happy. The baby was healthy and adorable. It could happen.

But so could bad things, and even though she'd agreed to try for one last child, she still couldn't help worrying. Their last try when she was in her thirties had ended in a miscarriage. Who was to say this wouldn't?

Miscarriage wasn't the only possible problem. The older you got the riskier pregnancy became. She would be forty-four in a couple of weeks, and if she got pregnant it would be considered a geriatric pregnancy. *Geriatric* at forty-four. It was a disgusting term. But biologically accurate. Forty-four wasn't exactly old, but it wasn't young, either. Menopause was right around the corner, which in terms of reproduction was old age. The fertile years would be gone. This was their last chance.

Suddenly, she didn't feel like singing.

She wished this romantic Labor Day getaway didn't have any underlying purpose, wished they were just two people in love spending time together. In fact, she wished she'd already gone through menopause, wrapped things up early like her mom had. Then they could have fun, just the two of them. They'd have grandbabies to play with and spoil in the future. Maybe that should be enough.

But it wouldn't be enough for Max.

They checked into the hotel, then took a walk on the beach before the September sun set. They dined at a restaurant with a gorgeous view. They drank champagne, and she got a little tipsy.

"Might as well enjoy it now," Max said.

Yes, because once she was pregnant, she wouldn't be drinking. The sun was setting outside the restaurant, and a waiter was starting to light candles on the tables. She suddenly felt cold and shivered.

"Come on, let's get back to the room," he suggested. *Let's go make a baby.*

Back in the room, Max didn't simply work on making a baby. He worked on making her almost go out of her mind with pleasure. *And in the Sexual Olympics, Max Turnbull brings home the gold.*

And it looked like nine months later they'd be bringing home a new member of the family. The missed period and the home pregnancy test confirmed it.

Max was excited.

Michelle was too scared to be excited. What had they done? More to the point, why had they done it? Why had she let him talk her into this?

She asked herself the same question twelve weeks later but this time it wasn't prompted by worry. This time it was filled with bitterness.

Watching the snow through the car window as they made their way back home from the hospital, Michelle felt as if a million ghostly spirits were circling them. Spirits of all the babies who never made it safely out of the womb.

She choked back a sob, and Max laid a hand on her leg. "It'll be okay," he said.

But it wouldn't.

The cause of the miscarriage had been chromosomal abnormality. Translation: old eggs. They'd waited too long to make that final try for the boy Max wanted, and nature had punished them. Or maybe it was God.

No, it was Max who'd brought this on them.

Back home she couldn't get warm. Clothes still on, she piled on extra blankets and curled into a ball in their bed. He slipped in beside her, wrapped an arm around her and snugged her up against him.

It didn't make her feel any better.

Nothing made her feel any better.

"We'll get through this," he said.

How? How did you get past the feeling of loss, the anger? She said nothing.

He kissed her cheek and whispered, "I love you."

She knew she needed to say the words back to him, but they wouldn't come out. She wasn't sure she loved him. She wasn't even sure she loved herself.

Her mother brought her chicken soup and the kind of comfort and empathy she specialized in.

"I'm sorry, darling," she said. "I know it's not easy. To lose a baby is to lose a dream."

"I knew we shouldn't have tried," Michelle said miserably.

"Life is all about trying," her mom said. "If your father and I hadn't kept trying we'd have never had you. Or our granddaughters," she added, a subtle reminder that Michelle had been blessed with three healthy children.

The ones she had didn't make the loss of this one any easier.

Max brought home takeout for dinner the next night, and they both sat at the kitchen table and picked at their food. "We shouldn't have waited so long," he said at last.

Was he blaming her?

"We shouldn't have even tried," she snapped. "You shouldn't have pushed me." She'd been well aware of the possible complications and hadn't wanted to risk it. It was his selfishness that had led to this loss and heartbreak. "I told you I'm too old."

"You're not that old," he insisted. "And I thought you wanted the baby, too."

"Because I finally went along with you?"

He glared at his kung pao chicken. Then he shoved away the plate, tipping over a carton of chow mein in the process, and left the table.

She sat looking at the spilled mess and wished she'd shoved it in his face.

Later that night he apologized, but she didn't. She had nothing to apologize for.

The girls circled the wagons around her. Julia did her chores without being nagged, trying not to rock her mother's emotional boat. Shyla bought Michelle's favorite ice cream. Audrey texted and called several times during the week to check on her, and each time Michelle told her she was fine.

She wasn't. She was exhausted, both physically and mentally. Getting dressed was a chore. Why bother? Why bother with anything or anyone? She wished Max hadn't told people about the pregnancy. It was like he'd jinxed them.

Audrey offered to bring over DVDs of her favorite movies and keep her company, but she declined. She didn't feel like laughing at Steve Martin, and she didn't want to watch Sabrina fall in love. She especially didn't want to have to wear a brave face in front of her too-perceptive firstborn. It wasn't a comfortable fit.

It wasn't comfortable having to be around her husband, either, to try and have any kind of rational conversation. She went to bed before he did and pretended to be asleep when he said her name. She stayed there in the morning, eyes tightly shut, until he left for work.

Julia was out one night and she was in the living

room, wrapped in a blanket and watching some mindless reality show on TV, when Max joined her on the couch and put an arm around her.

"Chelle, come on, talk to me," he pleaded.

"What do you want me to say?"

"Something. Anything."

The tears were stinging her eyes. She pressed her lips together, shook her head. There was nothing to say.

"We had to try."

She shrugged out from under him. "No, we didn't." She kept her gaze forward but could see his frown out of the corner of her eye.

"It would have been fine if we'd just tried earlier, like I wanted," he said.

Like *he* wanted. As if it was her fault that she'd worried they couldn't afford another child, that she hadn't jumped on board with his plan to try one more time for a mini me for him.

"The business was still struggling," she reminded him. How easily he forgot that money had been tight.

"The business has done fine. You could have trusted me, Chelle."

She glared at him. "I did finally trust you, and look what happened. I knew better. I knew deep down it was a bad idea, but you wouldn't listen."

"I'm sorry," he said, his voice rising.

If he was sorry, why was he yelling? "It doesn't matter now. It's all too late. And it's all your fault."

He stiffened and pulled away. She returned her attention to the TV screen, pretended he wasn't there.

Finally, he left, and in that moment she scrubbed all the things he'd done right over the years and all the things she loved about him from her mind. Her misery was on his shoulders. He'd been the instigator, the one who'd kept insisting it would be great to have one more kid, that it wasn't too late. She'd carried that child long enough to fall in love with it, and then she'd lost it, and it was his fault. His selfishness had brought them to this, and she couldn't forgive him.

The snow mixed with rain that they'd seen when they first left Maple Valley had become more hefty as they'd gotten onto Highway 18, turning into fat flakes, adding to what had fallen the previous day. Much of the white stuff had been pounded away by traffic, but the new snowfall was quickly recoating the road. The snow was swirling madly around them.

Michelle checked the weather on her phone. Not good. It was dumping in the mountains. The Washington State Department of Transportation tried to keep the pass open for travelers, usually doing travel-blocking things like avalanche control at night. But sometimes, they couldn't if there were accidents or there was a heavy amount of snow in a short period of time. Further checking, both on her phone and out the car window at the thick cloud of white flakes flying around them and piling up everywhere, told her there was a pass closure coming 'round the bend. They might not make it over before that. She wished they hadn't stopped for coffee.

"I'm famished," Shyla announced as the sisters drove into Reno. *The Biggest Little City in the World* proclaimed the iconic sign over the strip. The city wasn't a glitz giant like Las Vegas, but it had a rustic feel to it that Audrey found appealing, and all the mountains surrounding it, especially the Virginia range, which lay to the east of the city, gave it a picturesque backdrop.

Shyla hadn't done any research on where to stay on their trip or the amount of miles they had to cover, but she had researched restaurants and casinos. She dragged Audrey into a casino that Shyla had assured her would be great fun to check out. The Rawhide Casino was off the main drag and was sure to have lots of atmosphere. And who knew? Audrey could end up meeting some hunkaroo cowboy there.

Or not. "Where did you learn about this place?" Audrey asked in disgust as they walked inside.

"Online," Shyla said. "The diner's supposed to be great."

"According to the owner's mother?"

"Ha ha. It's one of those places the locals all go to, and locals always know the best places to eat."

"I bet this one never made it into any brochure, and if it's on the chamber of commerce website, that's probably because money changed hands," said Audrey.

It had no hotel attached, and Shyla had been right about one thing. It appeared to be strictly for locals. No high rollers here. Only low rollers. It was dingy and smelled like smoke.

The diner had a fragrance all its own. It smelled like grease and heart attacks.

"Seriously?" Audrey said as they stood at the entrance to the casino's restaurant. Somehow she'd pictured them eating a slightly more upscale lunch. In a slightly more upscale establishment.

"It's got great atmosphere," Shyla insisted. She made a sweeping gesture in the direction of the casino's slot machines. "Look at all those cowboys, pardner."

Audrey rolled her eyes. A couple of nice-looking men were in there, but for the most part she saw scruffy losers.

"Oh, please," she said.

"I know what you like to read. I know you like cowboys."

"I like my cowboys in a book," Audrey said. "Where they have jobs. And muscles."

And they behaved and came to their senses by the end of the story. Not like certain men in real life.

"I bet those guys have jobs," Shyla insisted, "and—"

Audrey cut her off. "I wouldn't give those tools the time of day, let alone my phone number."

"You're such a snob," Shyla said in disgust.

"There is such a thing as standards," Audrey said in response.

"Fine if you want to be a lemming and follow the crowd," Shyla taunted.

Audrey heaved a long-suffering sigh. "Okay, let's see if we can find something edible on the menu."

They did succeed in that department. Cholesterol be damned, the hamburgers were great. Of course, after they ate, Shyla wanted to try her hand at the slots. "After all, we're in Reno. I thought we were going to have some fun along the way."

"We should get back on the road," Audrey said. "We're behind schedule."

"What are we, a railroad? We'll be fine. Come on."

"You have no concept of time."

"Oh, stop already. We've got plenty of time."

Audrey would have liked nothing better than to get her sister in a headlock (which she'd had no problem doing when they were kids) and drag her out of the casino. They were a little too old for that, though, so she opted for compromise.

"Okay, half an hour," she said.

"Forty-five minutes," Shyla bargained. "Loosen up."

"Forty-five minutes. But no more," Audrey added, pointing a finger at Shyla for emphasis. "I'll be back."

"See you in an hour, Terminator. Where are you going while I'm having fun?"

"I'm going to take a walk and actually see something of the city."

"Good idea. I was going to suggest you take a hike," Shyla said with a smirk.

"Very funny," Audrey replied and took her irritable self out of the casino.

The air was sharp and crisp, which called for brisk walking with her gloved hands in her pockets. The streets were clear, but wafers of snow from an earlier, light snowfall still lay scattered along their edges, a little bit of winter seasoning in an area mostly known for its desert heat. She found plenty to see, including a huge climbing wall on the edge of the Whitney Peak Hotel, which towered over the top of the Reno Arch. At a hundred and sixty-four feet tall, the thing looked as terrifying to her as a mountain. Julia would happily scurry up it like a little squirrel. Shyla, too, but rock climbing there or anywhere would never make Audrey's bucket list.

She decided not to do the river walk along the Truckee River, instead checking out The Row, the central underground walkway connecting the city's three major casinos. *Shyla would love this*, she thought as she passed the many shops and restaurants decked out with greenery. They should have eaten somewhere there.

And her sister could have just as easily lost her money in
the glitzy Circus Circus or Eldorado. Well, she'd wanted
local color. She was sure getting it. A pretty ugly color
compared to what Audrey was seeing.

As for color, there wasn't time to check out all the
murals scattered around the city, but she was entranced
by the ones she saw. *We should have allowed a full
day here*, she thought as she stood in front of an atmospheric mural featuring horses with the Untamed West
as a background.

Maybe she'd have to come back. The open spaces and
wildness surrounding the city appealed to her.

Of course, at the moment anywhere but where she
was living appealed to her. (Not that her pride would
ever let her admit it to her mom.) LA now felt like a
constant reminder of the fact that she'd left her home
state for a relationship mirage. Life there wasn't so fun
after getting dumped. It had been six months, but the
wounds still smarted.

A change of scenery, a change of lifestyle—would
that do it? She sighed. Probably not. The problem with
going someplace new was that wherever you went, there
you were.

No, no, no. That was all wrong. She could take herself anywhere, darn it all, because she wasn't the problem. He had been. Wherever she went she could start
over.

She paused in front of a pawnshop. All the sparkling
jewelry in the window caught her attention. So many
diamond rings. What was the story behind them? How
many breakups and buckets of tears were represented
in that display case?

She and Dennis hadn't gotten to the ring stage, but

with all the tears she'd shed, one would have thought they had. She'd been sure that was the direction they'd been headed. How could she not have been when he said things to her like, "You are amazing" and "I am one lucky SOB to have found you." She'd felt the same way.

A lucky escape, she reminded herself. But even with lucky escapes you could get banged up pretty good. And in the end, realizing that he didn't really appreciate her, didn't want her… She pushed back the tears. He didn't deserve any more than she'd already given him.

"I wasted a lot of Ina Garten recipes on you," she muttered.

A middle-aged man in a Western-style suit and boots walked by. "That's a good one, little lady, if you got a ring weighing you down," he said in passing.

"Thanks," she murmured. No ring weighing her down. Only memories of her failed relationship. Too bad you couldn't pawn those.

She checked the time on her smartwatch. She needed to return to the casino and collect Shyla. It was time to get going.

She found her sister at the slot machines, but she wasn't exactly concentrating on playing. Instead, she appeared to be shooing away one of those atmospheric cowboys she'd pointed out earlier. *Fake cowboy*, more like. Jeans and a Western shirt did not a cowboy make, especially when you were wearing tennis shoes. Especially when you had a beer gut. He was being an offensive pest while a sunbaked old geezer who looked like he might have ridden the range a few lifetimes ago lounged at a nearby machine, enjoying the show.

SHEILA ROBERTS   111

Oh, no. Nobody messed with Shyla, not on Audrey's watch. With narrowed eyes, she marched over.

She was approaching when she heard Shyla say, "Your keeper's probably looking for you, so why don't you take it on the arches?"

"Now, that's not very friendly," said Mr. Fake Cowboy, leaning a hefty arm on her shoulder. He bent lower and looked about ready to stick his tongue in her ear, and she shrugged him off. But of course, that wouldn't stop him from trying again.

Yep, here was a prime example of primate. "Hey!"

Audrey's commanding voice got his attention, and he turned and blinked in surprise. Then his eyes lit up like mini slot machines, and he grinned.

"Well, now, who we got here?" he said, straightening up.

"Big Billy Goat Gruff," cracked Shyla, grabbing her purse.

"Ha! That's a good one," he said.

"But I had this under control," Shyla informed Audrey.

"Yeah, I can tell," Audrey said to her. "Come on, let's go."

"Hey, now. What's your hurry, sweetheart?"

The dude closed the distance between Audrey and himself, and it sure wasn't like a scene in a novel that turned you all tingly when you read it. He smelled like beer and sweat. Gram would have politely said, *Somebody didn't use his dew drops.*

"Not in the mood," Audrey said in a voice that would have told anyone with half a brain to back off.

"I bet I can get you in the mood. Stay and play, sister," he said, reaching for her hair.

He was right in front of her, perfectly positioned and asking for it. So she let him have it, the old knee-to-the-crotch move.

He doubled over with a yelp.

"Impressive there, little sister," said the old lizard. "I was about to step in, but I could see you had it handled."

"Always," said Shyla. As they left, she said to Audrey. "I had things under control, Wonder Woman."

"Oh, really."

"I just didn't want to make a scene."

"Neither did I, which was why I didn't drag you out of there by your hair. Good grief, Shyla. How long had that crap been going on?"

"Not long. He stopped by and asked if I was winning right before you thundered on the scene. Which I wasn't, darn it all. Anyway, he decided he needed to stick around and give me pointers. I'd have had him gone in a minute without resorting to assault."

"Uh-huh."

"I would have," Shyla insisted. "Shit, Audrey. What did you think he was going to do to me right there in the middle of the casino?"

"Who knows?"

"You should never have let Mom talk you into watching *Thelma and Louise* with her."

"I wasn't trying to be Thelma."

"Louise is the one who shot the guy," Shyla corrected her.

"So Mom got you to watch it with her, too."

That brought a reluctant smile. "No, it was Gram. Family tradition."

"Don't we have the interesting ones."

"Oh, well," Shyla said and linked her arm through

Audrey's. "I'm glad you've got my back. And I'll have yours, too, if you ever need it. Which you won't," she added and sounded almost disappointed. "You're a better Louise than the one in the movie."

"Yeah?"

"Yeah. You didn't shoot anybody, which saves us from having to run for our lives and drive off a cliff. I'm really not up for that."

Audrey grinned. "Me, neither."

"So, how about checking out a couple of pawnshops before we leave? We can get some great bargains on jewelry. It'll be almost like checking out *Pawn Stars*."

"Those guys are in Vegas."

"Well, this is almost Vegas," Shyla argued. "Reno, Biggest Little City in the World. Casinos and gambling, people losing money at the tables, pawning all kinds of valuable stuff."

"And then other people swooping in like buzzards and getting it."

"That's me, Betty Buzzard. Anyway, since when are you not up for a bargain? Did you learn nothing about smart shopping from Mom and Gram?"

Audrey shook her head. "I looked in the window of one while I was waiting for you, and that was enough for me. It was depressing. All those abandoned engagement rings. I couldn't help wondering what they'd say if they could talk."

"They'd probably say *She should never have put me on her finger*. Losers happen."

"Don't I know it," Audrey said bitterly.

"So do winners, and you're gonna be one. That ring is out there somewhere just waiting to find your finger."

"I guess I didn't get the memo."

"Not to worry. I already had a talk with Santa. He's on it."

"No way am I trusting a man who never shaves and wears the same red suit all year long."

Shyla giggled. "That was pretty good. But you shouldn't make fun of Santa. He might bring you a lump of coal for Christmas instead of your perfect man."

Audrey gave a snort. "There is no such thing."

"Oh, yes, there is."

"Honestly, you are so naive sometimes. Life's not like a Hallmark movie, you know." Which was a shame, because Audrey had come to love them.

"And it's not always like a slasher movie, either. With that attitude you probably wouldn't recognize your perfect man even if Santa dropped him right in your bed," Shyla scolded.

That produced another snort. "Yeah, well, I dare him to."

"You are asking for a Santa smackdown. I sure hope I'm around to see it."

"A Santa smackdown?" Audrey repeated. "What's that?"

"You being made to eat your cynical words, that's what. Now, come on, back to business. One pawnshop."

Audrey heaved a sigh. "Okay."

They went inside the one where she'd looked in the window. It offered everything from tools and musical instruments to electronics. And, of course, jewelry. While Shyla ogled the rings, Audrey drifted around the shop. She paused in front of the collection of guitars, remembering the last time she'd heard her mother sing. It had been at her mom's cousin's second wedding. One of Mom's other cousins had played the guitar, and Mom

had sung some old song about white lace and promises.
It had been beautiful.

She missed her mother's singing.

Audrey frowned and rejoined her sister, who was
trying on an amethyst ring.

"What do you think?" Shyla asked, holding out her
hand for inspection.

"It's pretty."

"And it's my birthstone."

"Mom gave you one with your birthstone."

"When I was sixteen."

"So it doesn't fit anymore?"

"I lost it. Don't tell Mom."

"Guess you'd better buy that one, then," Audrey said.

It was what her sister wanted to hear. "I think so.
Can't beat the price," Shyla said and whipped out her
charge card.

"Now can we go?" Audrey asked as they left the store.

"Now we can go," Shyla said, giving her a grin and
a shoulder bump.

They reached Audrey's Toyota, and Shyla held out a
hand. "Here. Give me the keys. It's my turn to drive."

"Oh, no. I like my car. And even if I don't have a
man in my life, I still want to live."

"Stop being such a control freak. It's a major sign
of insecurity."

"I am not a control freak," Audrey insisted.

"Then, let me drive. You need a break." Shyla wag-
gled her fingers. "What? Chicken?"

"With you behind the wheel? Cluck, cluck."

"We're going to be in the middle of nowhere. What
do you think is going to happen? I'm gonna hit a tum-

bleweed? Or an armadillo? Except this isn't Texas so we're at least safe from that."

"They have them here, and they're on the rise," Audrey informed her. "But we probably won't encounter one. They're mostly nocturnal, and they tend to hibernate in their burrows a lot in winter."

Shyla shook her head. "Leave it to my sister to know. Anyway, now that we've eliminated the threat of an armadillo accident, I think you can trust me to drive for a couple of hours. And I want to pull my share."

"You are. You're paying for the gas."

"Come on, Audrey," Shyla said, losing patience. "I'm not sixteen anymore, and I'm not going to kill us."

Audrey got the point. She did still tend to fall into those old birth-order patterns and treat her sister like the baby.

"Okay, fine," she said, handing over the keys. Then couldn't help adding, "But don't speed."

She was pretty sure she heard her sister swear under her breath as she walked around to the driver's side.

"We're getting Starbucks before we hit the road," Shyla announced as they roared away from the curb. "And no arguments," she added with a wink.

"You're not going to drive crazy like this all the way to Winnemucca, are you?" Audrey demanded. Maybe there was something to be said for keeping those birth-order behaviors in place after all.

"Gotta make up all that time we lost, right?" Shyla said with smirk.

"I knew I shouldn't have given you the car keys," Audrey said. With her sister at the wheel, who knew what would happen?

8

Hazel and Warren were in a diner taking a lunch break when a young couple walked in and took a table nearby. They were both bundled in winter coats and boots and torn jeans. There was a time when torn jeans meant you were poor. Now it meant you were stylish.

A silly style if you asked Hazel. But then, who was she to talk? In the eighties, when she was in her thirties and thought she was hot stuff, she'd worn jeans with her high heels…and shoulder pads in her dresses and jackets that made her look like a linebacker. And big, big, big hair. She had a few photos in the family album that she would never let see the light of day. Then there were leg warmers. Couldn't forget those if you were going to aerobics class, because nothing accented a leotard and tights and tennis shoes like leg warmers.

Yep, she couldn't judge.

But darn, she had been sexy back then.

"I sure miss my youth," she said, coveting the girl's smooth skin. *Someday you, too, will have wrinkles. And thinning hair. No waistline. Leg dandruff.* She sighed.

"You're still as beautiful as the day I first saw you," Warren said.

She shook her head at him. "Your vision's not that great anymore."

"You're a beautiful woman," he insisted.

Love saw what it wanted to. But then, when she looked at Warren it didn't bother her that he had a paunch and that his hair was even thinner than hers and all gray. He was still her man and a wonderful man at that.

"I can still see you on that first night we met, out on the dance floor in that red disco dress."

She'd noticed him, too. She'd gone to the club with some friends and spotted him when he first came into the bar, a tall husky man in stylin' brown bell-bottom pants and a neon green shirt. Yep, the 1970s hadn't been the best fashion decade, either.

He'd come right up to their table and crashed the party. She'd laughed when he told her someday she was going to marry him. "Says who?"

"Says me," he'd replied. "You wait. I'll be the best thing that ever happened to you."

"You've got a fat head," she'd said.

But he'd also had a great smile and a big heart. And he'd been right. He was the best thing that ever happened to her. She'd thought she'd marry a well-educated man, had always pictured herself with a teacher or a banker. Instead, she'd wound up with a man who'd decided a high-school diploma and trade school was good enough for him, and he'd turned out to be smarter than anyone she dated in college.

Warren had always been a big man on so many levels. Sometimes she wished she could turn back time simply for the privilege of reliving the happy life she'd enjoyed with him.

"I envy those two," she said, looking at the young couple. "They have so many adventures ahead of them still."

"So do we," Warren said.

She hoped so.

The diner was pretty much empty, so it was easy enough to tell who Warren was talking to when he called over to the couple. "Where you kids headed?"

"On our way to see her parents," said the man. "We just got engaged," he added, and she held up her left hand to show off the tiny diamond in the ring.

"Well, congratulations," Warren said.

They both beamed and thanked him, then returned their attention to each other.

"Ain't love grand," Warren said. He fished his wallet out of his back pocket and signaled their server, a trim woman who didn't look much older than the couple at the nearby table.

Babies. They were all babies, Hazel thought wistfully.

"Are you ready for some dessert?" asked their server.

"I'm full," Hazel said.

"Guess not," Warren said to the woman. "We'll take the check." He pulled out a fifty-dollar bill and handed it over. "Meanwhile, though, I want to pay for that couple over there. Keep whatever's left for your tip."

The woman's eyes lit up. "That's really sweet of you."

"It's the season," Warren said.

That was Warren. He'd been paying it forward before anyone ever thought up the idea. "You are a good man, Warren Turnbull," Hazel said as the woman moved away to get their check.

He chuckled. "That's what I keep tellin' ya."

Hazel's phone lit up to announce a text.

"Don't tell me, let me guess. It's the kids," said Warren.

"Julia's checking to see how we're doing."

"Tell her we're doing great," he said and downed the last of his coffee. Warren took it black, no sugar added, because he claimed sweetener was for wimps. He also took it decaf, which he complained about, but too much caffeine was not good for a man whose heart tended to race. Without his meds that was the last thing they needed.

She wished they'd had the doctor call the prescription in for the nearby drugstore and delayed long enough to pick it up. But Warren took the attitude that delays of any kind were unacceptable. "I'll be fine till we get to St. Maries," he kept assuring her.

Except she didn't really feel assured. She should have put her foot down and insisted.

"Bad enough our kids fuss over us. Now we got the grandkids in the act, too," he grumbled. "What do they all think is gonna happen to us, anyway?"

"Anything can happen on a road trip," Hazel said. That sounded ominous. She put another packet of sugar in her tea.

"I don't know why they worry," he said with a frown.

"They think we're old."

Compared to their kids and grandkids they were. Funny how age was such a subjective thing. When Hazel was a young woman, people in their fifties seemed ancient, and seventy was as good as dead. But she was seventy, and she didn't feel any older than she had at fifty.

Until she looked in the mirror. That was always a

bit of a shock, as if she'd entered a fun house where the mirrors were distorted. Gray hairs, wrinkles, a saggy neck—she didn't want them. Where was the cosmic return counter? *Surely there's been some mistake*, she'd say, *because the way I feel certainly doesn't match the way I look.*

"Hazel, we ain't that old," said Warren, as if he'd read her thoughts.

In Warren's mind he was still forty and in his prime. But he wasn't. His reflexes were slowing. He was also starting to get a little forgetful.

Of course, so was she. People's names flew out of her mind at the most inopportune times. Or she'd forget the name of a movie they'd recently watched. Once she even forgot the fancy way she tied her favorite neck scarf when she was getting dressed for church. After a moment she'd remembered, but the experience had given her a jolt of terror. Every time she forgot something, she was sure she was getting Alzheimer's. Who knew? Maybe she was.

Were the kids noticing things she and Warren weren't? It was so easy to shrug off little signs of future big trouble. Maybe it was time to stop shrugging and get practical. Rethink doing some of the things they used to do so easily.

"We aren't as sharp as we used to be," she said to him.

He scowled. "We're also not staring into space, drooling, either. Tell her not to worry."

Hazel dutifully texted, We're fine. Then she said to her husband, "There does come a time when kids have a right to worry."

"Well, it ain't yet."

She thought about him forgetting his blood thinner. *Sooner than we like to think.*

But he had a point. Even though they weren't kids anymore, they weren't completely in their dotage.

She still couldn't help wishing they'd opted for staying home where it was safe.

Their server returned with the check. "Looks like the weather channel was right after all. Here comes that snow they were predicting."

Snow! If only they were already in Idaho.

It was more than the awful driving conditions putting Michelle on edge. It was the close proximity of her husband. The anger and resentment hung around them, a miasma of resentment and bitterness. How far they'd sunk from what they once had. Her mind drifted back to when she'd first met him.

Michelle had been running from six o'clock on, serving up burgers and fish and chips and beer, and her feet were killing her. And the macho loser who kept hitting on her was irritating her. Not that she couldn't handle him if he got out of hand, but still, it was like having to keep shooing away a mosquito.

If it wasn't for the tips—a hundred a night—she'd quit. But she didn't want to until she was done with school. It was her last quarter, and come the middle of June she'd have an AA in liberal arts, finishing the two-year degree with a 3.8 GPA. Not that it would lead to some impressive corporate career, but that was okay. She'd figure out where she wanted to go from there eventually. One thing she knew for sure: she wasn't going to keep working at Balls and Brews. More like Beers and Leers.

"I really hate this job," she said to Lindsey, another harried waitress.

"It's not that bad," Lindsey said. "A lot of cute guys come in here."

Michelle rolled her eyes. "None I want to hang out with. They're all proles."

"Oh, yeah? You must not have seen what just walked in a few minutes ago. He's seated in my section."

"Unless he looks like Rob Lowe, I'm not interested."

"Funny you should say that. They could be brothers."

"You're hallucinating. None of the regulars look like that," Michelle said.

"This one's a new regular."

"Same old new. These guys are all alike—burping contests, baseball stats and crass jokes."

"You know what your trouble is? You're a snob," Lindsey said.

"No, I'm not. I just don't want to settle. If a guy doesn't zing me, what's the point?"

Lindsey shook her head. "With all the cute guys who've hit on you, I think you're zinger's broken. But that's okay with me 'cause if this one hasn't been grabbed I'm taking him."

Michelle just chuckled as her friend grabbed her orders and hurried off. She wasn't looking for the kind of guy who haunted Balls and Brews, crass bozos who drank too much, laughed too loudly and talked dirty. She wanted someone with some class.

And he had to be kind. And easy to talk to. And looking for a real relationship, not a one-night stand, and certainly not a live-in girlfriend. No way was she going to lower her standards.

So far nobody she'd met, either at work or at school, had measured up. "You're asking too much," all her friends told her. She didn't think so.

On her way back to one of her tables—a four top of guys who were entertaining each other by trying to dangle their spoons off their noses—she caught sight of Lindsey's latest customers. She immediately knew which man Lindsey had been talking about. He did look like Rob Lowe. Her heart gave a little squeeze, and she almost tripped. Zing!

Okay, so he was gorgeous. So what? Gorgeous was nothing more than window dressing. Zingy window dressing, but still. Great-looking as he was, he was probably conceited. *Don't even go near there*, she told herself.

"We need a refill, gorgeous," said one of the guys, holding up their empty beer pitcher.

"You got it," Michelle said, forcing herself to smile. She hated it when men she didn't know called her *gorgeous* or *babe*. But she always let it slide. A chilly waitress never got a good tip.

She delivered a check to two tables, then hurried to get the beer. Thirsty customers remembered slow service, and they didn't tip well, either. She had the beer and was passing a table of rowdy regulars when a hefty man at one of her tables tried to get her attention by making a tipsy grab for her arm. She pulled away. "Be with you in a—"

The sentence went unfinished as she collided with six feet of solid male. Her pitcher sloshed up a wave of beer onto her sports jersey that then rivered its way down to her waist. And there he was, Mr. Gorgeous, looking horrified.

"Oh, man. I'm so sorry," he said.

"My fault," she said. Eww. She hated beer, hated the smell of the stuff, and now she'd just been drenched in it.

Not his fault, though. She was the one who'd run into him. He'd probably been on his way to the men's room, obviously minding his own business.

He grabbed a napkin from a nearby table and handed it to her. "This isn't really gonna help, is it?"

She made a feeble dab at her drenched chest. "It's the thought that counts."

"Oh, man," he said again.

"It's okay, really," she assured him. "All part of the job. Enjoy your meal."

"Not sure I can now."

"Try," she said and gave him a smile. She went back for a fresh pitcher, feeling all yucky and clammy. And something else. Zinged.

Michelle's supervisor found her another jersey, and she got back to work, glad that with the smell of greasy fries and beer in the place, none of her customers would notice the smell of her eau de Budweiser that still lingered on her. They probably wouldn't have cared anyway.

She tried not to look in the direction of the table where Rob Lowe Junior sat, but she couldn't seem to help herself. Every time she looked his way, she saw him looking at her. He'd wave and smile, and she'd feel her cheeks sizzling. *Stop looking!* She couldn't.

She was about to go on break when the hostess delivered a napkin with a note on it. *Let me make it up to you. Dinner? Do you like Italian?* It was signed *Max*. Max, what a cool name.

She showed it to Lindsey. "Think I should go?"

"I think you're a fool if you don't," Lindsey said. "Darn. If you weren't so nice I'd have to hate you. I've been flirting my ass off with him and getting nowhere."

"I guess you should have spilled beer on yourself," Michelle said.

"If I'd known that was what it took, I'd have jumped in barrel of it."

Michelle wrote her number on a napkin and had Lindsey deliver it. This would probably go nowhere. He'd turn out to be all looks and no substance. But maybe not. He'd already shown that he was a nice guy. He called the next afternoon, and before she knew it she had a date for Sunday.

Max came to her house, met her parents, told them he was from Oregon and studying business at the University of Washington. A man with goals, and obviously smart. He was quick to add that he didn't normally spill beer on a girl to get her attention.

"Not that he did," Michelle said. "It was my fault."

"Well, you enjoy yourselves," her mom said and smiled at Michelle as if to say, *Looks like you might have found a good one.*

Michelle thought the same thing as they strolled along the Seattle waterfront, looking for a place to eat.

"Sorry the Italian place was closed. I guess a lot of restaurants close on Sunday," he said.

"It's okay. Everybody needs a day off once in a while," Michelle said.

So instead of Italian they wound up at Ivar's Fish Bar, eating fish and chips. "There's something you never get where you work," he said and laughed. "So far I'm not making a very good impression."

He was making a fabulous impression. "It's okay," she said. "I happen to like fish and chips." And she liked Max.

"How did you end up working at Balls and Brews?" he asked. "Somehow, I picture you working someplace more, I don't know, high-class."

"Like?" she prompted.

"Canlis."

"That is definitely a step above where I am now. A lot of steps."

"I bet you don't see yourself working as a waitress at all, though. Maybe a scientist?"

She shook her head. "Never liked dissecting frogs."

"Running a company?"

"Sounds stressful."

"What would you like to do?"

She shrugged. "I don't know. I'm not sure what a liberal arts degree is going to get me."

"Educated," he said, and she smiled.

"I really haven't figured out my future, but I think I'd be happy with a simple job in retail. I don't need a high-powered career."

"What do you need?" he asked.

"To be happy. I'm not out to set the world on fire, just to make my own corner of it a better place."

"I'd say that sounds like a winning goal," he said.

"It's where I am now."

"A good place to be."

They strolled along the waterfront, checking out the various attractions like Ye Olde Curiosity Shop, where he bought her a set of Russian nesting dolls.

"Are you like that, several versions of the same woman?" he asked.

She shook her head. "What you see is what you get." She suddenly wished she was more complex, an ambitious woman of many talents.

"I like what I see," he said, and his smile sent a charge of electricity through her chest.

"Never mind me. Tell me about yourself," she said. *Are you as wonderful as you seem?*

"Not that much to tell. My old man's proud of me, I will say that. He never went to college, and he's pretty stoked that I'm going to be graduating this year. It took a while. I worked for a couple of years first and saved up."

"I'd say you have plenty to be proud of," Michelle said.

"I'm doing okay. So," he asked, "you got any brothers lurking around who are gonna threaten to beat me up?"

"One, but he's going to college in California, so you're safe. You'd like him."

"Yeah? Would he like me?"

"Absolutely." *What's not to like?* she thought.

"I never got a brother or sister. Sometimes I feel like I missed out."

"You did," she said. "Family is important."

"Yes, it is. So's finding the right person."

A week later, when he brought her home from their second date—this time a drive all the way to Snoqualmie Falls for brunch—and kissed her, she knew she'd found the right person. When his arms went around her, every nerve in her body came to life, and the touch of his lips melted her. Max Turnbull was the best thing that ever happened to her.

After that they were inseparable. Being with him

filled her with happiness, and she knew—just knew—
that the love they had was too big, too strong to ever die.

With just one life-changing event, they'd gone from
that to...this. Michelle could almost hear her mother
saying, *When there's a problem, everyone plays a part
in making it.*

She could feel her defenses rising as if her mother
was right there next to her. Max had played the biggest
part in their problem, not her. She shut her eyes, trying to hide from the mental picture of her own angry
self. Honesty demanded she open them. *You played
your part.*

She still was.

Grudges. You could bury grief, try to move forward, go through the motions, but a grudge was a different matter. Grudges refused to stay underground and
popped up when least wanted—when you were at a
party and your husband made a stupid joke about your
collection of vintage china growing out of control; when
you were at a garage sale with your mother-in-law, and
she asked how you were doing; when your husband
wanted to have sex, and the very idea turned you off.

When your emotions were swinging all over the
place, and you were starting to get hot flashes.

When he started meeting his friends at the local bar
after work on Fridays. Like he was in some episode of
that old TV show, *Cheers.*

When you were empty nesters and should be doing
things together and planning exotic vacations, but he
kept working longer hours, and you realized it was yet
another example of how selfish he was.

Grudges always pointed fingers away from you,

never at you. They kept score and kept adding points to the scoreboard. They knew you were right, and they always clawed their way back to life just when you'd thought you were done with them.

How could they stay buried when you kept them alive?

But darn it all, didn't she have a right to? Ugh. What was she doing here in this vehicle with him? And in these weather conditions? How was this all going to end? She was afraid to guess.

The snow was a thick curtain around them as Max crept the SUV farther up into the Cascades.

"We're never going to make it over the pass," Michelle fretted.

"We'll be fine," he said, but the words came out harshly.

"We shouldn't have stopped for coffee."

As if ten minutes made that much difference. "I was trying to do something nice, okay?" he snapped. Damn it all, what was the point? "Guess I shouldn't have bothered."

"I guess you shouldn't," she said, her words stiff.

"The real problem is that we didn't leave earlier," Max informed her. And that hadn't been his fault.

She gnawed on her lip, stared out the window as if expecting to see the Abominable Snowman jump out in front of them any minute. "I wish we'd left yesterday."

"I could have taken the day off. But it's too late now. We're stuck with what we've got."

"That's not my fault," she was quick to say.

"I never said it was." Were they going to get into it now, on a snow-infested highway with limited visibility? He gripped the steering wheel more tightly. "Look, let's try to make the best of this. Okay?"

"Okay," she said and fell silent. But the silence didn't last for long. "What if they close the pass?" she fretted again.

"We're fine," he assured her.

"They've closed the roads in and out of Leavenworth before," she argued.

"Chelle, cool it already," he growled between clenched teeth. She was going to drive him nuts.

He could feel the hurt his harshness had caused. A quick glance in her direction confirmed it. He saw her surreptitiously wiping at the corners of her eyes and felt like a shit. The cold bastard he'd become wasn't the man he wanted to be. He hadn't started out this way.

He'd dug deep, trying to be patient and understanding after they lost the baby, tried to help Michelle get past it even as he was struggling to accept the loss. He'd thought they would come together, that she would lean on him. Instead, she'd leaned as far away as possible, and this was what their marriage had come to.

Being stuck together in the small space felt like they were in a prison on wheels. How could they have fallen so far from what they once had? Moments like this, he supposed.

"Sorry I snapped," he said.

She sniffed and nodded. "Sorry I'm so tense."

It was the first time in a long time either of them had said that one little word to each other.

A pickup roared past them, hurling slush against the windshield, and Michelle let out a gasp. "That is so rude," she said.

"He thinks he's invincible." Even snow tires and all-wheel drive couldn't guarantee safety, though. Their SUV had both, but Max knew better than to disrespect Mother Nature and drive like a fool. "We'll probably find him slid off the road somewhere farther up."

"I wouldn't wish that on anyone," Michelle said. "Especially us."

It seemed she'd barely spoken when an eighteen-wheeler came around the curve from the other direction. It was obvious the thing was sliding out of control.

It looked like a scene from an action movie with the semi coming right toward them, road slush flying in all directions. Except, unlike in the movies, where such scenes were carefully planned and controlled, nothing in that moment was under control. If the semi hit them, they'd be done for.

"Max!" Michelle screamed and grabbed his arm as if he had super powers and could stop it from coming.

Max had always heard that your whole life flashed before your eyes before you died, but there was no time for that. He had his hands full trying to swerve out of the way. It was like being inside a video game, with everything going at warp speed: the truck, the snow, his wife next to him with one hand braced on the dash, the other with his arm in a death grip. His heart was pumping so fast it felt ready to burst. *Dodge the semi, save the woman and stay alive, and then you can go to the next level.*

They did dodge it, barely, fishtailing as he tried to maintain control of the vehicle. By the time they'd straightened out, his heart was going like a jackhammer. He shot a look over to Michelle. Her face was as white as the snow banking the sides of the highway.

"You okay, babe?" he asked. *Babe.* It had been a long time since he'd used that endearment.

She bit her lip, nodded and said in a soft voice, "We almost died."

That would have been it, the end of them. Even worse if only one of them had survived. If he'd died, he'd never have had a chance to make one last try to put things right. He'd have died with her hating him. The thought made him sick. It made him even more sick to think about her dying, about never seeing her again. What would the girls have done without their mother?

He shook off the morbid thoughts. "But we didn't," he said. *Thank God.* He reached over and laid a hand on her thigh in an effort to comfort her. And maybe to assure himself that they really were still alive.

She let out a breath and nodded again, then shut her eyes and lay her head back against the headrest. He caught sight of a tear glistening at the corner of her eye.

"Hey, we're all right," he said softly, patting her thigh. "We survived."

"I don't want to be here," she whimpered.

With him. He'd told her they'd be fine, and instead they'd almost died, had the shit scared out of them. It was one more thing to hold against him.

Their life-and-death moment had put his whole body on red alert. Adrenaline was coursing through him, making him feel shaky. *We're okay*, he told himself. *We're okay.*

If only that were true for them as a couple.

Her words stayed with him when he pulled off onto the designated chain-up area to put chains on the car. His hands shook as he wrestled with them. *We almost died.*

One life, one chance to get it right. How was he going

to do that when she blamed him for so much? When she'd just reminded him that she didn't want to be with him? He hadn't handled things well when they lost the baby, but he still wasn't sure what he could have done differently.

Since then, though? He hadn't done such a good job in the following months, either. Or years.

But damn, he'd tried. It seemed like the more he'd reached for her, the more she'd pulled away.

He'd finally gotten hurt and fed up and walled himself off. Now he wasn't sure how to pull down those walls. If only he was a Cyrano de Bergerac with a gift for sculpting words. If only he knew a Cyrano who could write some beautiful poem to her for him. He didn't. What they'd just survived was a wake-up call, but now that he was awake, he didn't know how to proceed.

They got off I-90 at Ellensburg and made their way north onto Blewett Pass, riding in silence.

By the time they pulled into Leavenworth he felt like he'd been beaten and left for dead. "We made it here okay. We're all right." He said it as much for himself as for her.

"I need a drink," she said.

"Me, too, but we can't afford to stop until we get the rest of the way over the pass." He was not taking the blame if they dawdled in town and then couldn't get out. "Check on the pass conditions and see if there are any updates."

She started searching on her phone. A moment later she swore.

"What?" he prompted. But he knew.

9

"The pass is closed," Michelle said miserably. "Highway 2 is closed. Everything's closed! How can that be? We just came through."

"Okay, now I really need a drink," he said and started looking for a place to park.

They were able to order a late lunch at Andreas Keller, a popular restaurant that offered authentic German food served to customers as they ate in booths shaped like giant beer barrels. It was all knotty pine, murals and solid food for people who didn't want to mess around on diets.

Their server was a fortysomething, round-faced woman wearing a dirndl and a friendly smile. Michelle's first words to her were, "Is it true the pass is closed?"

"Just a few minutes ago," the woman confirmed. She gave them a pitying look. "Were you on your way somewhere for Christmas?"

"We're on our way to Idaho to spend Christmas with our daughter," Michelle told her. There came the glisten of tears again. "I can't believe it's closed. We just now got through."

"Well, then, lucky you, because they're closing everything now. Too much snow coming down too fast. It's not safe. Nobody's getting in or out until it stops and they can clear the roads."

"Lovely," Michelle said sourly, swiping at her damp cheek with a napkin.

"I'm sure you'll be able to get out in time to get to your daughter's," the woman said. "Meanwhile, what can I bring you?"

"Beer," said Max. "And we'll have the schnitzel with pommes frites."

The woman nodded. "Absolutely. Oh, and while you're waiting you might want to call around and see if you can get a room somewhere before they all fill up. I suspect you're not the only stranded travelers in town."

"She's right," Michelle said miserably. "We're stuck here."

Stuck here. With him. He could hear it in her voice, and it was a double punch to both the ego and the heart. But what had he expected? Maybe that their near-death experience had affected her as strongly as it had him.

He pulled up the chamber of commerce site on his phone. Fortunately, there were plenty of hotels, motels and B and Bs in the town. They'd have no trouble finding a place.

Michelle was already calling one. "I'd like to book a room. For tonight." He could tell by her frown that they'd struck out. "Okay, thanks," she said. "Booked solid," she announced.

"I guess we shouldn't be surprised. This is a popular place. Probably a lot of people staying here on their way somewhere."

"On top of all the people who are stranded," she said and started punching in another number.

"Who are you calling? I don't want to duplicate you."

"The Alpen Rose Inn."

"Okay," he said. "I'll call the Bavarian Ritz. Sounds ritzy," he added, hoping to coax at least a reluctant smile with his pun. He failed.

He also failed to find a room. So did she.

"This is terrible," she said. Their server was back with their beers, and she started on hers like she was going to drain it all in one gulp.

"Don't give up. We'll find something," he said.

It took several more calls before they did. He scored a room at the Enzian Inn, the last one available. "We got one," he told Michelle. It probably wasn't a good idea to tell her that they were in the Bridal Room.

"Thank God," she said, letting out a breath.

"We'll take it," he told the woman making reservations.

"How many nights would you like?"

"Better make it for two," he said.

Michelle's brows lowered.

"In case we can't get out tomorrow," he said to her. In which case she'd probably murder him.

She texted Julia to tell her of the delay then ignored him as they finished their lunch. Afterward they silently made their way to the inn, which sat right on Highway 2 in all its Bavarian splendor.

Trimmed with a myriad of colored lights and with the snow falling all around it, the inn looked like it belonged in a snow globe. The lobby was decked to the hilt with an elegant Christmas tree as well as a sleigh filled with toys. Fir boughs and bows ran along the carved banister.

Max sneaked a look his wife's direction. She was taking it in with the kind of appreciation it was meant to inspire. Score.

"Wow," she said.

The old wow factor. Maybe it was going to turn out to be a good thing they were stranded in a fancy inn. Maybe he could try and find a way to explain how that near collision had affected him. Maybe he could make her see how short and tentative life was and convince her to reach back with him to a time when they had something good going.

If you had to be stranded, Leavenworth was the place for it. It was a town designed for fun and smiles, with enough shops to gladden the heart of any all-American girl, along with great restaurants and lots of good beer. And the wine shops were well stocked. Maybe he'd pick up a bottle. A romantic setting, some wine—good building materials for repairing a broken relationship. Well, for at least making a start. Hopefully.

When they opened the door to the room it practically cried out for wine. And sex. The king-size bed looked inviting, and the room had a fireplace to set the mood.

His wife's reaction didn't set the mood, though. It was a bucket of ice and a reality check. What they'd broken couldn't be repaired.

"One bed," she observed dully.

"I'm not sleeping on the floor," he informed her. "We'll have to tough it out."

They were back to snapping at each other. They were still alive, but obviously they weren't meant to finish their lives together.

It was a depressing thought.

In better times, they'd sure had no problem sharing

a bed. When they were first married they'd happily squeezed into an old iron double, an antique his great-aunt had given them for a wedding present. Oh, yeah, they'd had some great times in that old bed.

"I'm going shopping," she announced. The *without you* was implied.

He grabbed the TV remote and flopped on the bed. "Knock yourself out," he said bitterly.

The door shut, and she was gone, and he was alone in the fancy bridal room. There was nothing on he wanted to watch. He looked over at that stupid fireplace and swore.

Julia called her husband, catching him on break at the supermarket where he worked in the produce department. "The pass is closed, and Mom and Dad are stuck in Leavenworth. They're stuck there, and it's all my fault. You were right. I should never have asked everyone to come here."

"Too late to worry about that now," he said reasonably.

"Mom sounded mad. She and Dad are probably having a screaming match right now, thanks to me."

"If they're fighting, it's not your fault," he said. "Hey, what's for dinner tonight? Bag salads are on sale."

"Bring one home. It'll go with the spaghetti and garlic bread I'm making." Spaghetti was one of her specialties. Actually, it was her only specialty, and canned spaghetti sauce was her secret ingredient.

"Okay," he said. "Gotta go. And don't worry about your parents. They'll make it here fine."

She sure hoped so. "I wish I'd listened to you."

"Yeah?" He sounded pleased to hear it.

"We should have waited to do this in the summer."

"Oh, well. Too late now," he repeated cheerfully.

"I'm gonna hate myself if they don't make it here by Christmas. By the way, I told Mom I'd go ahead and bake the red velvet cake if she can't get out."

"Now *I'm* gonna hate you if they don't make it here by Christmas," he cracked.

"Oh, you are funny," she said, irritated. "I've got the recipe. I can handle it."

"Of course you can," he said. "I was just funnin' with you."

Some funnin', she thought after they were done talking. But he was right. Cooking wasn't exactly her gift. Baking for sure wasn't. Still, she could manage red velvet cake, for crying out loud. She had the recipe in the notebook of family favorites Mom had put together for her. So how hard could it be?

Caroline was still napping. She could go ahead and bake the cake right then and freeze it for Mom to frost on Christmas Day. It would be one less thing for her mother to worry about if the cake was already done, and it would be nice to show Mr. Funnin'-with-You when he got home that she could manage cake. Rub his face in it. Figuratively speaking, of course.

She pulled the notebook out of the drawer she rarely opened. Other than a ketchup stain on the page with the meat-loaf recipe, and a yellow mustard stain on the one with Mom's potato-salad recipe, the book was in pristine condition, attesting to the fact that it was mostly ignored. Bagged salad mixes and deli delights were Julia's best friends. And you couldn't beat those cookies the store's bakery made. She couldn't, anyway.

Of course, all the other women in her family could. They each had their specialties. Gram's was spritz and gumdrop cookies and her famous fruitcake cupcakes that she made every year for Christmas. Mom made chocolate chip ones that tasted as good as Mrs. Fields's, Shyla made a great peanut butter cookie, and Audrey, overachiever that she was, could whip up lavender sugar cookies blindfolded. She experimented with everything from anise to rose water and never had a kitchen fail.

Which explained why Julia hadn't bothered with baking. Or much of anything in the kitchen. Gino didn't mind that she couldn't make boeuf bourguignon or lemon meringue pie. He was perfectly happy with the her limited culinary repertoire—and between his grilling abilities and his mother's expertise, why bother, right?

Except, as she turned to the cake recipe and studied it, she began to wish she had spent more time with Mom in the kitchen. What a weird recipe, calling for vinegar and a whole bottle of red food coloring. A whole bottle—was that even good for you?

As if she'd ever stopped to worry about that when snarfing down her second piece for breakfast the morning after Christmas. Anyway, you didn't mess with tradition, no matter how much red food coloring was involved.

On checking her cupboard she saw she only had… none. She'd never seen anything colored red come out of her mother-in-law's kitchen so she suspected Lina would be little help. She didn't want to wake Caroline from her nap just to drag her to the store. She could have Gino pick some up. But darn, she knew she wouldn't have any interest in messing around in the kitchen come evening (unless it was with Gino). She put in a call to her neighbor and walking partner six houses down.

"I think I've got some," said Gabrielle. "Let me check… Hey, I do," she said a minute later. "I gotta pick up Kai at school in a few. I'll drop it by on my way."

"Thanks. You're a lifesaver," said Julia.

It turned out her friend was a semilifesaver as the bottle she dropped off was half-empty. It should still work. Julia got busy mixing her ingredients. The food coloring only turned the batter pink but oh, well. Pink was…festive.

Don't overstir after adding vinegar to the batter, Mom's directions cautioned. *You want the cake to rise.*

Hmm. Maybe she should put in a little extra baking soda just to be sure. And baking powder. There. Good to go. She greased the cake pans—a bridal-shower present, never yet used—and poured in the batter. Spanked the bottom of the pan like she'd seen Mom do to get out the air bubbles, then carefully laid them on the rack in the 350-degree oven and set the timer for twenty-five minutes. *Always check at twenty-five minutes*, Mom had written. *All ovens are different, and you want to make sure your cake doesn't get overdone.*

Julia sure didn't. Not when she'd be serving it to the kitchen queens.

Partway through the baking process she decided to take a little peek and see how her cake was rising.

Rising? It was a regular pink lava flow going everywhere. Over the pan, onto the rack, dripping down. Everywhere! Nooo!

Julia stood in front of the open oven waving her hands back and forth as if she could magically make what she was seeing disappear. It didn't. She slammed the oven door shut and turned the air blue, blue, blue. This kind of thing never happened to Mom.

Caroline had awakened, and Julia could hear her

starting to fuss. The pink lava would have to wait. Maybe what was still in the pan would be okay. She hurried upstairs to get her daughter, hoping when she returned she'd find something salvageable.

Her daughter had a poopy diaper. A very poopy diaper. It was a major cleanup operation. By the time they got back downstairs the cake was done. Really done. And the pink lava had turned to charcoal, and the charcoal was smoking, and the kitchen stank, and why the heck had she decided to bake the stupid red velvet cake?

She turned off the oven, then moved the high chair out of the smelly kitchen into the dining room where she fed Caroline some organic applesauce. After that she put the baby on a blanket on the living-room carpet with her favorite baby play gym and returned to the scene of the baking crime. She dumped the ruined cake in the garbage, scraped up as much of the mess as she could and set the oven to self-clean. Then she called Gino.

"It's burgers tonight and not spaghetti," she informed him.

"Oh? What happened to spaghetti?"

"I can't heat the garlic bread. The oven's in use."

"Yeah? What's in it?"

"The remnants of red-velvet disaster," she replied with a scowl.

"Huh?"

"I thought I'd go ahead and get the red velvet cake baked for Christmas."

"Uh-oh," he said.

"Yeah, uh-oh. It was a total fail," she said miserably. "I'm cleaning the oven now. I suck."

"You don't suck. You just..."

"Suck."

"Nah. So what if you can't bake a cake? We got a bakery at the store. Anyway, you're good at other things."

"Like what?" she said, in no hurry to lose her bad mood.

"I'll let you show me tonight," he said, and she could hear the grin in his voice.

Well, yes, there were some things she was good at.

"Just let your mom make the cake when she gets here."

"But what if she doesn't?" There was a crummy thought. Who'd invited that into her brain?

"Then, your gram will bake it. No worries."

"No worries," she repeated. And nobody had to hear about this little culinary disaster. She sincerely hoped she wouldn't be faced with the possibility of another disaster...of any kind.

"Now, don't you go fretting," Warren said to Hazel as they left the diner. "You know I'll get us there safely. Remember, I grew up driving in the stuff."

Hazel hadn't. She was a Seattle girl, born and raised, and with its more temperate weather, the city had never gotten that much snow. It had been a rare treat for her as a child and something she hadn't had to deal with much as an adult. She never considered herself very good at driving in it, and she didn't like riding shotgun in it much better. Whenever it snowed she stocked up on groceries and holed up, happy to enjoy the view from inside her house.

"It's hardly coming down at all," he added.

"Who knows how hard it will be coming down before we get to St. Maries?" she said. The sooner they got to Julia's house, the better she'd feel.

They got in the car, and she fastened her seat belt and took a deep breath. She regarded the white flakes dancing in a gray sky. Ugh. First Thanksgiving and now Christmas. She was seeing a future filled with road trips and wasn't sure she liked what she saw.

"I wonder if it's time to move," she mused as they pulled onto the highway.

"Move?" He made it sound as if she'd suggested they each cut off a leg.

"Closer to Max. Or to a retirement home." Someplace where she didn't have to clean—a small living room and bedroom, eating dinner in a dining room instead of cooking endless meals. That would be nice.

"He's not that far. And I like where we live."

"But there comes a time when you have to make changes. We really don't need as much house as we have. Something smaller. I wouldn't mind living in a retirement home, either."

"You can't want to live in one of those," he said in disgust. "There's nothing but old people in 'em."

"We *are* old people, and there's nothing wrong with that."

"I don't want to be stuck in some giant building with people living on top of each other. Getting put on a bus to go to the store," he said.

"Having medical care handy."

"Our doctor's plenty handy. And there's nothing wrong with me."

"Nothing that a heart ablation wouldn't fix."

"My medicine works fine."

How many times were they going to have this discussion? "It's not a guarantee that you won't have a stroke."

"Nothing's a guarantee that I won't have a stroke."

"Getting your heart fixed so you don't have the A-fib issues would be a vast improvement."

"I'm fine, hon. You worry too much."

That was what women who were married to stubborn old men did. She clamped her lips shut and looked out the window, preferring the scenery to her husband's stubborn face. She loved him dearly, but there were times when she wanted to throttle him.

The procedure would fix his heart, yet she couldn't get him to make the leap. Warren feared hospitals as if merely entering one was a death sentence. Which was odd, since they'd been in hospital emergency rooms often enough—always because his heart was jumping around and shooting his blood pressure through the ceiling. He now had pills for that, but it was still scary when it happened.

"You did remember to pack your metoprolol, right?" she asked.

"Of course I did." He sounded insulted.

She didn't bother to point out the blood-thinner fiasco. Was he telling a big whopper to save face?

"I wouldn't forget that," he added.

"Just like you wouldn't forget your blood thinners."

He said nothing.

The snow insisted on accompanying them as they drove on Route 10 North toward Walla Walla. If only it would stop.

Funny how much she'd loved those rare snowfalls when she was a child. She remembered one year when they actually had enough for her to use the sled that her older brother had given her. What a thrill it had been zipping down Queen Anne Hill's Eleventh Avenue on that sled. She'd brought it out again when Max was a child, and he and his friends had enjoyed it as much as she had, taking it to a nearby park that offered a perfect hill for sledding. As long as you didn't have to go anywhere, it was wonderful. Snow days, the sound of laughter as children played in the front yard, making snowmen, taking an evening walk in it.

Now that she was older, it was a menace, not a delight. And the last thing she wanted at this point in life was to take a walk in the snow, as she had no desire to slip and fall and break a hip. The best medical advice for seniors was *Don't fall*.

What was the best advice for seniors when it came to driving in the snow? *Don't do it!*

They should have gone to Seattle and then driven to Julia's with the kids. It might have been awkward, considering what was going on with Max and Michelle, but at least it would have been safe.

"I've got this. We're fine, Hazel," Warren said firmly, reading her thoughts.

"I didn't say we weren't." It was too late to say anything.

"I know you didn't, but I can see you gripping the armrest."

She released it to prove to him that she was perfectly fine. And she was. They were. Good grief, she was such a sissy. At the rate she was going she'd soon be afraid of her own shadow.

The flakes were heavy and piling up, and visibility was bad. Horrible driving conditions if you asked her.

Not that Warren would. He considered himself capable of meeting any challenge.

Except… "Deer!"

10

The deer bounded right in front of them as if determined to be hit. Warren tried to swerve, but it was too late. They collided with a horrible thud, rocking the car and sending the poor animal flying.

At first Hazel was too frightened to do anything but gasp. Then, as Warren pulled off to the side of the road, she found her voice. "The deer!" she cried.

"My car," Warren moaned.

"Never mind the car. We probably killed that deer."

"Not on purpose."

She looked back to where the deer lay. Could they possibly help it?

"Don't go over to it," he cautioned, reading her mind again. "It could still be alive, and you could get hurt."

"As if that poor animal is in any condition to hurt anyone," she said, her voice trembling.

He took a deep breath. "I'm sorry, hon. If I could have avoided it I would have." He laid a hand on her leg. "You okay?"

She nodded. "You?"

He nodded as well. "Call 9-1-1. We need to report this."

She did, informing the dispatcher that the deer was not on the road, blocking traffic. "I think it's dead," Hazel whimpered.

"These things happen," the woman said and promised to send someone out right away.

Of course, accidents happened, but not to Warren and Hazel. Again, she looked back to where the animal lay. If it wasn't dead it was surely dying. She felt ill.

Warren crossed his arms over the steering wheel and laid his head on them, and suddenly she had more to worry about than the deer. "Are you all right?" she asked.

He heaved a great sigh and sat up. "I'm fine. Damn thing," he muttered.

"Poor thing," she corrected. "It's not like the deer set out to ruin our day."

"You're right. Bad luck all around." He heaved a sigh and pulled his phone out of his jacket pocket. "I need to take pictures of the car for the insurance company."

She got out along with him. The cold made her pull her coat tightly around her. The deer was a couple of yards away, still not moving, and she wanted to cry.

"I'm sorry," she said to it. It was a doe. Did she have a fawn somewhere, wondering when Mommy was coming home?

Warren came around the front to her side of the car, and they stood together, looking at the front-right bumper. It looked like the car had been in a demolition derby. They'd be lucky if they could drive it to the next town. She suddenly felt very tired.

Then hopeful when the animal's legs began to move. But still it was unable to stand. Maybe she could help it.

"Don't go over there," Warren said.

A highway patrol officer showed up. "We didn't mean to hit it," were the first words out of her mouth.

"Of course you didn't," he said.

"I think it's still alive," Hazel told him.

"I'll go inspect it for injuries." He motioned to the car. "You're going to need to get this vehicle someplace to have it looked at. Call a tow truck. I'll wait with you till it gets here," he said, then offered the name of two companies in the area.

"Thank you," she breathed. Having another human being with them on this deserted stretch where it was nothing but trees and snow—and an injured animal— helped calm her somewhat.

But the calm was short-lived. Warren looked pale. How Hazel wished they'd stayed home.

The tow truck arrived and took them away before she could learn the fate of the deer, and Hazel had to content herself with the hope that the officer had called the proper authorities to try and help it.

"Are you sure you're all right?" she asked Warren as they rumbled down the road.

He waved away her concern. "Stop worrying."

That wasn't an answer.

"That deer did a number on your car," the mechanic informed them when they got to the garage.

"How bad? We need to get on the road," Warren said to him.

"We're on our way to our granddaughter's for Christmas," Hazel added.

"Whereabouts you headed?" he asked.

"St. Maries," Hazel said.

"Well, we'll take a look, but don't get your hopes up.

You're probably gonna need to get a rental car to take you the rest of the way."

"Great," Warren grumbled.

The mechanic was right. Their car would be going nowhere soon. Ten minutes later Hazel and Warren were loading their suitcase and bags and presents into a taxi, and in another fifteen minutes they were at a Hertz car rental.

"Would you like a compact?" asked the rental agent.

"No, we'd like a tank," Hazel said.

No tanks were available, but they did get an SUV. Another twenty minutes and they were on the road again. The whole ordeal had only set them back an hour or so. The poor deer had definitely gotten the raw end of the deal.

She still didn't like the way her husband looked. "Warren, you don't look good," she said.

"Hitting that damned deer got my ticker going."

Just as she suspected. The A-fib was back. Who knew what kind of hit his heart had taken. "Pull over. I'm going to get your metoprolol."

He complied, a sure sign he really wasn't feeling well. Hazel unbuckled her seat belt and got in the back where they'd put the suitcase. She dug out his toiletries bag. Warren laid his head back against the headrest and closed his eyes. This wasn't good. She should have known that jolt of adrenaline would kick off his A-fib. She should have forced him to take his medication the moment they'd come to a stop.

As she pawed through the toiletries bag she found all kinds of items—his shaver, his aftershave, deodorant, a half-used roll of antacid. But where was the stuff he needed?

"Where's the metoprolol?" she asked, trying to push down the rising panic.

"Isn't it in there?"

"No. You told me you packed it." She was ready to slap him. Except she was too worried.

"I guess I didn't. I thought it was in there somewhere."

If she'd made him double-check last night, they could have asked the doctor to call in a prescription for that as well as his blood thinner. Hindsight was always twenty-twenty.

Once again, she kicked herself for not being more stubborn than the stubborn man she'd married. "It'll settle down," he said and sat back up.

"I'll drive," she said.

"The temperature's dropping, and it's gonna get slick."

"I can manage."

His eyebrows took a dip. "I can drive."

"So can I."

"Not as good as me, and you hate driving in snow."

"I hate riding in snow with a husband who could end up having a heart attack while he's behind the wheel. Get out of the driver's seat," she commanded.

"This is stupid," he muttered after they'd changed seats. "I can drive."

But even as he said it, he laid his head back on the headrest and shut his eyes. Suddenly, Hazel wasn't feeling great, either.

She brought up the nearest hospital on her phone, St. Anthony's in Walla Walla, and got Google Maps going.

"What are you doing?" he asked, suddenly suspicious.

"Getting us to the hospital."

"Hazel, I'll be fine."

"Yes, you will. Once the doctor sees you."

"Come on," he protested.

"Don't argue with me, Warren. I'm not in the mood."

He knew better than to do that, but she could also tell that he simply wasn't feeling up to it—yet another sign that they needed to visit the emergency room.

She should have been used to this. They'd been through it before. Him not feeling well, his blood pressure shooting up. Racing to the ER. Each time she worried that it would be the last. Each time the medical staff got his heart under control. Each time he later checked in with his doctor after the episode. All was well that ended well.

How well would things continue to end, though? It seemed like this was happening with increasing frequency. And now here it was happening, and they had no medication for him to take to help it. What if he had a massive heart attack? The very thought made her want to cry. She set her jaw and tightened her hands on the steering wheel.

She wished she could have floored it, but the weather wouldn't permit that. All the way to the hospital, she kicked herself for not having called 9-1-1 from the car-repair shop. Should have, could have. Dumb.

Alone in the bridal room. *Great irony,* Max thought miserably. His marriage was shot, and this trip was a disaster. It seemed like every word out of his mouth lately made him look like a bastard.

Of course, Michelle had thought he was a bastard long before *lately.*

He didn't want to be. He didn't want to be the enemy any more, yet he had no idea how to bring about a peace accord. He should have stuck it out with the counseling.

Now it was too late. They'd already agreed on a divorce. How did you pull back from that?

In those movies she loved to watch, a grand gesture always did the trick.

But the grand-gesture department had been closed for way too long. They were well beyond flowers and candy, that was for sure. Those hardly counted as grand gestures, anyway.

So what could he do? Open a vein? Crawl to her on his knees through the snow? Maybe he would, if he could even figure out where she'd gone.

He had to do something. He switched off the TV, donned his coat and left the room, hoping that somewhere out there he'd find inspiration.

He finally found it at Östling Jewelry Design, where he confessed to Margaret, the designer, "I'm in deep shit."

She showed him a ring she'd designed: a blue sapphire nestled in a thick gold band with three small diamonds on each side to add to the sparkle. It wasn't cheap. But then that stupid bike, the big metal last straw that he'd bought, hadn't been either. Dumb-shit him.

"It's a variation on my Omega designs," she told him.

Omega, as in the last. His last chance to get it right. He pulled out his charge card. Paid for it. Left the shop.

And then wondered what kind of fool he was to think that any gift could buy Michelle back.

Once Hazel and Warren got to the emergency-room admitting desk, things went fast. Couple the word *heart* with anything, and medical staff always moved quickly. Within minutes Warren had a thin, plastic bracelet on his wrist, and they were in a small room with a nurse who was taking both his medical information and his blood pressure. Next came the electrocardiogram and the news that he would be with them for a while. Hazel had become an expert at reading that screen, and she could see by the jumping squiggles that his heart wasn't happy.

So could the doctor. A room with a bed was found for Warren. Blood tests were taken, intravenous fluids started, and he was hooked up to a heart monitor. Everyone was calm and competent, which Hazel took as a good sign. The nurse showed Warren the call button and handed him the remote for the TV hanging in one corner of the room, and they were settled in.

"I'm going to find us a room for tonight," Hazel informed Warren.

It would be a long time before they got to it. She knew they would be at the hospital for hours, with him under observation. In addition to being given something to calm down his heart, the doctor would prescribe the medicine they'd left behind. He'd be given a discharge summary and told to consult with his own doctor when they got home, and that would be that. As had been done before, maybe this doctor would suggest Warren look into getting a heart ablation. He'd thank the doctor and let everything the man said go in one ear and out the other. And she'd keep bracing for the day he finally had a fatal heart attack.

"I'm sorry I forgot my medicine," he said humbly.

"That makes two of us."

"It'll be okay," he said softly. Warren's favorite phrase. She'd have it put on his tombstone.

This was not the time to be thinking about tombstones. She could feel the tears gathering.

"One of these days it won't be okay," she snapped.

"I'm going to call the kids and let them know what's going on."

"Don't do that," he protested.

"Max will want to know. And Julia needs to know that we won't be getting to her house anytime soon."

"Well, then, tell Julia, but don't bother Max."

Hazel knew what was behind that request. If his son heard that they'd hit a deer with Warren at the wheel, he'd be ready to confiscate his father's license. In some ways, that would be fine with her. But, really, what had happened to them could have happened to anyone, no matter the driver's age.

"If I tell Julia, he's bound to find out, so I may as well tell him," Hazel said.

Warren made no reply to that, just frowned and began channel-surfing. She got busy looking for a motel where they could spend the night once he was finally released. She hoped she could find someplace not far from the hospital. She was wrung out and all she could think of was finally flopping onto a nice, soft bed. She suspected she'd sleep soundly no matter who wound up occupying the room next door.

Once she'd secured a room reservation with a very late check-in, she went in search of a bathroom. She found one and locked herself in. An accident on the road, the car trashed, Warren in the hospital emergency room yet again—the stress of it all came on her like an avalanche. She put down the toilet seat, sat down and indulged in a good cry. If only they were already in St. Maries, enjoying hot cocoa with Julia's little family.

Julia. Yet another thing she needed to do. She dried her eyes, went back out into the hallway and called her granddaughter.

"Sweetie, I'm afraid Grandpa and I aren't going to get to your place as early as we thought we would."

"Why is that?"

"We had a little accident."

"What?"

"Don't worry, we're fine. But we hit a deer."

"Oh, no. Is it okay?"

"I don't know." Hazel doubted it, but at least she could hope.

The poor thing. Alas, deer knew to run from predators such as mountain lions and bears. But the two-legged kind that came at them in cars were something they couldn't fathom.

"That's awful. But you guys are okay, right?"

They would be once the doctors got done treating Warren.

"Pretty much," said Hazel. "Our car is in bad shape, and we had to get a rental," she continued, then decided to leave it at that. There was no sense panicking her granddaughter.

"That sucks. How's Grandpa?"

It was no secret that Warren took medication for his heart. "He's doing fine."

"What do you mean he's doing fine? Where are you guys?"

"We're in Walla Walla."

"Where in Walla Walla?" Julia pressed.

Hazel gave up on dodging the question. Her youngest granddaughter was a persistent little thing. "We're at the hospital."

"Oh, no," Julia said weakly. "Oh, no, oh, no, oh, no, oh, no." The words came out with increasingly rising volume.

"Now, don't you worry. Grandpa's okay," Hazel said in an effort to calm her. "He came off without his heart medicine is all, and his A-fib kicked in. The doctors are taking good care of him, so don't worry."

"Yeah, right."

Hazel could hear the sob in her granddaughter's voice. "No, really, he's going to be fine. You know this has happened before."

"But you never hit anything before. Or got stuck someplace," Julia fretted.

"We really are fine, a little shaken, that's all. Anyway, I wanted to bring you up to speed because I knew you'd worry when we didn't show up."

"*Would* worry? I'm worried now! This was a stupid idea. I should never have made you guys all come here."

"No, it was a lovely idea. You know we all want to see your house."

"I want you to live to see it. Oh, man, I'm such a jerk."

"No, you're not."

"Does Daddy know?"

"There's no need to worry your parents. We'll be fine. Honest."

"Really?" Julia said dubiously.

"Yes, really," Hazel said, as much to herself as to Julia.

"Be careful. And if Grandpa doesn't feel good, don't drive. We can send someone to Walla Walla to get you. In fact, we probably should."

"Oh, no. Your grandfather would have a fit. He'll be good as new by tomorrow, so don't you worry." *Like I am.* What if the doctors couldn't get his misfiring heart under control this time?

"Okay. But if he's not better tomorrow, please call me," Julia said.

"I will," Hazel promised.

Julia ended the call with her grandma, hugged baby Caroline and proceeded to rain tears all over her. What had she done? What kind of fool dragged her family through miles of snowy roads to see her at Christmas? A selfish one, that was what kind.

Unsettled by her mommy's tears, Caroline also began to cry.

"Oh, baby, I'm sorry," Julia said and sniffed. She began to rock back and forth, patting Caroline's back to soothe her. "It's okay, it's okay. Everything's going to be okay."

But what if it wasn't?

Oh, bad thought to have. That started the tears all over again. "It's all right, it's all right," she said, this time to herself.

What if it wasn't? What if...?

She veered away from the what-if. If any more bad stuff happened to her grandparents, she'd never forgive herself.

And poor Daddy. No matter what Gram said, he needed to know. She put in a call to him, barely giving him time to say hello before starting yet a third round of boo-hooing.

"Julia, what is it?" he demanded.

She suddenly wished she'd told Mom and made her break the news. Better yet she should have let Gram call Daddy when she was ready. But it was too late now, so like a sinner late for the confessional, she rushed on.

"It's Gram and Grandpa," Julia wailed. "They're in the hospital, and it's all my fault."

Hazel ended the call and sat for a minute, staring at her phone. Should she call Max? Maybe she shouldn't. After all, what could he do? It was probably best not to worry him. She decided not to. Bad enough she'd had to tell Julia what was going on. Warren would be fine. They'd be fine.

She was on her way back to Warren's room when her phone rang. Max. Julia must have alerted him.

Sure enough. "I just talked to Julia. What's going on?" he demanded.

Of course Julia had called her father. "Don't worry, darling. We're fine."

"You hit a deer, Dad's in the hospital, and you're fine. Tell me another lie."

"No, we are. Your father forgot to pack his medicine, and his A-fib started. I thought it was best to get him to the hospital. But they're taking care of him. I only wish I could convince him to get that heart ablation," she couldn't help adding. "But you know your father. He's so stubborn."

There was silence on the other end for a moment. "I don't like this."

"*You* don't like it. It's no picnic here, either."

"You guys should have ridden with us."

"Yes, we should have," she admitted. "But that's life. We're okay now, so don't worry." *And take your own advice, Hazel*, she thought.

"You should stay put," Max said firmly.

"We're certainly not going to do that and miss Christmas with all of you." Warren would be determined to press on. And even though she was feeling fearful, she knew she wanted to, as well. With everything that had happened, she needed to get to her family.

"It can be a belated Christmas. Once the pass is clear, I'll come get you guys and take you back to your house for Christmas there."

She heard no *we* in that sentence. Oh, dear. The anxiousness she was working so hard to keep at bay found a new weak spot to attack.

"Your father would never stand for it," she said, directing her focus to the problem at hand. To be treated like some sort of invalid would kill Warren more efficiently than a heart attack.

Her words inspired another long silence. "I don't like it," Max said again.

"We'll be all right, really. At this point what else could happen?" Was it tempting fate to say that? She hoped not. "Darling, I've got to go. You and Michelle be careful on the road. You should almost be there by now."

"We're not. We're stuck in Leavenworth. The pass got closed."

He didn't sound happy about it. Michelle probably wasn't, either.

"I'm sure the highway will get cleared in time," Hazel said. "And maybe you two can enjoy a little romantic interlude in the meantime."

Max gave a disgusted snort.

How to respond to that? Hazel decided there was no way to and settled for telling him she loved him and would see him soon. Then, after their call ended, she sent up a quick prayer that something good would come of her son and his wife being stranded together. It was, after all, a season to celebrate miracles.

As she walked to Warren's room, she tacked on another plea: that her husband would be fine and they would make it safely to those they loved.

Shyla was driving and Audrey was trying to relax—hard to do when someone else was at the wheel of her car—when Julia texted.

M & D are stuck in Leavenworth. Snowed in. And G & G hit a deer and it's all my fault.

Audrey snagged on what had happened to the grandparents. Fear gave her heart a vicious squeeze, and she gasped.

"What's wrong?" Shyla demanded.

"Gram and Grandpa hit a deer," Audrey said.

"What? Are they dead?"

Leave it to Shyla the drama queen to suggest that horrible possibility.

Except that was the first thought that had come to Audrey's mind, as well. They OK? she replied.

G is in the hospital in Walla Walla. Heart.

Audrey read it to Shyla.

"He's had a heart attack!"

A-fib, Julia continued. They're treating him. Poor Gram.

Poor all of them if they lost their grandpa. Audrey abandoned texting with her sister and put in a call to her grandmother, her hand shaking as she did.

"Hello, darling," Gram said.

She didn't sound hysterical. That had to be a good sign.

Unless she was simply putting on a brave face. "Are you guys okay?" Audrey demanded.

"Yes, we're fine. Grandpa forgot his pills, and his heart started acting up. The doctors have it under control now."

The tide of panic rising in Audrey began to recede. "You're sure?"

"Yes. Warren, say hello to Audrey."

A moment later her grandfather was on the phone. "Hello there, lovely," he said.

He didn't sound too bad. "Are you sure you're all right?" Audrey pressed.

"Yeah, I'm fine. We hit a deer, and it put my darn heart into overdrive."

"Did the airbags deploy? Do they have broken ribs?" Shyla wanted to know.

"Airbags don't always deploy when you hit a deer," Audrey explained.

"Ask them," Shyla insisted.

Grandpa had heard her. "No, the airbags didn't deploy. But the animal sure did a number on my car."

"Your car probably did a number on it," Audrey pointed out.

"Yeah, not exactly a win-win. Here, I'll put you back on with your grandma."

Gram was on a moment later. "You see, dear? He's fine. They're keeping him here for a while to make sure, but he's already feeling better. The wonders of modern medicine. How are you girls enjoying your road trip?"

"So far, so good," Audrey said.

"Good. You two watch for animals. And don't go crazy in Reno."

"We're long past Reno," Audrey assured her. "Next stop Winnemucca."

"I hope you have a nice hotel room reserved," Grandma said.

"We do," said Audrey.

"Be careful, anyway. There are all kinds of weirdos out there," Gram cautioned.

"You guys be careful, too," Audrey said, then they exchanged *I love you*s and goodbyes.

"Those two are too old for road trips," she said once the call was ended.

"Don't let Grandpa hear you say that."

"I know. He thinks he's indestructible. But he's not."

They rode in silence for a while. Shyla finally said in a small voice, "First Mom and Dad, and now this."

"We don't know for sure that Mom and Dad are finished," Audrey said.

"It sure doesn't look good. Can you imagine next Christmas with them not together?"

Audrey didn't want to.

"And Grandpa. I hate the thought of losing him. Or Gram."

"Same here. Funny how easy it is to take people for granted, to assume they'll always be around," Audrey mused.

It was easy to take a lot of things for granted. Like her parents' marriage. Growing up it had been the bedrock of her life. No matter what was happening at school, no matter how insecure she might have felt as she navigated her nerdy way through the jungle of teenage relationships, she'd always known she could count on her family being solid, her parents holding them all closely together. Now, looking at her parents' relationship through adult eyes, she saw how unnervingly easy it was for the earth to shake and solid ground to crumble.

Rather like what had happened with the relationship she'd had with Dennis. One minute they were on solid ground, the next the earth was shifting beneath her.

"If only life came with a guarantee," she said.

"Yeah, if only," Shyla agreed. "I guess you have to simply trust that good things will always come out of bad, even if you don't see it right away."

So far Audrey hadn't seen much good come out of her breakup and said so. "But that was very philosophical," she complimented her sister.

"And true."

"For you," said Audrey. Good grief. When had she become such a pessimist?

"For you, too. I'm betting on it."

"Yeah, well, I already saw back in Reno how good your luck is," Audrey taunted.

Shyla just chuckled and pressed down harder on the accelerator.

"Hey, slow down. Somebody needs to make it to Julia's in one piece."

"We'll be fine," Shyla said. "Julia's probably going nuts, though. First Mom and Dad stuck in Leavenworth, and now Grandpa in the hospital."

The reply Audrey got from their mom when she decided to text her was short, merely telling her that the pass was closed. If you beat us there, you're in charge of the cake, Mom finished.

"At least everyone's alive and well," Audrey said.

"And Leavenworth's a great place to be stuck." Shyla smiled. "It's pretty romantic there this time of year. This might be exactly what Mom and Dad need."

Maybe. They could hope.

11

Michelle tasted another sample at Schocolat, one of her favorite shops in the little Bavarian town. Delicious as their candy was, it did nothing to sweeten her mood. It only made her think of all the times Max had bought her chocolates, starting with their first Valentine's Day as a married couple.

Michelle came home from work to find a giant red heart filled with chocolates sitting on the kitchen table. She smiled as she picked up the note sitting next to it.

The world is full of sweet things, but nothing is as sweet as you.
Love, Max.

Teary-eyed, she ran her fingers across the box. What a guy.

She set the grocery bag filled with goodies she'd bought for him on the counter—his favorite beer, teriyaki beef jerky and barbecue potato chips—then called her cousin in Olympia to brag.

"That is impressive," said Charlotte. "Does he know he's set a dangerous precedent?"

"No. Should I tell him?"

"You'd better warn him."

"I don't think he needs warning."

"Yeah, yeah. Mr. Wonderful can do no wrong."

"Other than leaving his dirty socks lying around, you're right, he can't."

"Trust me, at some point he will," Charlotte said. "They bring their A game when they're after you, but it doesn't last."

"I can't believe I'm hearing this." Charlotte had only been married three years longer than Michelle and Max.

"Sorry to burst your bubble, but it's true. Men are all selfish."

Not her dad. And not Max.

"There's always a hidden agenda, especially when they bring you gifts."

"For Valentine's Day? There's no hidden agenda there."

"Of course there is. He wants to get lucky."

"Well, so do I. Since when don't you like sex?"

"Since I had a baby. I'm a mommy zombie, and by the end of the day I'm exhausted, and the last thing I want is sex. Carl's not up nursing the baby at two in the morning. He's getting a good night's sleep every night, so he's ready to take up where we left off. And when I don't want to, he gets all pouty."

"He should understand about you being tired," Michelle said.

"He should, but he doesn't. He expects me to be ready to do it whenever the mood hits him."

"Maybe the mood will hit you tonight. It is Valentine's Day, and I'm sure he'll get you something."

"I'm not holding my breath. Once you have kids and bills, the romance dies."

And Happy Valentine's Day, Michelle thought as she hung up. Bills and babies and no romance. Was that what she had to look forward to?

She called her mother and related her conversation with Charlotte.

"Oh, honey, their relationship was rocky before they even got married. You know that."

"It was still unnerving to listen to her. I don't want to end up like them."

"You won't. Now, tell me. Has Max gotten you something for Valentine's Day?"

"Yes. A big box of chocolates. I found it sitting on the kitchen table when I came in. He must have brought it over on his lunch hour."

"What a darling! See? You two will be fine."

Yes, they would. Of course they would.

That night they broiled steaks for dinner and drank cheap champagne. But first they had wild, crazy sex on their secondhand living-room couch. "I love you, Chelle," he said afterward as he played with her hair.

"And always will, right?"

He looked at her in surprise. "Of course. Why would you even ask that?"

She shrugged. "I don't know. People do fall out of love. Charlotte and her husband are already having problems."

"Your cousin's a ditz, and he's a jerk, so that's not surprising. And that's not going to be us."

She smiled. "Yeah? How do you know? Prove it."

"I will," he said. "I'll give you the biggest box of chocolates I can find every year for Valentine's Day for the rest of our lives. It'll be like…"

"The swallows returning to Capistrano," she said, joking.

"Yeah, that. Or the sun rising every morning."

Now, were those the words of a selfish man?

Max had given her chocolates every year after that, but after they lost the baby the gesture felt hollow. She never opened the box. Her cousin had been right. All men were selfish. It sat on the counter for two weeks until she found it in the garbage. Max had gotten the message. *Don't want anything to do with your candy or you.*

The next year there was no box of chocolates on the table. And even though she knew it was her doing, that he'd gotten hurt and given up, she still held it against him. Because that was what grudges did. You nursed them, and they got big and strong.

"Darling, why should he get you more when you insulted him the last time he did?" her mother had asked reasonably during their last mother-daughter shrink session before Mom died. "You have to let go of this resentment."

"I have," Michelle had lied.

Of course, she hadn't. It was too handy to keep her husband in the role of villain. He deserved it. He'd never taken the blame for what happened. An *I'm sorry* wasn't enough unless it was accompanied by an *It's my fault.* And it was his fault. He'd pushed and pushed her until she'd finally caved and he'd gotten his way, and look what had happened.

Anniversaries became a sick joke, even when they invited Audrey and Shyla along as buffers. Their big twenty-fifth had been a farce: dinner with their family and her brother at a nice restaurant and champagne toasts as if all was well. Her smile had been forced, and she and Max hadn't said one word on the way back home.

"At least we made it twenty-five years," he'd said as they pulled into the garage. She'd said nothing in response, and he'd sighed and gotten out of the car. She followed him in, shoving aside the memory of all those happy anniversaries when they'd gone out to dinner and then come home and made love. Things had been different then. They'd been different then.

She remembered their last anniversary. She'd told him she didn't see the point in doing anything. Counseling had failed, and they were barely speaking.

"Why go out and pretend we want to be together?" she'd said.

"I guess you're right," he'd said through clenched jaws.

She'd felt a small thrill of triumph, seeing his hurt. And to think he'd once said she was sweet. She wasn't sweet at all anymore. She was nothing but a bitter-bricklayer.

She should have listened to her mother. How she wished the woman was still with her, to guide her out of the abyss into which she'd plunged herself. *God knows she tried*, Michelle thought. Even their last conversation had included one last attempt to get Michelle to see the truth.

"Oh, Mama," Michelle sobbed as she sat by the bed as her mother lay dying. "You're too young for this." It wasn't fair that the cancer had come back so quickly. They should have had more years together.

"We die when it's time," her mother said. The words came out softly, pushed out by a weak body. "I'm ready to see your father."

It was wrong to want to hold her back, but to let her go…how could she? Her mother was her best friend.

"I know you do," Michelle managed, "but what am I going to do without you?"

"You have your husband." Her mother closed her eyes, took a shallow breath. "Hang on to him. You need each other."

"Husbands aren't the same as mothers," Michelle protested.

Mom managed a weak smile. "They usually last longer."

Michelle could think of several snotty retorts to that, but she kept her mouth shut. This wasn't the time.

"You've been a good daughter. I couldn't ask for better. Now it's time to work on being a good wife."

A good wife? She'd been a good wife!

"I love you," her mother said, then sighed and fell silent.

"I wish I loved myself," Michelle murmured.

But her mother didn't hear. She was gone.

Michelle bought a small box of mixed chocolates to give to Hazel and left feeling depressed. This would be the last Christmas she bought a gift for her mother-in-law, the last one they'd all spend together.

It was Max's fault. Max's fault, Max's fault. That had been her mantra. But she knew she'd been the real murderer of their marriage, with her resentment and unforgiveness. He'd reacted with resentment of his own and become her accomplice. Every time they'd almost reconciled, they'd run into that wall. Now look at them.

Life is about trying. Her mother's words grabbed her by the heart. She hadn't tried to save her marriage. The only thing she'd worked hard to save was her justification for her resentment and bitterness.

Every wise woman buildeth her house: but the foolish plucketh it down with her hands. Her grandma had quoted that Bible proverb in the wedding card she'd given Michelle along with a place setting of her Fiestaware. *The most important thing you'll ever build is a good relationship with those you love*, she'd written beneath it. *Be a good builder and you'll be happy.*

Oh, Grandma, how I've failed, she thought. It seemed every woman in her family was wise except her.

When she was young she'd just wanted to live a good life and make people happy, to make her corner of the world a better place. She'd started well, but now she was a failure. She'd wound up miserable and made the person closest to her miserable, as well. Here she was, managing a Hallmark store while living a life that looked like a Hallmark movie that had been kidnapped by Tim Burton. *The Nightmare After Happy.*

Roofs and sidewalks were frosted with snow. Children were sliding down the hill at the far end of the street where the little park was located, and their delighted cries danced on the air. She could smell roasting chestnuts. The people she passed as she walked down Front Street were all smiling and happy. It was like being inside a greeting card. She wished she could feel that happiness, wished she could tap into the festive feeling of the place.

In the town square, a band was playing Christmas music. "Joy to the World." It was Christmas, but she had no joy. It was one of her favorite carols, and she had no voice.

People tended to think marriages broke up because somebody cheated. But that wasn't always the case. It was little things being turned into big things, big things being seen as insurmountable. It was letting one loss multiply until you lost everything.

Even cheating could start with something much more mundane—a slow erosion of closeness, a perceived hurt that wouldn't heal, followed by another and another— a million little beestings until the relationship finally went into anaphylactic shock and died.

She'd felt so grateful after that close call with the semi, grateful that they were alive, the two of them. It was almost like a message from God. *Giving you a second chance here.*

Max obviously hadn't gotten the memo and didn't want to keep trying. Who could blame him? She wouldn't want to give herself a second chance.

The coffee gesture had been a thoughtful one. Why hadn't she been more gracious? Why hadn't she refocused when they were in the restaurant, taken a moment to be grateful, taken a moment to say she was glad they were alive? If she'd pulled the dark curtain away and suggested that they'd been wrong to pull the plug on their marriage, would he have reacted differently when they got to the room?

He hadn't exactly reacted with joy at the sight of it, a sure sign he had no interest in reviving their love. She hadn't been able to stand it, had refused to sit in that room and cry in front of him, but maybe she should have.

She was crying now. How she wanted to reach out and snatch some of the happiness floating around her and share it with Max. She didn't want a divorce. She wanted their life back. She wanted him. And now it was too late. She was like Scarlett O'Hara, realizing she wanted Rhett, that she'd loved him all along, only to find her realization had come too late.

Lovely as all the shops were, she had no desire to continue exploring them. The one thing she wanted couldn't be found in a shop. She turned back to the inn, her steps slow.

Inside, the place was decorated so beautifully. It was a shame she couldn't appreciate it. Christmas had once been her favorite holiday.

With a sigh, she let herself back into the room. There was Max, sitting on the bed where she'd left him.

But his body language was different. He'd been surly when she left, reaching for the TV remote, but the TV was off and he was slumped on the side of the bed, his cell phone discarded next to him. His hair was sticking every which way, as if he'd been running his hands through it.

A sense of foreboding climbed onto her shoulders. What had happened since she left him? Surely nothing with the girls. They would have called or texted her. But something had upset him, something more than her storming off.

"Max, what's wrong?" she asked. And then, before he could answer, she knew. It had to be his parents. Something awful had happened to them.

"Dad's in the hospital. The folks hit a deer and trashed their car and it triggered his A-fib."

Sick dread crept up her throat. "Oh, no. Is he okay?"

"Mom's putting a good face on." He gave his thigh an angry slap. "I knew we should have gone and picked them up."

"You know your dad wanted to drive."

"Well, we can't always have what we want, can we?" he snapped.

Her emotional reflex demanded that she retaliate in kind, but she stopped herself. This wasn't about him and her. This was a wounded man lashing out. And hadn't she done her share of that? She'd seen where it had gotten them.

He started for the door, his mouth clamped tightly shut. He was withdrawing into himself, as he always did, going to go nurse his wounds far from her. Not even remotely surprising, all things considered.

Yet after the life-and-death moment they'd shared, she knew she couldn't let him leave without her doing something. She'd been the first to move away. She needed to be the first to move closer.

"Max," she said softly and took a step toward him.

He shook his head and left the room.

Michelle stood for a moment, indecisive. Should she go after Max or give him time to process what he'd heard? She decided to call Hazel and get the details of what was going on firsthand.

Hazel answered on the second ring. "Hello, dear."

In the background, Michelle could hear voices. Hospital staff?

"Max told me about your accident, but he was a little short on details," she said. "Are you still at the hospital?"

"Yes, the doctor's talking to Warren right now."

"But he's okay, right?" Michelle pressed.

"Yes. They've given him something, and his heart's settled down."

"He already takes medicine for his heart." Had it stopped working?

"He does. But he forgot it at home. His doctor had called a prescription ahead for us in St. Maries, but that didn't do us any good on the road."

Michelle could almost see her mother-in-law frowning at her husband in disapproval. She couldn't help but feel for Hazel, who had been after him for several years to do something to get his heart repaired.

"They're keeping him here for a while for observation," Hazel continued. "It looks like we won't get any farther than Walla Walla today."

"Maybe you should stay put."

"I told Max that won't happen. Dad's already champing at the bit to get going."

"I hope you can find a way to take it out of his mouth."

"You know your father-in-law."

Yes, she did. Once Warren set his mind to doing something, there was no dissuading him. He'd always been a powerhouse, a self-made man who'd built a successful business. He prided himself on his ability to overcome obstacles and was probably already minimizing his condition to both the doctor and his wife.

"How are *you* holding up?" Michelle asked.

Hazel's sigh said it all. "It's been a long day so far. We had to leave our car at a garage and rent one, and I've been dealing with the insurance agency and finding a place for us to stay tonight. Once we finally get out of here and into our motel room, I'll sleep like a log."

"I'm glad you're all right," said Michelle.

They could have been injured. Or worse. She and Max should have gone and picked them up. It would have been a detour, but so what?

Hazel sounded done in. It was clear to Michelle that the time was fast approaching when they were going to need more support with the challenges of life. She and Max needed to consider moving closer to the folks so they could help them.

Except they weren't going to be together anymore. They were in no position to help anyone when they couldn't even help themselves. Look how troubles rippled out.

"We're fine," Hazel said. "I told Max not to worry."

How could he not, after hearing his parents had taken a hospital detour? Poor Max.

"I need to go, dear. I want to hear what the doctor's saying to Warren."

"Of course. Be careful," Michelle said.

As if they weren't. Accidents were called *accidents* for a reason. Nobody ever planned on having one.

"We will be. See you soon."

Hopefully, yes, Michelle thought after she'd said goodbye. At least for the moment both Hazel and Warren were being taken care of. Now, what to do about Max?

Even though Michelle's in-laws had survived their encounter with the deer and Warren was being treated at the hospital, it was still unnerving to realize they could have been killed. The terror Michelle felt when she thought that eighteen-wheeler was going to take out Max and her was still so fresh in her mind she could shut her eyes and see the moment play out, feel the sick horror of it. An animal leaping in front of you wasn't quite as terrifying as a transport truck coming your way, but the suddenness of it would certainly be awful. It was a wonder Warren hadn't had a full-on heart attack.

It was also hardly surprising that Max would be upset by the news that his dad was in the hospital. Although Warren's heart condition was nothing new, it still worried Max when Warren's heart acted up. Any time could be the last time.

Max was devoted to his parents. She knew it was killing him to be stranded so far away and unable to help. Where was he? Did he need consoling? More to the point, would he accept any attempt at consolation by her?

She wanted to console him. And that desire spoke volumes.

They could have died back on Highway 18, two strangers sharing the same car. What a sad ending to their story that would have been. And yet, after being in love, after raising three girls, building a life together, they were contemplating another sad ending. Maybe not as quick, but equally wrong. When she stacked the hurts against the good years they'd had together, the perceived wrongs she'd been clinging to so tightly against all the rights, it was…humbling. Humiliating.

She wouldn't blame him if he wanted to split up, but she would blame herself if she didn't attempt to put them back together again. She had to make the effort.

"Life is about trying." Hearing herself say the words felt as if she was working to remaster a foreign language long forgotten.

She would master it. She wanted her husband back. She wanted that happy life she'd set out to have, the one she once did have with Max.

First, though, she had to find him. Where was he? What was he doing?

There was only one way to find out. She grabbed her coat and went in search of him. She'd check around inside the hotel first, and then if he wasn't there she'd start combing the streets.

She wasn't surprised to find that Max wasn't in the main lobby or any of the other cozy nooks in the hotel. He'd look for anonymity, someplace where he could be miserable but blend in unnoticed. It was too cold to walk around outside for long, which meant he'd gone to ground somewhere. She began a systematic search of the bars in town.

"There's a procedure that could help you," the doctor said to Warren, and Hazel held her breath, praying that her husband would be open to this doctor's advice.

"So I hear," Warren said with a frown.

"You could be a good candidate for a heart ablation. There's a cardiologist in Bremerton, Washington, who does them. His name's Segerson, and he's a rock star. People come from all over to him."

It wasn't the first time they'd heard that name. "Our doctor back home recommended him," Hazel said.

"It would be worth considering," said the doctor.

"Yes, it would," Hazel agreed.

Warren said nothing.

"We'll get you out of here soon," the doctor promised, then left.

So did Hazel.

"Where are you going?" Warren asked her.

"I need..." *you to come to your senses.* She didn't say it. She was simply too tired to argue. "Some water."

Away from his room, she leaned against a wall and cried softly.

A gentle hand gave her a start, and she turned to see a young nurse in turquoise scrubs looking at her with concern. "Are you all right, ma'am?"

Hazel sniffed and nodded. "It's been a long day."

"Is there anything I can get you?"

A hypnotist? That was what it would take to convince Warren to get the heart ablation.

"No, I'm fine," Hazel said and managed a weak smile. She wiped her eyes, grabbed some toilet paper from a nearby bathroom and blew her nose and then went back into his room.

"I'm sorry I'm messing up our trip," he said.

"You're not just messing up our trip. You're messing up our lives," she snapped. It looked like she wasn't as tired as she thought.

The conversation went no further as another nurse entered the room. Hazel sighed and sat back in her chair and settled in to wait until the doctors deemed Warren recovered and ready to go on his way. The conversation wouldn't have gotten any further, anyway.

The sisters were halfway to Winnemucca with nothing but sagebrush and power lines for company when the car began to swerve and list to the side and go thumpity-thump.

"What are you doing?" Audrey screeched.

"Nothing," Shyla screeched back.

"Slow down!"

"I am!"

They slowed down, the car ka-thump-thump-thumping as they went.

"I think we've got a flat," Shyla said.

"I told you not to short-cut through that empty lot back in Reno," Audrey scolded. "We probably picked up a nail."

"You don't know that," Shyla retorted. "Maybe your tire was worn out."

"I just bought new all-weather tires two months ago," Audrey snapped. "Stop the car before you ruin the tire."

Shyla pulled off the road, and they got out of the car. One of the right rear tires was deflated, its bottom flat along the ground.

"It's definitely flat. But you've got a spare, so we're good," Shyla said.

"Yeah? When was the last time you changed a flat?"

"Uh, never? But not to worry. I'll call roadside service."

Shyla took her phone from her purse. Looked at it. Scowled. "I have no bars."

12

"Of course you have no bars," Audrey snapped. "We're in the middle of nowhere."

"Well, you have to know how to change a tire. You know everything."

"The last tire I didn't change was when I was sixteen, and Dad was showing me how and wouldn't even let me jack up the car."

"Same here," said Shyla. "But it can't be that hard. Pop the trunk."

They got the trunk open and the jack and the tire out and put together the jack. But then the process became a mystery.

"You don't know where to put that thing," Shyla said, as Audrey worked on puzzling out how to get it secured safely under the car.

"If you don't shut up I'm going to tell you where you can put it," Audrey growled.

"If you do it wrong the car can fall on you. That much I remember from my session with Dad."

Audrey frowned and set the jack down. "Great."

"Of all the places to have a flat," said Shyla miserably. "Why couldn't this have happened in Reno where there were people? And cell towers."

"And bathrooms," said Audrey. "I'm going to have to pee pretty soon."

"Peeing at the side of the road. Gross," Shyla said in disgust. "I'll burst before I do that."

"You just might if you keep drinking. You've almost polished off the last bottle of water."

"So what? I have to stay hydrated."

"We don't know when or how we're going to get help. We need to make that last, so don't drink any more."

"Can you not be so bossy?"

"Can you not be so immature?"

"Hey, you're not Mom, and it's about time you stopped acting like you are," Shyla shot back at her.

"What's that supposed to mean?" Audrey demanded.

"You know what it means, Miss In-Charge-of-the-Universe. Last I checked, God didn't need a replacement, so you can step down from your throne."

Her sister's words hurt. Okay, so Audrey liked to be in control, so she was a little bossy. So sue her. She'd spent a lot of time watching over her younger sisters when they were growing up, both on the playground and after school at home when they were all older and Mom was working. She was used to being in charge, and she liked being in control. She liked to plan, and she liked things to go according to plan. There was nothing wrong with that.

She suddenly wanted to cry. But she didn't want to apologize. She leaned against the car and glared at her sister. "How about a little appreciation for all the trouble I went through to plan this trip?"

Shyla rolled her eyes.

"Or maybe for the fact that I tried to be a good sister to you when we were growing up, even when you were a stupid little twit? And who broke Buddy Morton's nose when she caught him harassing you behind the baseball backstop when you were in eighth grade? Where you two shouldn't have been, I might add."

Shyla must have seen the tears in her eyes, because she suddenly lost her scowl, and her features softened. She came alongside Audrey and put an arm around her shoulder.

"I'm sorry," she said.

Okay, so maybe Audrey did want to apologize after all. "Me, too," she said. "You weren't always a twit," she added.

"And you're not that bossy. Well, actually, you are, but I love you anyway. And at least if we die out here we'll be able to die not mad at each other."

"Let's not joke about that," said Audrey. Someone would come along.

But not before nature called. "I can't put it off. I have to pee," she said miserably and walked around to the side of the car. Even with the car between her and the road, with no living thing in sight, she still felt exposed.

"There is no way I'll be at the side of the road doing that," Shyla claimed.

Half an hour later, when not a single car had passed them, she was peeing at the side of the road. "This is disgusting!"

"No, disgusting is being stranded here." The temperatures would drop come nightfall; then they'd have more to worry about than a flat tire. The very thought made Audrey pull her coat more tightly around herself. She marched over and picked up the jack. She was not going to let a simple piece of equipment defeat her. She could figure this out. It was simply a matter of logic.

She was saved from going into battle with the jack when a truck came in sight.

"Thank God my pants are back up," said Shyla from the other side of the car.

Next thing Audrey knew, her sister was in the middle of the road, waving her hands frantically.

The truck slowed. It appeared to have one person in it. A man. Hopefully, he wasn't a rapist or a serial killer. Audrey swallowed down her fear and stepped up to join Shyla. If he was, he'd have to take them both down.

The truck was red and a little dusty, but it looked fairly new. *Livingston Construction* was painted on the side of it. Serial killers didn't run around in pickups with a company name on them, right?

The man stepping out of it looked like the kind of cowboy Shyla had promised they'd see in Reno. He was tall and lean, wearing jeans and a shirt with a shearling-lined suede jacket over it. He wore a Stetson over brown hair. And boots, not tennis shoes. He had lovely brown eyes and a square chin with a cleft in it. He looked exactly like what Audrey would ask Santa for if she was placing an order.

Audrey's mouth suddenly felt dry.

"Looks like you ladies are having some trouble," he said and smiled. It was the kind of smile that not only moved his lips but also shined out from his eyes.

It made Audrey's heart flutter. Serial killers didn't smile like that.

Oh, wait. She'd read about Ted Bundy. He'd been charming, and he'd probably had a great smile, as well.

"We had a flat," Shyla said, stating the obvious.

"No cell service out here," Audrey added. "Otherwise we'd have called roadside service." As if that wasn't also obvious.

"Not much of anything out here." He pointed to the jack in her hand. "Mind if I help?"

"Please, be our guest," Shyla said.

Audrey handed it over, hoping he wouldn't use it as a weapon against them. *Oh, stop already*, she scolded herself.

"We really appreciate you stopping," Shyla continued. As if he'd had a choice with her standing in the middle of the road.

"Always glad to help someone in need," he said, then bent over and set the jack under the car in an area that Audrey realized was probably meant to hold it.

Of course, that was how you did it. She gave herself a mental kick for her moment of insecurity.

"You're like a gift from Santa," continued Shyla, the flattery queen.

If ever there was a gift from Santa, this man looked like it. No ring on the finger. But he probably had a girlfriend. Had to. He was too good-looking, too nice, not to. Anyway, what would she have in common with a construction guy? The men she dated were white-collar types.

Yeah, and how had that been working out?

"Just doing what anyone would do," he said.

"We thought we were going to die out here," Shyla told him, making them sound like drama queens.

"It is a pretty deserted stretch, but someone would have come along eventually," he said as he worked. He made jacking up a car look easy.

Which it was. Audrey could have done it with a quick YouTube refresher course. If they'd had cell reception.

"I should know how to change a tire," she said,

watching him. What a ridiculous thing to say. But she should. "My dad showed me how when I was sixteen. Sadly, I've never gotten a lot of practice. I buy new tires on a regular basis."

And he needed to know all that because? Next she'd be informing him that she went to the dentist regularly. She could feel her cheeks catching fire.

"My sister's very organized," put in Shyla.

"Well, you know what they say. *The best laid plans of mice and men*," he said.

"We really do appreciate you stopping," Audrey repeated as he got to work unscrewing the lug nuts. *And we really appreciate you not being an axe murderer.*

"Happy to help. Where are you ladies headed?"

"Winnemucca," said Shyla.

He looked up at Audrey. There was that smile again. "Yeah? Got family there?"

"No, just passing through," Audrey said.

"We're on our way to St. Maries, Idaho, to see our sister," Shyla added.

"Everybody's on their way somewhere about now," he said.

"How about you?" asked Shyla, taking the words out of Audrey's mouth. No, make that her brain, which was turning to mush before her very eyes. Why couldn't she think of anything smart to say beyond telling him her car maintenance habits?

"My folks have a place in Winnemucca. I'm headed there to see them."

"Where are you from?" Audrey asked, determined to make rational conversation.

"From the North Pole," quipped Shyla. "Of course. Santa sent him to help us."

He chuckled at that. "Right now? Tahoe. I'm remodeling my grandparents' place on the lake. It's been in the family for years, but with all the fires lately, the family's decided to sell it."

"Kind of sad to sell something that's been in your family that long," Audrey said.

"Yeah, it is. I've got a lot of good memories from summers at that place. But life's about change. Adapt or die." He pulled the tire off and inspected it. "There's your problem," he said, pointing. "You ran over a lag screw."

Audrey frowned at her sister, the shortcut queen, but Shyla was conveniently looking the other way.

"Like I said, the best laid plans," he repeated. "By the way, my name's Russ."

"Livingston?" Audrey asked.

"How'd you…?" Then he looked over at the truck and flashed her that million-dollar smile again. "Well, duh."

"I'm Audrey Turnbull," said Audrey. "This is Shyla."

"Nice to meet ya. Where are you two from?"

"I'm from LA," Audrey said. "Shyla lives in San Francisco."

"City girls, huh?"

"Is that good or bad?" Shyla asked. It sounded an awful lot like flirting, and Audrey knew on whose behalf she was doing it.

Subtle. She sent her sister a warning look. *Stop already.* Then she turned her attention back to their rescuer. "For the moment, anyway. But really we're small-town girls. Well, sort of small," she corrected herself. "Where we grew up is pretty populated now. It seems like most of Western Washington is."

"Yeah, so I hear. I also hear it's a great state."

"It is," Shyla said. "Something for everyone."

"But you're both in California now," he pointed out.

"Well, sometimes you find something in another state. Or someone," Shyla said. "I did."

"I didn't," Audrey muttered.

He looked over his shoulder at her, and she felt herself blushing for no logical reason. "You're probably serving a life sentence in LA," he said, which showed what he thought of big cities. "Lots of friends."

"A woman can always make room for more," Shyla told him. "Right, Audrey?"

Oh, for crying out loud. Why not just call out *Here, hottie, hottie.* Audrey shot another frown at her. "Right."

"So how'd you end up in LA?" he asked.

"Long story," Audrey said. No way was she going to tell a stranger that she'd been stupid enough to follow her boyfriend there.

"Ah," he said in response. "None of my business, of course. I'm a nosy bugger."

He had the new tire on and began lowering the car. Another minute and he'd be on his way. She'd handled their conversation all wrong, but oh, well. Nothing could come of a chance meeting on the roadside.

"Good as new," he said as he picked up the flat tire and walked to the trunk with it.

Audrey followed him, carrying the jack. Shyla stayed at the front of the car, giving her sister a chance to... what?

She couldn't give him her phone number unless he asked. That would look tacky.

Really, there was no reason for him to ask. They lived in two different states, for Pete's sake. She was on her way to see her family, he was on his way to see his.

He shut the trunk. "Good to go."

"Thanks again for your help," she said.

"No problem. Since I'm going that way, I'll follow you into town."

"You don't need to." They weren't completely helpless, after all.

"May as well, since we're going the same way."

"Okay," she said and headed for the driver's side of the car. She was driving the rest of the way whether Shyla liked it or not.

"Thanks," Shyla called and got in. "Did you give him your phone number?" she asked as they pulled out.

"No."

"Why on earth not?"

"He didn't ask."

"Seriously? What the heck were you doing back there?"

"Thanking him."

"And sending off *I'm not interested* vibes," Shyla said in disgust.

"I was not."

"I swear, opportunity could bang on your door and you wouldn't hear it."

"What should I have said? 'I think you're cute. Are you my gift from Santa?'"

"You could have. You should have. Instead, you were making me do all the work for your gift. Santa's probably giving up on you right now," Shyla said in disgust. "I was doing a better job of flirting with him than you were, and you were the one he kept looking at."

Audrey shrugged. "It wasn't meant to be."

"Maybe it was, and you were too chicken to take a chance."

"Okay, so I was growing feathers," Audrey admitted.

For sure she was. There was something about getting dumped that messed with a woman's confidence.

"Just because one relationship didn't work out doesn't mean the next one won't," Shyla said gently.

"You're right," Audrey said with a sigh. "My head knows that. I guess my heart hasn't gotten the message yet."

"Oh, well. Maybe we'll run into him in town."

"I doubt it. Unless he decides to stay in our motel instead of going to his parents' place."

Opportunity lost. Had it been banging on her door? She'd never know.

A few more minutes and the town of Winnemucca came in sight. Being located along I-80 as well as US Highways 93 and 40, it was an important regional transport center, serving both the mining and ranching industries. It looked like a town that would serve those industries: hardworking and simple. It had a few casinos with only a dusting of glitz that said *Throwback Thursday*, establishments that wouldn't bring tourists to town but where you'd pop in to enjoy some local flavor.

"This place has a cool history," Audrey said. "You know, Butch Cassidy's gang robbed the First Bank of Winnemucca in 1900."

"Leave it to my sister to know that," Shyla teased. "That is dope, though. It all looks kind of frontiers-y. We should check out one of the casinos later. We might get lucky."

"Like you did in Reno?" Audrey teased.

"Sometimes you lose, sometimes you win."

"The odds are always in favor of the house."

"You never know. Somebody has to win once in a while. And after getting rescued from death in the desert, I'd say we're pretty lucky."

They pulled into the motel parking lot and waved out

their windows at their escort, and he saluted them with a toot on the horn and kept on going. Audrey watched as he turned into a gas station, filling up before finishing the trip to his parents' house, of course. Goodbye, nice man. Goodbye, opportunity. *Sorry I blew it, Santa.*

Oh, well. Life went on. Maybe somewhere down the road she'd meet someone.

Or not. At the rate she was going she was never going to find her perfect match, her soul mate. There were too many men out there who couldn't keep up with a smart woman, too many insecure losers. All the good ones were taken.

May as well face it. Opportunity did only knock once, and if you hesitated, it went on to the next door. She was going to end up alone. Julia was married and starting a family, happy in her new home, adored by her in-laws. Shyla had found her man. She'd be the next one planning a big wedding. And then she'd have kids. Audrey would...wind up being the favorite aunt. One day one of her nieces would ask, "Aunt Audrey, how come you never got married?" and she'd have to answer, "Because I didn't open the door when opportunity knocked."

Okay, enough, she scolded herself. She shoved aside the idiotic thoughts and said, "Let's get checked in. Then find someplace that serves cosmos and has a menu with lots of carbs." Carbs fixed everything.

"Like a casino," chirped Shyla.

The desk clerk had a welcoming smile for them and got busy on her computer when Audrey gave her name. Then the smile became sympathetic.

"I'm sorry. I'm not finding anything under that name," she said.

13

"That's impossible," Audrey informed the desk clerk. "I made the reservation a month ago online."

"I'll check again," the woman said.

Checking again didn't change anything.

"Are you sure you completed the final step in the reservation process?" the woman asked.

"Of course I did," said Audrey.

"I'm sorry. I'm not seeing your reservation," the woman insisted.

How could that be? Audrey cast back to the moment she made the reservation. Wait a minute. Had she? Her boss had called, wanting to discuss an important detail of her latest assignment. It had been a long conversation. Had Audrey made that final step?

Of course she had. She dug out the form she'd printed. "Here."

The woman looked at it, then at her. "I'm sorry. It looks like you booked with a third party and weren't really on our site, and somehow the reservation didn't get completed."

"What?" Audrey snatched back the printed page and studied it. "It says my reservation is confirmed."

"There must have been a mix-up," said the clerk.

"On your end," Audrey said, irritated.

Small hotels had less reliable IT systems and could lose reservations, especially those made through a third party. She should have called the hotel and spoken to someone in person. But still, this was not her fault.

"Oh, well. Mistakes happen," said Shyla, the peacemaker.

Her sister was right. *Let it go.* "Can we get a room now?" Audrey asked.

The woman pressed her lips together as if she was fighting back the desire to cry on their behalf. "I'm so sorry. We don't have any left."

"Rooms?" Shyla echoed in disbelief.

"No vacancies," the woman confirmed. "Someone got the last one only a few minutes before you walked in."

"Unbelievable," Audrey said between clenched teeth.

"I'm sorry," the woman said.

"That makes three of us," Audrey said. "I can't believe this," she ranted as they hauled their carry-ons back to the car.

"Stuff like this happens," said Shyla, the philosopher.

"Not to me!" Audrey prided herself on being organized, smart, on top of things. This was...wrong.

She popped the trunk and heaved in her carry-on. Once Shyla's was in, she slammed the trunk shut. Then she got back inside, took out her cell phone and started searching for another motel.

"Well, this is fun," said Shyla, plopping back into the passenger seat.

"Don't worry, I'll find us something. There are nineteen motels in this town. They can't all be full," Audrey said.

Maybe they could. She struck out six times in a row.

"Great. We're going to end up spending the night in the car," Shyla predicted. "We'll freeze to death."

Audrey couldn't blame her sister for panicking. Afternoon was on its way out the door. Once it got dark, the temperatures would drop. Sleeping in her car was something she'd never done and never wanted to. Would the local police come by and give them a ticket for vagrancy?

No, no, no. That was not going to happen. She was going to make sure of it.

"We'll be okay. I have a dozen more places to call."

She was on hotel number sixteen when Shyla got a text.

"If that's Mom tell her we're fine," Audrey instructed.

"It's not Mom. It's Milton, and we're not fine."

"I'll find us someplace," Audrey said between gritted teeth.

Shyla's fingers were flying over her phone's keyboard. Audrey could only imagine what she was saying. *My know-it-all sister screwed up.* It was the truth.

"Milton says we should keep driving," Shyla reported a minute later after her phone dinged with another text.

So the nonpresent boyfriend was now an expert on travel? "Milton isn't here. How does he know what we should do?" Audrey demanded.

"*I* think it's good advice, because we're not exactly on a winning streak here, are we?" Shyla said, glaring at her.

"I'll get this sorted out. Chill."

"I'm already chill, and by midnight I'll be sleeping in this car and the world's biggest ice cube."

"The car has a heater."

"I don't want to sleep in it," Shyla said, her voice rising.

"Me, neither," Audrey said, punching in the number for another motel on her phone. "Will you quit panicking!" *Like I'm doing.*

"I'm getting us an energy drink," Shyla announced. "We might have to drive all night."

"No! Those are bad for your heart. Everybody knows that."

"Well, everybody also knows you'll freeze to death if you try to sleep in your car in this weather," Shyla retorted.

"We will not. Just keep your butt glued to the seat for a minute, will you?"

Shyla obliged, but she scowled and began texting again.

A perky voice came out of the phone and greeted Audrey.

"Do you have any vacancies?" Audrey asked.

She didn't need to tell her sister the answer. She knew her face said it all.

"That does it," Shyla said, shoving open the car door.

"What are you doing?" Audrey demanded.

"Coming up with a creative solution to our problem," Shyla informed her and started for the grocery store.

What did she think she was going to find there, a heated tent? Audrey called after her, "I'll find someplace."

"So will I," Shyla called over her shoulder and marched off to Ridley's Family Market.

"Don't buy anything!" Audrey hollered out the window. They wouldn't need it. She'd find them a room.

Somewhere.

Over the rainbow.

All she got in answer from her sister was a certain finger pointed heavenward. If they were still kids Audrey would have shouted *I'm telling Mom.* She was still tempted, but she didn't have time. She had to find someplace for them to stay. Okay, what was the next town after Winnemucca?

Five minutes later she'd hung up from her third luckless call and looked over to the grocery store to see her sister standing in front of it holding a large piece of cardboard with something printed on it. Oh, no. What had Shyla done?

Audrey sped over to the market and parked the car in a nearby space. As she got out, she could see Shyla talking to an older woman who was bundled in a long winter coat. She could also see what her sister had written on that piece of cardboard. She'd managed to scrounge a Sharpie from someone and had written in large letters *Help. Need a Place to Stay.* Oh, no.

She got to her sister in time to hear her telling the woman, "I don't need money."

"There's no need to be ashamed. We all need help once in a while," the woman said to Shyla. She fumbled in her purse and brought out a wallet.

"No, really. My sister and I are stranded, and we just need a place to stay."

"Of course you do," the woman said. "And food." She

pulled out a bill and shoved it at Shyla's gloved hand. "Now, promise me you won't spend this on drugs."

"Don't take that," Audrey commanded her sister.

"I'm not," said Shyla, putting her hand behind her back.

"This is no time for false pride," the woman told her.

A man came out of the store carrying a plastic shopping bag. He looked about the right age to be retired and was wearing a heavy coat and a cap. And a disapproving frown.

"Erma, you shouldn't be giving money to panhandlers," he said.

"We're not panhandlers. We're stranded," Shyla protested.

"That's what they all say," the man said, scowling at her. "You know you're not allowed to panhandle out here."

"But we don't have any place to stay," Shyla protested. "There's no room at the inn." She was almost wailing.

"I'll find something," Audrey said between gritted teeth. "Come on." This was beyond embarrassing.

"If you don't leave, I'm reporting you to the manager," said the man.

Shyla didn't budge. "What is wrong with people?" she demanded. "There's not a single motel with a vacancy anywhere in this town. Do you want us to freeze to death in our car?"

"Will you stop?" Audrey hissed, grabbing her arm.

Another man joined them. He was wearing slacks and a shirt. No coat. No bag of groceries. So, not a shopper. "I'm sorry, but there's no soliciting in front of the store," he said. With that voice of authority, he was probably the manager.

"We're not soliciting," Shyla protested. "We need help."

"You need to leave," the manager or whoever he was said.

Great. Shooed away for panhandling. Audrey could feel her cheeks tingling, and it wasn't from the cold.

"These poor girls need money," protested Erma, the Good Samaritan.

Yet another customer, a man with a beer gut stuffed inside a parka, stopped and joined them. "Con artists," he informed the woman. "They pretend to be broke down and needing money for gas. Then they go buy drugs."

Now Audrey's face was on fire.

Shyla's was pretty red, too. "We do not do drugs," she said, incensed.

"Ladies, please. You need to move along," the manager said. Even more firmly. He wasn't smiling.

If the scene wasn't so pathetic and humiliating, Audrey would have laughed. Instead, she started hauling her sister back toward the car.

"We're not scammers," Shyla insisted.

"Will you come on?" Audrey hissed again.

Shyla dug in her heels. "No. I'm working on a plan B."

"To make us look like con artists? Are you out of your mind?"

"Well, you're not having any luck. Somebody's got to do something."

"I am doing something," Audrey snapped. "If you'd just be patient."

"Have you found a room?"

"Not yet."

Shyla turned and held up her sign again. "Help!"

Audrey snatched it away. "Will you stop that! You're going to get us arrested."

"Are you ladies okay?"

They both turned around at the sound of the familiar voice. There stood Russ Livingston in all his glory, holding a reusable shopping back full of groceries.

"No, we're not," Shyla said pitifully.

"We've just run into a small complication," Audrey said, refusing to look pitiful.

"Yeah, like no place to stay."

"There was a mix-up on our reservation," Audrey explained.

"Every place in town is booked. What's with that?" Shyla demanded.

"Well, it is the holidays," said Russ.

A middle-aged couple walked past. "Merry Christmas, Russ. Good to see you back in town," said the husband.

Russ gave them a quick salute and said, "Merry Christmas to you, too."

The beer-bellied man had something to say also, as he walked past. "Don't let those two take you in."

The other man echoed his advice, and Erma tried one more time to give Shyla money.

"Thank you, but we're fine," Audrey said. "Merry Christmas."

"And to you, as well," said Erma. "And don't buy drugs."

Audrey swore under her breath.

Russ chuckled, then sobered. "I think I can help you with your problem."

"You own a B and B somewhere?" Shyla asked hopefully.

"Even better. My folks can put you up at their place."

"Oh, we couldn't," Audrey protested. First they had him changing their flat, and now they were bumming rooms off his family. The leech sisters.

But why, exactly, she was hesitating to take him up on his offer she wasn't sure. Russ Livingston obviously wasn't a serial killer, and he was offering a solution to their problem. Mom had drummed it into all of them that it was better to give than to receive, and you shouldn't take advantage of people's kindness, but this was a case where it would for sure be better to receive, since they had nothing to give.

"Yes, we could," Shyla said and glared at her.

Her sister was right. This was no time for false pride. "We'd be happy to pay," Audrey offered.

"And deprive my mom of a chance to do a good deed? Good luck with that. We're not far out of town. You can follow me. I'll call the folks and tell them we're coming."

"Thank you," the sisters said in unison.

"You almost blew it again," Shyla scolded once they were back in the car. "What were you thinking?"

"That I could work this out."

"It did work out. Let's be grateful for that. And for heaven's sake, opportunity is back at the door again. Don't be stupid."

That was Audrey's line. She'd used it enough on her sisters when they were growing up. Rather humbling to have it thrown back at her.

"No stupidness," she promised.

"Good," Shyla said with a grin. "And you can thank me now for finding us a place to stay, 'cause if I hadn't stood in front of the door at Ridley's with my sign, we'd have been turning into ice sculptures."

In a heated car. Her sister, the drama queen.

"That is very interesting reasoning," said Audrey. She'd have found them a place to stay eventually. They'd have driven until they found something. The humor of the situation hit her, and she giggled. "You panhandler, you."

"That was rude," Shyla said. A moment later her frown righted itself to a smile, and then she, too, began to giggle. "That old woman was trying so hard to be a Good Samaritan and give me money."

"You had her concerned. I'd say that was some good acting."

"I wasn't playing a panhandler," Shyla said, incensed. "I just wanted to do my part. We were in a mess."

"We were," Audrey admitted. "And that was my bad. And you know what?"

"What?"

"There's no one I'd rather be in a mess with."

"Same here," said Shyla. "And now, on to the next great adventure."

Russ's parents' place was a ranch, and the house was big and impressive, with a three-car garage and painted red to match the barn nearest it. The house had a long porch running across the front of it, and right on cue Christmas lights strung along the wood railing winked on in welcome as the last of daylight bowed out to darkness. A swing occupied one end of the porch, while on the other, two white wooden rockers invited people to sit outside and enjoy a sunset. Big and welcoming as it was, it certainly looked like it could serve as a bed and breakfast. Outside the barn was a corral, and Audrey could envision Russ out there, breaking in some wild horse.

"Wow," breathed Shyla. "I guess they have room."

An Australian cattle dog came to greet Russ as they walked toward the house, tail wagging. "Hey there, Lucky," he said and bent to give the dog a good rub.

The dog took a nip at Shyla's heels as they followed Russ onto the porch, making her yelp.

"Lucky, stop!" Russ commanded, and the dog slinked off. "Herding instincts," he explained. "Sorry about that. He's really very friendly."

"I'll take your word for it," Shyla said.

Russ's parents had the door open before he could even turn the handle. Both were slim and fit-looking, him in jeans and a Western shirt and boots, her also in jeans, topped with a red sweater. She had slippers on her feet made to look like a pink Cheshire cat. Mrs. Livingston's smile was just as big as that famous feline's.

"Welcome to our home," said his dad. "I'm Tom, and this is my wife, Vera."

"It's so kind of you to take us in," Audrey said.

"We weren't looking forward to sleeping in our car," added Shyla.

Audrey resisted the temptation to insist that they'd have found someplace. Maybe they would have, but who knew? And she didn't want to sound ungrateful.

"That would be awful," said Vera. "I'm glad our son rescued you."

"For the second time today," said Audrey. "He found us earlier stranded with a flat tire."

"That's our boy, Sir Galahad," said Tom.

"We've got the guest room all ready for you," Vera said.

She led the way up hardwood stairs accented with a rustic wood banister. "I've got chili on the stove and

French bread, but if you don't like that, we can have something else."

"Oh, no, that's fine," Audrey said. "We don't want you to go to a lot of trouble."

"No trouble at all. We enjoy having company." She stopped at a door across from a bathroom and opened it, showing off a gigantic bed with a quilt on it. Two wooden nightstands stood on either side, and an old-fashioned dresser with a mirror was parked against one wall. "It's not the Hilton, but I promise the bed is comfortable."

"It's charming," Shyla assured her.

Audrey pointed to the bed. "That's a beautiful quilt."

"Thank you," said Vera.

"Did you make it?" Audrey asked.

"Guilty as charged. I have a slight fabric addiction," Vera quipped.

"So does my grandma," Audrey told her.

"Does it run in the family?" asked Vera.

"I'm an addict, too," Shyla told her.

"Shyla has the sewing-and-crafting gift," Audrey said, quick to give credit where it was due.

"My sister has other talents," Shyla said. "She speaks a million languages—"

"French and some Spanish," Audrey qualified.

"Does sudoku puzzles for fun, always wins at Trivial Pursuit and should have her own cooking show."

Okay, this was overkill. "I like to cook, but I'm not that special."

"Yeah, you are," Shyla said.

Vera smiled. "It's lovely to see sisters who think so highly of each other."

"Most of the time," Audrey said.

"When we're not fighting," Shyla said, adding a smile to show that the fights were never that bad.

"I have a sister. I know how that goes," Vera said. "I'll let you freshen up and then come on downstairs and join us in the family room for some hot buttered rum. That other rascal of mine should be getting home from work any minute."

"Two for the price of one," Shyla said after Vera had left.

"Oh, stop," said Audrey. "And don't be embarrassing me like that anymore."

"Why not? It's guaranteed you won't brag on yourself."

"I don't need to. I am who I am."

"Nothing wrong with telling these people who you am," Shyla said, copping an attitude.

"They'll figure it out. And either they'll like me or they won't."

"Of course they'll like you. Don't be so irritatingly philosophical," Shyla said in disgust. "But you do like Russ, don't you?"

"What's not to like?"

Shyla grinned. "That flat tire was meant to be."

"There's no point in trying to make something out of this," Audrey said. "It's only a chance encounter."

"Two chance encounters, and now we're staying with his family. Come on, sissy, read the graffiti on the wall. This beats meeting someone in the grocery-store produce department."

"Yes, but if you meet someone in the produce department it usually means you live in the same neighborhood. We don't even live in the same state."

"It's not as if you're on opposite coasts," pointed out

Shyla. "And what are the odds that we'd run into the same man who changed our tire just when we need a place to stay? Come on, Santa's working hard for you. Give him a chance."

"Only if you promise not to act like one of his elves. No obvious maneuvering, no more bragging or embarrassing hint-dropping. No nothing."

Shyla gave Audrey her most serious look and crossed her heart. Then added, "But don't go screwing it up. At least let the man know you're interested, because he's obviously interested in you."

Was he? Really? Or... "He's just being nice."

"You know as well as I do that a man who's just being nice doesn't look at a woman the way we've both seen this one look at you. And, may I remind you, it was you he was interested in when he was changing our tire? I could have been a cactus for all the attention I got."

Audrey had to smile at that. "Bugs you, doesn't it?"

"It would if I hadn't already found the most perfect man ever. You'll have to settle for second best," Shyla teased.

Russ Livingston was as far from second best as a man could get.

They freshened up and started downstairs. On the stairs they encountered another hottie coming up them. He was almost as tall as Russ and had similar features but was a little heftier. His hair was a rusty red, and he had a dimple when he smiled, which he did as he stopped right in front of them. The Livingstons had certainly made a couple of beautiful boys.

"You must be the sisters," he said. "Nicest thing my bro's brought home in a long time. I'm Rand," he added.

"Hi," said Shyla.

"I'm Audrey, and this is Shyla," Audrey said. "It's really great of you guys to put us up for the night."

"Stay as long as you want. It'll give me something nice to look at instead of that ugly brother of mine." He held up grease-stained hands. "I smell like a car jock. Be down to join you as soon as I've cleaned up," he said and kept on going, taking the stairs two at a time.

"Wow, a regular cuteness bonanza," Shyla whispered as the sisters went on down the stairs.

The family room was a monster of a space, with thick throw rugs over a hardwood floor. A love seat and some chairs were arranged around a coffee table, all pointed toward a roaring fire in a stone hearth. The mantel had been dressed up with greens and pillar candles in red mercury glass. On another side of the room stood a pool table. A small table was set up by the window and held a half-finished puzzle.

Tom Livingston stood in front of the fire, warming his back. "You probably just met Son Number Two. The boy's a genius with cars. Just opened his own repair shop in town," he added in a proud-papa voice.

"Pretty awesome to have your own auto mechanic in the family," Shyla said. "We could use that. We're all girls."

Audrey was about to add *Not that girls can't repair cars*, but Tom beat her to it.

"I wouldn't want to get all greasy," Shyla said, wrinkling her nose. "And I'd probably drop an engine on my foot."

"I think they have winches so you don't have to worry about that," Audrey said. Then to Tom, "You have the perfect HGTV home."

"Built it myself," he said. "With the help of my brothers and my sons."

"That is amazing," Audrey said.

"No, *that's* amazing." Tom pointed to his wife, who was entering the room bearing several steaming mugs. "This woman is the best thing that ever happened to me."

"We were blessed to find each other," Vera said, smiling at him.

With the looks they were exchanging they could have been newlyweds. It had been too long since Audrey had seen her parents look at each other that way.

The thought made her sad, but she brought up a smile and a thank-you for Vera as she took a mug of hot buttered rum from the tray.

Russ came in right behind her and set a charcuterie board of brie cheese, sliced salami, crackers and olives on the coffee table in front of the couch by the fire. His hat was off, and her fingers itched to play with the brown curls grazing the back of his shirt collar.

"This buttered rum is my wife's own recipe," Tom bragged.

"Not all that original," said Vera. "Once upon a time maybe, but these days you can find a recipe for anything and everything on the internet."

"It's still the best," Tom insisted. "So our son tells us you ladies are on your way to see family."

"We're sure trying to get there," Audrey said. "I still don't know what went wrong with our reservations."

"No matter. All's well that ends well," Tom said.

"I'm just glad Russel ran into you when he did," put in Vera.

"He's been our guardian angel today," Audrey said.

Just then his brother entered the room. "Angel Russ, huh?"

Russ pointed a warning finger at him. "Don't be a smart-ass."

His brother gave a half smile and helped himself to a mug.

"My boys are both angels," Vera said, beaming on them.

"Shows how much she knows about our teen years," said Russ with a wink.

"They were adorable," Vera insisted. "Both nice boys. Every girl in town chased after them."

Audrey could well imagine. Rand was cute and had the bonus of a super personality, just like Shyla. Russ was tall and lean, and she was willing to bet had been a skinny guy. Maybe a basketball star. With beautiful eyes and a killer smile. Yes, the girls probably drooled every time he walked past.

"But nobody caught us," said Rand.

"Yet," said his father. "Amy Richardson is sure making an effort."

To catch which one? And was she succeeding? Audrey hoped for more of these important details, but none came.

"I'm waiting for someone to nominate me for *The Bachelor*," said Rand. "Is that show still on?" So, not him.

"Who knows?" said his brother. "There are better ways to meet women than going on TV and making a fool of yourself." Here, he looked at Audrey. So maybe the mysterious Amy was after his brother and not him. A girl could hope.

Although it would be stupid to. A chance meeting,

one short evening together—nothing was going to come of this. Plus, nice as he was, Russ probably wasn't the scholarly type. If he was, he'd have been working some white-collar job. She needed to hold out for a college professor or a brain surgeon or member of MENSA— someone, anyone, who wouldn't feel threatened by a smart woman, someone who wouldn't label her a *know- it-all*.

She sighed inwardly. Why were there so many inse- cure men out there?

Michelle finally saw Max at Stein, a unique beer hall that offered a myriad of beers on tap as well as food. He was at the end of the bar, hunched over a beer. Next to him sat a woman who looked to be somewhere in her thirties. Highlighted hair, red lipstick, wearing jeg- gings and boots and a V-neck sweater that was trying to contain her cleavage. She was leaning in close and looking concerned.

The place was packed, and as she approached it was impossible for Michelle to hear what the woman was saying, but her body language said more than enough. Michelle's eyes narrowed as the woman touched his shoulder with perfectly manicured hands. Michelle had never bothered much with manicures: between garden- ing and housework she was too hard on her nails. She suddenly wished she had gotten a fancy mani for the holidays, something with lots of holiday red and little snowflakes.

She got to them just in time to hear the woman say, "We all need to find comfort somewhere."

"Don't worry, he will," Michelle said. "I'm his wife. Scram."

The woman blinked in surprise and pulled away her hand. "He said he was getting divorced."

"We are," Max said gruffly.

"Not yet," Michelle said. "You're sitting in my seat."

"Bastard," the woman spat. She took her beer and vacated, and Michelle slipped in next to him.

"She hit on me," Max was quick to say.

"Which showed excellent taste on her part."

His eyebrows shot up. Then lowered. "Very funny."

"I was being serious. Max, I'm sorry about Warren. I'm sorry about a lot of things," she added.

He stared into his nearly empty glass. "They could have been killed."

"So could we. But none of us were. We're all right."

His response to that was a grunt.

They both sat in silence for a moment. Until he finally said, "I hate that I can't get to them."

"I know. Me, too. But they're okay."

He nodded. Downed the last of his beer.

"Max. About what you said to that woman."

He didn't look at her. "Don't start up on me. Not after what I've just gone through with my parents."

"I know, my timing sucks. But, Max, I've been wrong. I'm not ready to give up on us."

At her words he turned his head and stared at her. "Say again?"

"I know we agreed."

"I don't blame you for wanting out. Look, if I could go back in time I'd never have pushed to get pregnant. I know that's where this all started. I know you never forgave me."

"I should have," she said softly. "I'm sorry."

"You were right. We shouldn't have tried for another.

I should have been happy with the girls. I was happy with the girls," he quickly added.

"I know you wanted a boy, too."

"I already had more than any man deserves."

"Do you still think that?" she asked.

He nodded, turned to look at her, his expression earnest. "I really don't want to split. But the way things kept unraveling, especially these past couple years…and when you said you wanted a divorce…" He frowned. "What kind of a shit would I have been if I'd said no? I'd already let you down a lot."

"I've blamed you for so much. That was wrong."

He pushed his palms into his eyes. It hid the tears but the tremble in his voice couldn't. "I'm sorry, Chelle. I'm so damned sorry."

She held him as he cried silently, his big shoulders shaking. It was something he never did, something he hadn't even done—at least not in front of her—when they lost the baby. He'd been too busy trying to console her. Consolation she'd rejected in the end.

He took a swipe at his eyes with the back of his hand. "I never could say anything right, do anything right."

"Oh, Max, I'm sorry." She took his face in her hands. "We belong together, for better or for worse. I think we've been through the worst."

"I'll make it better. I promise."

"Me, too," she said. "I really want to try again. Can we?"

In answer, he pulled her to him, nearly toppling her from her stool and kissed her like a starving man.

"Let's get out of here," he said.

14

The Livingston family radiated good cheer and kindness, and the love between Mr. and Mrs. Livingston was plain in every smile they exchanged during dinner, in the way he praised her cooking and in the way she bragged about how smart he was.

"Nah, she's the smart one," he said. "We didn't have two pennies to rub together when we first got married. Thanks to my lady's money management, we don't have to worry about how to pay the bills."

"You're the one who built the ranch up," she said.

"But you're the one who picked the right stocks."

Arguing about who was the best—it was so cute. And touching. Obviously, those two had formed their own mutual-admiration society. That was the kind of relationship Audrey wanted someday. It was the kind of relationship she wished her parents still had.

The bragging switched to their sons. "Rand here is the car genius," said Mr. Livingston. "And Russel—"

"They saw the truck, Dad," Russ said in an obvious effort to stop his father from continuing.

"Yeah, but not it's not just any construction company," Mr. Livingston said. "Right now he's building restaurants."

Interesting. Audrey looked at Russ. "Restaurants?"

He shrugged. "I've got a couple of partners. I design and build the space, then they take over and manage the restaurant, and I get a share of the profits."

Designing and building restaurants. Okay, that was seriously impressive.

"Wow," Shyla said, echoing Audrey's thoughts. "Are you an architect or something?"

"BA with a major in architecture. I spent some time at a drawing board. But I like getting out and getting my hands dirty, too. Worked construction every summer when I was in school."

"You must be busy all the time," Audrey said.

"Not so busy I can't make time in my life for people I like," he said and smiled at her.

That smile set her heart on fire. And other body parts, too.

Of course, neither the words nor the smile meant anything. They were simply two people on the road to Christmas, stopping for a little conversation before going their separate ways with a friendly wave.

After dessert—red velvet whoopie pies, otherwise known as fat bombs—Mrs. Livingston said, "Okay, men, time to bring in the tree." She turned to the sisters. "I hope you girls won't mind keeping us company while we decorate our tree."

Oh, no. They were intruding on family time. "We don't want to be underfoot," Audrey said, ready to go hide in the guest bedroom.

"But we are expert ornament-hangers," put in Shyla.

"Good, 'cause I'm all thumbs at that," said Rand.

"Every year Mom makes me help, and every year I break something."

"So you are both needed," Mrs. Livingston said to Audrey. "And, frankly, it's nice to have some women helping. Sometimes there is too much testosterone in this house," she said with a teasing smile.

The men all carried their dishes to the sink, and Audrey jumped up and took hers, as well as the empty bread platter, and followed them. As they left, she and Shyla remained to help with the rest of the kitchen cleanup.

"I can't tell you how much we appreciate you taking us in," Audrey said to Mrs. Livingston.

"We really are happy to. We love having company."

"And we love being company," Shyla quipped. "I don't know what we would have done if your son hadn't come along."

"I'm sure you'd have figured out something," Vera said.

The vote of confidence was nice and was more than Audrey had gotten from her sister. In spite of Shyla's panicking, she'd have found them a place somewhere. Although, she had to admit, the place where they'd wound up was more special than any motel could have possibly been.

"I was working on it," Shyla said, making Audrey roll her eyes.

"She was standing at the grocery store entrance with a cardboard sign," Audrey explained. "And, by the way, where did you get something to write with?" she asked suspiciously.

"On the aisle with the pens and notebooks and stuff," Shyla said. "And I paid for it. I got the cardboard from one of the men working in the produce section. Anyway, I thought it was a creative solution to our problem."

"Yeah, I know the store manager was impressed," Audrey said in disgust.

"You got in trouble with the store manager?" Vera asked.

Her question called for a recap of the afternoon's adventure, which had their hostess laughing and both sisters, too.

"The look on your face when that woman made you promise not to spend the money she was trying to give you on drugs," Audrey said. "I should have told her you're a chocoholic and you'd be blowing the money on Dove dark."

"I can't believe she thought that," Shyla muttered.

"I'm glad Russel came along when he did," Vera said. "Although, I'm sure someone would have come to your rescue. We have good people in these parts."

It sure looked like it.

The living room was large but not quite as big as the family room. The floor was hardwood, partly covered by a big area rug, and yet another fireplace took up one wall, its mantel also decorated for the holidays. The collection of family pictures atop a large cabinet, which Vera said held a TV, made it feel more intimate. "I don't like the TV taking center stage, so we hide it," she explained.

Audrey drifted over to look at the pictures. Most were of the brothers at various stages of childhood, sitting on Santa's lap, probably brought out specially for the season. Another showed the whole family, seated in front of the Christmas tree. Vera sat with her sons on both sides of her, and Tom stood in back, leaning over them all with his arms on his sons' shoulders. Off to the side, a cat was sneaking into the picture. It was in a double frame, and the picture next to it showed the tree in the process of toppling, with Tom trying to grab it. A furry blur was in the process of jumping from a branch.

Vera came to stand next to her. "That was what we like to call our *National Lampoon* Christmas. Our cat, Mortimer, hadn't learned his Christmas manners yet. Tom did manage to catch the tree, but I lost several of my favorite ornaments. That was the same year the oven went out halfway through cooking the turkey."

"We had a similar problem last year when our power went out. What did you do?" Audrey asked.

"Cut off the meat and barbecued it. It turned out great. Which just goes to show that you never know what good things can come out of seeming catastrophes."

"For sure," put in Shyla, giving her sister a look that dared her to complain about the flat tire.

The men brought in the tree, a balsam fir, and the room suddenly smelled like Christmas.

Audrey inhaled deeply and smiled. "That smells wonderful."

"There's nothing like a live tree," Vera said.

As the brothers worked on getting the tree set up in the living room, the family joked back and forth and shared more memories of Christmases past. There was no underlying tension, no looks from either parent that hinted at discontent, no comments that needed to be dissected and worried about. No gray cloud hanging over the gathering.

It had been that way with Audrey's family once, and she and her sisters had nested in the security of knowing their parents shared both love and happiness. If only they could find their way back to that. She had a sudden longing to talk to her mom.

She took a moment to text her. How are you and Dad doing?

Audrey wasn't sure she wanted to hear the answer to that question considering the tension she'd felt between them at Thanksgiving, but she couldn't stop herself from asking.

While she waited to hear back from Mom she also sent a quick text to her grandmother. Is Grandpa out of the hospital yet?

Staying a little longer but expect to be out of here by ten. Long day but we are good, came the reply.

"You texting Gram?" Shyla asked.

Audrey nodded. "Grandpa's still in the hospital, but he's all right." She was aware of Mrs. Livingston politely pretending not to hear as she sorted through one of the boxes of ornaments. "Our grandparents hit a deer on their way to our sister's. They weren't hurt, but it triggered his A-fib. They had to take a detour to the emergency room."

"How awful to have something like that happen at the holidays," said Mrs. Livingston.

Tom came in with another box of ornaments. "Remember that time we hit an elk? Totaled my truck," he told the sisters.

"Better your truck than us," Vera scolded. "And the poor elk. It was awful. I'm glad your grandparents are okay," she said to Audrey.

"I wish I'd hear back from our parents," Audrey said. "They're stuck in Leavenworth. Our whole family is supposed to be meeting at our sister's house for Christmas. I hope we all make it."

"I'm sure you will," said Mrs. Livingston.

Audrey nodded. "We will." Why hadn't Mom texted her back yet?

15

Their clothes were scattered on the floor, and Max and Michelle lay in that comfy bed in each other's arms. He felt like he'd just run a marathon...and come in first. That was the best sex they'd had in years. No, ever. Not just because it had been so long since they'd had it, but because they'd come together knowing how very tenuous life was and how lucky they were to still be alive. They'd been given a second chance, and they'd taken it.

Her gorgeous long hair was half in her face. He brushed it aside and kissed her forehead. "That was amazing."

"Yes, it was," she agreed. "Oh, Max, I wasted a lot of time being angry."

"And I wasted a lot of time feeding that anger. I'm sorry," he said. He really couldn't say it enough.

"Me, too. It was so easy to blame you for everything that wasn't right."

"I didn't do enough to try to get us back to where we needed to be," he admitted. "And I did my share of pulling away." *Stupid male pride*, he thought. In the end, what did it get you?

She sighed. "Experts are always talking about how you need to communicate, but they forget to tell you that all the communicating in the world doesn't do any good without forgiveness, without someone being willing to take the first step to change things for the better."

He felt like he'd tried to change things for the better, at least at first, but she'd been having none of it. Water under the bridge. He kept his big mouth shut.

A good plan because, really, the one thing that could have made things better would have been for him to say *I'll take the blame*. He hadn't said it, and his reward had been to watch her love for him slowly die. She'd kept up the pretense of a solid marriage for the girls, but the only thing solid had been the wall she'd built between them.

If not for this road trip they'd still be ready to take that final step right over the cliff. The End. He'd almost lost her. He drew her closer and kissed the top of her head. She smelled like the rose-scented perfume she favored. He'd always loved it on her. He'd always loved the way she felt in his arms, too. He'd almost lost that forever.

"I've missed holding you like this," he said. "Missed... us."

She snuggled against his chest. "I can't believe how close we came to blowing it." She looked up at him. "Do you think we were supposed to have that near accident?"

"What?"

"You know, like a bit of a Christmas miracle."

"I don't know," he said. When he thought of miracles he thought of what he'd learned in Sunday school when he was a kid: Jesus walking on water, feeding the

multitude, healing lepers. Nearly getting creamed by a
semi sure didn't fit that category.

"I feel like it was a wake-up call," she said.

"It about woke the shit out of me."

She chuckled. "I guess sometimes it takes something
so dramatic to turn us from a bad decision."

"I guess you're right," he said. And if that was the
case, then thank God for their close call.

"Are you hungry?" Michelle asked.

"For more of you."

She smiled. "There's plenty of time for that. Let's get
some food and have a picnic here in the room."

A picnic. Her words made him smile.

They got dressed and walked outside. The afternoon
dusk had been the signal for the town to turn on its
Christmas lights, and now everything was lit up like a
holiday-movie set. The snow was still falling, and instead of the curse they'd thought it to be, it now was
pure magic.

They found both blue and Havarti cheeses as well as
aged prosciutto in the Cheesemonger's Shop and picked
up a bottle of Riesling at the Icicle Ridge Winery. They
bought a loaf of German brown bread at Homefires
Bakery, then completed their picnic feast with two iced
Lebkuchen hearts from the Gingerbread Factory.

"Whole hearts again," Michelle said and smiled up
at him.

"By the way," he said as they strolled back to the
hotel, "I'm selling the bike. You were right. It was a selfish purchase."

The relief on her face confirmed that he'd made the
right decision. "Really?"

"I'm thinkin' we can use the money to do something special next year. Maybe a Caribbean cruise?"

"For sure a Caribbean cruise," she said and wrapped her arm through his.

I'm the king of the world, he thought, remembering the famous line from the movie *Titanic*. He'd thought the movie was sappy, but in that moment he sure knew how DiCaprio's character felt.

Back in the room they spread out their food and started the fire in the fireplace.

"I'm so glad we got snowed in," she said as he opened the wine. "Good thing we stopped for coffee."

"Good thing we got a late start," he said, handing her a glass. "Here's to all the things that went wrong."

"That are turning out right."

Yes, they were.

And things turned out even more right when they were able to book a sleigh ride. It was the kind of thing he knew she'd like—bundled up, just the two of them in a sleigh, gliding through a winter wonderland, the bells on the horses' harness jingling. The trees were heavily frosted with snow, and the air was crisp and clean. But it wasn't the scenery that he was enjoying, it was the nearness of her. He pulled her closer to him and kissed her cheek, which had been chilled by the mountain air, and it sent a thrill through him. Suddenly, all he could think of was getting back to their room and falling onto that nice soft bed with her in his arms.

"That was wonderful," she said to him after they'd thanked their driver and left.

"Yeah, it was," he agreed. So was being back together again.

Later, after another go 'round in the bed, she grabbed

her phone as he looked for a movie for them to watch on TV. He heard her chuckle.

"What?" he asked.

"We got a text from Audrey. She wants to know if we're all right."

He smiled and put an arm around her. "Tell her we're trying to make the best of things."

She smiled and texted, We're having a wonderful time!

The tree was up and gaudy with ornaments, lights and tinsel garlands, and the boys' stockings had been hung along the mantel. ("They still expect those to get filled every year," Vera had explained.) Vera had also hung mistletoe in the family-room doorway, sending a sly glance Audrey's direction.

With the decorating done, the sisters and their hosts were about to start a game of Trivial Pursuit when Audrey got her mother's text. She read it twice, trying to decode the message. Was Mom being sarcastic? Was she covering up the fact that they were miserable? No, she couldn't be, not with an exclamation mark at the end of the sentence.

She showed it to Shyla, who nodded and smiled. "Looks like our family is keeping Santa busy this year."

If her parents fell back in love again, it would be more than a Santa thing. It would be a holiday miracle.

Us, too, she texted back. Although with her mom having such a good time she didn't expect to get any kind of reply.

"How shall we play this?" Mrs. Livingston asked as she set the board out on the coffee table in the living room. "Girls against the boys?"

"Bring it on," said her husband.

"I should warn you, Audrey always wins," Shyla said to him.

"Not against the Livingston men," Rand warned, smiling. "Russ is the king of Trivial Pursuit."

Well, thought Audrey, *this is where the interest dies*. She'd look like a brainiac show-off, and he would be done.

He shouldn't, though. A smart woman shouldn't be a threat to a man who was secure in who he was. Was Russ one of those rare specimens? Or was he like her ex, threatened by a woman who was as smart as he was? She'd soon find out.

The game raged, with the women easily getting a brown wedge for literature. History was a slam dunk, also. But they couldn't come up with an answer for the science question, which stumped even Audrey.

"What amphibian did Pliny the Elder suggest be tied to the jaw to make teeth firmer?" Rand read again from the question/answer card. "I bet my bro can answer."

"We give up," Audrey said. "Let's hear it."

"A frog," Russ said with a shrug as if it was no big deal.

"Now, that's impressive," said Shyla and shot yet another look Audrey's direction. *There. Is this gift from Santa smart enough for you?*

"Not really," Russ said. "It's pretty much a matter of logic. How many amphibians were common and small but sturdy enough to try and use like that?"

"Of course," said Rand. "First you have to know who Pliny was."

"He was an ancient Roman, a naturalist. I think he

was born around 24 CE. Or *AD*, depending on which you prefer," Russ said.

Audrey found herself gaping. This man knew stuff. He was a regular fact-magnet.

Catching her staring, his cheeks reddened as if the flames from the fireplace had suddenly reached him. "I'm kind of a history geek."

"I think you've met your match, sis," Shyla said.

Maybe she had.

An hour later the women had won the game. "Poor boys," teased Mrs. Livingston. "It's always so hard on the ego to lose."

"We don't mind letting you win once in a while," her husband teased back.

"We're secure in our manhood," added Russ with a smile.

Maybe he was. What a refreshing change.

"Hey, and I never claimed to be a brain," said Rand. "I'm better at pool than Trivial Pursuit. Anybody want to play?"

"Ooh, yes," said Shyla. "I'm a regular pool shark."

Russ turned to Audrey. "How about you?"

"I'm afraid I'm not very good," she said.

"Well, then, how about a Trivial Pursuit rematch?" he suggested.

"I'm out of here," said his father. "Come on, my darling, let's go up to bed and watch a movie," he said to his wife.

The parents drifted off to their bedroom, and Rand and Shyla went to the family room to play pool.

Which left Audrey and Russ to stoke the fire in the living room and stay on the couch, getting sucked into the world of trivia. It was a close game, but she won again.

"Thanks to the easy sports question," she said in an effort to sound modest.

"I don't mind losing," Russ said.

"So is it true, then?" she asked.

"Is what true?"

"That you're secure in your manhood?"

He draped his arms over the back of the couch, looking very much like a man comfortable in his own skin. "I am."

"Then, that makes you a rare gem," she told him.

"Why? Because I don't mind losing at Trivial Pursuit? It's only a game."

"I know some men who would hate being beaten by a woman. At anything," Audrey said.

"Yeah? Isn't that thinking outdated?"

"Not for everyone."

Russ studied her. "I get the impression you're thinking of a specific someone."

"I am," she admitted. "I had a pretty insecure ex."

"Couldn't stand being with someone smarter, huh?" She sighed.

"Any man insecure enough to be threatened by a smart woman doesn't deserve her."

"Who are you?" Audrey said, feigning awe. Actually, she was only half feigning. This man was almost too good to be true.

"Considering the last twenty-four hours, I'd say I'm one lucky guy for having met you."

Heart-flutter time. Could Russ Livingston get any closer to perfect?

"How about some eggnog?" he suggested. "Got plenty of rum on hand."

"That sounds great," she said.

She accompanied him to the kitchen where he poured them generous glasses of eggnog with just the right amount of rum, then they returned to the living room and planted themselves on the couch and talked. And talked. And talked some more.

She told him about her job, and he talked again about his. They compared holiday memories and talked about favorite traditions.

"Getting the tree set up, for sure," Russ said. "It means Christmas has started. When we were kids the tree went up a lot earlier, but with me on the move for the business and not able to be home for as long, Mom always waits."

"Your mom is an awfully sweet woman," Audrey said.

"She sure likes you," Russ said. "But then, what's not to like?"

"Oh, there's plenty," she said.

"Yeah? I don't believe it."

"Just wait till you get to know me." Oh, crap. Maybe she shouldn't have said that. Here she was, talking like they were on their way to something when he was probably just being a good host and this was it, as far as they went.

"Looking forward to it," he said.

Or maybe not. Maybe he really was as into her as she was into him. His smile sure seemed to say as much. The moment wrapped around them, warm and promising. Russ Livingston was so easy to fall for, so easy to talk to.

So easy to look at. He had such lovely, broad shoulders. And pecs. She was sure he was sporting a six-pack under that shirt. And that lovely, smiling mouth of his... She was tempted to lean over and kiss him.

"So how about you?" he asked. "Favorite holiday tradition?"

Okay, no kissing. She brought her mind back to the subject at hand. "Baking," she said. "It's Christmas when we start baking cookies."

He grinned. "Oh, yeah. I like cookies."

"What else do you like?" she asked.

"Hanging out with people I care about, watching a good documentary, going for a ride on one of our horses and just being out in nature."

Horses, huh? "Believe it or not, I've never ridden a horse," she confessed.

"You haven't lived till you've ridden a horse," he said.

"I'd be afraid I'd fall off."

"Riding a horse is probably safer than riding in a car. Although, I don't have the statistics to prove it. You'd look great on a horse, by the way."

She wasn't sure she liked the idea of being on a horse, but she did like the fact that he thought she'd look great on one.

"I guess that's part of why I'm big on open spaces. I think I'm more of a country boy than a big-city kid," he said. "I mean, I don't mind a small city. But LA…"

"So you wouldn't move to LA for a woman?" Oh, no. She was fishing, and it was so obvious and pathetic. Where was the duct tape? She needed to tape her mouth shut.

He smiled. "I didn't say that." He had the sexiest smile, showing off perfect teeth and deep dimples. That mouth of his was full and strong and looked capable of doing amazing things. "When you love somebody, you make sacrifices."

Okay, it was official. He really was perfect.

"I'm not from a big city," Audrey said. "And I don't need to live in one. I actually followed my ex to LA. That was a mistake. Both the city and the ex," she clarified. "I mean, LA's not bad, and I like my job and the nightlife. But sometimes I feel so...lost." Was she sharing too much? Probably.

"Understandable. You thought you had a solid relationship, thought you knew where you were going."

"Obviously, I didn't know as much as I thought I did. Maybe I'm not so smart after all," she said with a rueful grin.

"You know, part of being smart is being able to analyze your choices and see where you've gone wrong."

"Has anyone ever told you that you have an amazing gift for knowing exactly what to say?"

He chuckled. "No. More like I'm usually told to shut up already." He sobered. "I know you're anxious to get to your family."

Not as anxious as she should be.

"But I kinda wish you were staying here another night."

"You've all been great."

"Never mind the rest of them. What about me?" he said with a laugh.

He was into her! "You, too." *Oh, be bold.* "You especially."

"Yeah?"

"Yeah."

"Think you might want to see more of me?"

"Definitely. Unless..."

"Unless what?"

"How stiff is my competition?"

"What competition?"

"Someone named Amy?"

He smiled and shook his head. "She's been after Rand since high school."

"And how many girls have been after you since high school?"

"Not that many. I was a scrawny dork."

He'd sure filled out fine since then.

His gaze dropped to her lips. He lifted it, looked at her with the age-old question in his eyes. *May I?*

She leaned toward him. *You may.*

They were mere inches apart when laughter and footsteps invaded the room. Nooo.

Embarrassed, Audrey pulled back so fast she almost gave herself whiplash.

"Your sister is a pool hustler," Rand said. His brows pulled together at the sight of Audrey and his brother. They probably looked like two teenagers who'd just been caught fooling around under the bleachers. "We interrupting something?"

"Yes," said Russ. "Go away."

"Fine," Rand said, pretending to be insulted. "Didn't want to hang with you anymore tonight, anyway. Some of us have to get up and go to work in the morning."

"I'm tired. Think I'll go to bed," said Shyla. "See you later, sis."

She'd go to bed, but not to sleep. Audrey would be getting the third degree from her sister, Santa's newest elf, as soon as she got upstairs. The way Russ was looking at her she'd be giving Santa a thumbs-up.

"Now, where were we?" he murmured after they'd left.

"Seeing more of each other," she murmured back.

"Ah, yes." He slipped an arm around her shoulders and touched his lips to hers.

Whoa, holiday magic! She was the string of holiday lights, and he was the electrical outlet. She slipped her fingers into her hair and kissed him back for all she was worth. Merry Christmas and Happy New Year!

"Even if I'm not going to luck out, it looks like my bro is," Rand said as he and Shyla started upstairs. "You're sure it's serious with that boyfriend of yours, by the way?"

"It is." Rand was a great guy and lots of fun, but it was Milton she wanted to spend the rest of her life with. "Looks like you'll have to let that local girl catch you," she teased.

"Or see if I can find your clone."

"Ha! There's only one of me."

"Well, that's a shame. I'm glad for Russ, though. He's never really found a woman he connected with, but I'd say him and your sis are connecting pretty good. Too bad you guys have to take off tomorrow."

Hmm. Did they? Really?

Once in the guest bedroom she sent a text to Julia. Might be delayed.

WHAT?!!!

Don't freak. Will be there for Christmas but I think Audrey's met Mr. Perfect, and Santa and I have some work to do. Stay tuned.

Kk, but you guys better be here Christmas Day.

We will, Shyla promised.

A text came through from Milton. How's Winnemucca? She told him about their adventures and how they'd been taken in by a local family, then couldn't help adding, Both bros are hot, just to keep him on his toes.

How hot?

Superhot.

She received an entire string of frowny-face emoticons in response, followed by Hot for you?
One is, of course. Oh, she was evil. Hehe.
The little dots jumping on the screen told her he was busy typing. Seriously?
Okay, it wasn't nice to be mean. Until I told him I was with the most amazing man in the world.
That earned a string of smiley faces.

One is crazy about Audrey, though.

Who wouldn't be?

Shyla read it and frowned.

Not me, of course.

Okay, he could live another day.

Hope it works out.

It will. She was going to make sure it did because her big sister deserved to be happy.
Audrey entered the room just as she hit Send. Oh, yeah, that smitten smile and those daydreaming eyes said it all.

"Did Santa come through or what?" Shyla teased.

"Maybe," Audrey said, obviously hedging her bets. "It's too soon to tell. We hardly know each other."

"Yeah? It looked like you were getting to know each other pretty good. So did he kiss you? Don't lie to me. I can tell by that sappy expression on your face that he did."

"He did," Audrey admitted.

"And did it jingle your bells?"

"Oh, yeah. He is a fabulous kisser."

"Let's see. Smart, kind, good with his lips. You hit the jackpot."

"I don't know. We'll be out of here tomorrow, and he'll forget all about me."

It was always a shock to Shyla how someone so pretty and smart could be so insecure and stupid when it came to men. "Right. Has he asked for your phone number?"

Audrey shook her head.

"He will."

"Oh, well," Audrey said with a shrug. "No matter what, it's been a great day."

Tomorrow's going to be great, too, Shyla thought. She had a plan. Hehe.

Audrey was still sawing logs the next morning when Shyla pulled on her clothes and sneaked out of the room. It was a good thing her last boyfriend had been a mechanic and a classic-car freak. She'd learned a few things from him. Double hehe.

She could smell coffee and hear voices coming from the kitchen down the hall as she crept down the stairs. The family was already up. She should talk to Mrs. Livingston, ask permission before pulling this stunt, but really it was always easier to ask forgiveness than permission. Such supernice people wouldn't have a problem with letting two stranded sisters stay another night. Two stranded sisters with a car that needed work.

She was like Mrs. Bennet in *Pride and Prejudice*, maneuvering behind the scenes to throw the couple together. Mrs. Bennet had used a horse. Shyla was using the modern-age equivalent. Jane Austen would be proud.

It was nip-your-nose cold out, but the sky was clear. A pretty day for horseback riding. Or camping in front of the living-room fireplace. Or both. Another twenty-four hours was sure to give what was sprouting between Audrey and Russ time to grow into something nice and healthy.

Shyla hurried to the car, got the hood up and had just stuck her head under when a deep voice asked, "Car problems?"

16

Shyla let out an "Eek!" and whirled around to see Rand Livingston standing behind her, a questioning eyebrow raised and a half smile on his face. "Umm," she said. She knew her face had to be as red as Santa's suit.

He cocked his head, smiling, still waiting for an answer.

"Okay, busted," she said. "I guess I'm not a very good sneak."

"You're a great sneak," he assured her. "I just happened to catch you 'cause I'm going into work a little early. What's going on?"

"I was trying to sabotage Audrey's car so it wouldn't start and we'd be here another day."

"I knew you couldn't resist me," he teased.

"I know. My poor boyfriend, right? Actually, even though it's tacky, I was hoping to get one more day here for my sister. With what's happening with her and your brother, one more day would really help love on its way."

"That it would. So what were you planning?"

"To steal the distributor cap if I can find it."

"Good luck with that. They stopped using those in the late nineties."

"No wonder I can't find it. Darn."

"Not to worry. I can mess things up for you."

"Not too much," she cautioned. "It's got to be fixable so we can get on the road tomorrow morning."

"No problemo." He leaned over the engine and began messing around with things. It only took a moment before he straightened up and said, "Okay, good to go. Or not go. But you guys will still be on the road first thing tomorrow morning."

"What did you do?"

"Just loosened the battery cable. An easy fix."

"Thanks," Shyla said. "You are a real Santa's helper."

"Anything for my bro. Guess I'd better hang around for a while so I can give my professional opinion on what's wrong with the car. And promise to order the part it needs."

Wait a minute. "It's gonna need a part? I thought you just loosened the battery cable?"

"I did, but your sister needs to think I gotta send for a part."

"Genius," she said, and they bumped knuckles.

They started back to the house. "I hope your parents aren't going to mind us being here another day," Shyla said.

"Are you kidding? They love having company. And I know Russ is gonna love having Audrey around longer."

"I'm surprised your brother isn't with someone." He really did seem too good to be unattached.

"We Livingston men are hard to pin down," Rand joked. "Seriously, though, he had a girlfriend he was nuts about his first year in college. She pretty much used him, then dumped him. Stomped his heart good. He's been dodging women ever since."

That didn't bode well.

"But I think it's different with your sister. I haven't seen him this into someone since Sarah."

"The heartbreaker?"

Rand nodded. "She was a real piece of work."

"So what's your story?" Shyla asked.

"No big heartbreak. I'm just taking my time. I want to make sure I get it right so I can end up like my folks."

"A good idea," she agreed. "The right one is worth waiting for." She knew firsthand that life was amazingly great when you found the love of your life.

And maybe, just maybe, her sister finally had as well. Maybe the star of Bethlehem was still up there in the sky, watching over God's children. Maybe it had guided them to this place.

Hmm. Could you see the star of Bethlehem all the way over in Winnemucca? Was there even a star of Bethlehem up there anymore? She didn't know. Whatever had brought them here, she was glad it had.

They'd reached the house, and Rand was following her inside when they met his brother coming down the stairs. "Where were you two?" Russ asked.

"Just showing Shyla around a little," Rand said, saving her from having to invent some tall tale.

"Too bad you're not staying longer," Russ said. "We could take you riding and show you the rest of the place."

It took superhuman effort for Shyla to swallow her smug smile.

Vera Livingston insisted the sisters stay for breakfast, which was a feast—scrambled eggs and bacon, toast and pancakes with homemade blackberry syrup, along with orange juice and coffee.

"Wow," Shyla said, looking at it all. "This is great."

It was a lot more than the toast and coffee she normally had.

"What can I say? I'm used to feeding my big boys and their big appetites," Vera said.

Audrey helped herself to a small amount of everything, ate quickly and surreptitiously checked her smartwatch. Shyla knew she was getting anxious to hit the road. She was in for a surprise.

"We should probably get going," she finally said just as Shyla was about to reach for a second helping of eggs.

You're not going anywhere today. Hehe. But Shyla feigned innocence and, after helping clear the table, followed her sister upstairs to get their things.

Once they were back downstairs, the brothers carried their baggage out to the car. Vera and Tom threw on coats and walked them out.

"If you have time, stop and say hi on your way back through," Vera said. "We'd love to see you again."

"Thanks," Audrey said. "You've been great. We owe you big-time for taking us in."

"Nonsense," Vera said, waving away her thanks.

Russ handed Audrey a business card. "We never got around to exchanging phone numbers. Mine's on the card if you want to put it in your phone."

"I will," she assured him.

"Thank you so much," Shyla said. She hugged Vera and Tom and then got in the passenger seat. *Be seeing you soon...in about two minutes.*

Audrey, too, gave the elder Livingstons a hug, then said goodbye to Rand and a shy one to Russ and climbed in behind the wheel. Put her key in the ignition, turned it. Nothing. Tried again. Still nothing.

"What is wrong with this car?" she muttered.

"Maybe it needs a tune-up," said Shyla.

"I take it in to the dealership on a regular basis," Audrey said irritably.

Yes, Miss In-Control-of-Everything. Her red cheeks showed how much this humiliating moment was killing her. Shyla tried not to snicker.

Everyone gathered around the car.

Rand tapped on the window. "Pop the hood. I'll take a look."

Audrey popped the hood and got out, joining him there while the other Livingstons stood off to the side, waiting for the diagnosis from the expert. Meanwhile, Shyla was doing an excellent job of maintaining a poker face, if she did say so herself.

"Maybe it just needs a jump," Audrey said.

"No, that's not it," Rand said slowly, like a man making sure of his diagnosis.

"What else could be wrong?" Audrey asked.

"Fuel pump," said Rand. "Nothing that can't be fixed," he added.

"Oh, good," Audrey said, letting out the old sigh of relief.

"I can order a part when I go in to the shop, have it for you by tonight."

"Tonight," Audrey echoed. "But we were supposed to be at my sister's by tonight. Julia's going to go berserk."

Already did that, but she's on board now. "Well, at least we'll make it by Christmas Day," Shyla said.

"I know, but…" Audrey bit her lip.

"I'll text Julia and let her know," Shyla said, stepping away. Operation Santa's Helper is a go, she texted, then deleted the whole conversation thread as soon as it was sent.

"Meanwhile, you can stay with us," Vera said to Audrey.

"On Christmas Eve?" Audrey protested. "I mean, that's your family time."

"The family doesn't arrive till tomorrow afternoon so it's no inconvenience," Vera assured her. "We may have to have another Trivial Pursuit match. Meanwhile, make yourselves at home. Tom will get a fire going in the living room. It's more cozy in there. Then you ladies can plan how you'd like to spend your day. I'm sure Russ would be happy to take you riding if you like."

"Absolutely," Russ said, smiling at Audrey.

"I'm fine staying inside," Shyla was quick to say.

"How about you, Audrey?" Russ asked. "We've got some extra boots that should fit you fine."

"She's game," Shyla answered for her.

Audrey gave her the big-sister disciplinary look, but then managed a game smile for Russ. "Sure."

Tom went to light some logs in case anyone wanted a cozy day by the fire, and Vera disappeared into the kitchen to make fresh coffee.

"I can't believe this," Audrey muttered as the brothers took their suitcases back upstairs.

"I guess Santa had other plans for us today," Shyla said. "You can't mind getting another day with Russ."

"Of course not. But we're supposed to be at Julia's. Her head's gonna blow off," Audrey predicted.

"Don't worry. She's fine."

"I can't believe this. How could this happen? I just had the car in for a tune-up."

"It's okay. We'll get an early start tomorrow and be there in plenty of time for Christmas dinner, so you can chill now," said Shyla. Sounding like a certain calm, in-charge older sister. Oh, yeah, she was loving this role reversal.

"Unless Rand can't get the part for the car."

"He said he could, so don't worry."

"I'm going to check in with Mom and Gram," Audrey said and got busy on her phone.

Shyla watched her and smiled. Oh, she was good. *Just call me Shyla Claus.*

It had been a long day, and once Hazel and Warren finally got to their motel room she'd slept like the dead. *Like the dead.* Not a good idiom to use.

In spite of her sound sleep, she still had a stress hangover. She downed the last of her coffee and gratefully accepted another cup from their friendly server in the Denny's near their motel where they were enjoying a hearty breakfast. After filling the prescription the doctor had given Warren to tide him over until they reached their destination. Priorities!

"You sure you slept well?" Warren asked her. "You don't look so good."

"I don't feel so good. Your heart problems are killing me."

He stared at his plate of half-finished pancakes. "I'm sorry, hon."

"I am, too. I'm sorry you won't do something to fix this. I was sick with worry yesterday, Warren. Sick." Her lower lip began to wobble, and a rising tide of tears made her eyes sting. "I don't want to lose you."

He reached across the table and took her hand. "You won't."

"How do you know?" she challenged.

"I just do."

Wishful thinking. "You could increase the odds of staying around if you'd just have that heart ablation. Oh, Warren, don't you want more years together?"

He patted her hand. "Of course I do."

"Then, please, for me, make an appointment with that heart surgeon when we get home."

"I'd do anything for you. You know that."

They'd had this conversation before. He'd said those same words, followed by the word *No*.

"Except this one thing," she said bitterly.

She knew how much he feared hospitals, how scary the idea of having an operation was to him. Surgery would extend his life and make the quality of that life so much better, it would make hers better, too.

"Please, do this for me. I can't even begin to tell you how scared I was yesterday."

He sat staring at his plate.

"Warren, you are afraid of the wrong thing," she pressed. "You're afraid of a procedure that's going to help you in the long run, when what you should be afraid of is having a heart attack. And a blood clot."

"I have medicine for that," he said stubbornly, pulling away his hand.

She raised an eyebrow. "Like you had on this trip?"

He frowned.

"You could be off somewhere by yourself without your medication and have a problem and wind up having a stroke. You know as well as I do that every minute matters. What if nobody got to you in time? What if you wound up paralyzed? What if you died? Do you really want that? Do you want to do that to me?"

"Of course I don't," he said earnestly.

"Then, fix this. Give me more good years with you. Please. I honestly can't go through this again, Warren."

He sighed heavily. "Okay, I'll make the appointment. It can't hurt to hear what the doc has to say."

She could hardly believe her ears. "Really? You promise?"

"I promise. I don't want to keep worrying you."

The tears spilled, and she smiled at him. "Thank you."

"No, thank you. For being such a good wife and caring so much about what happens to me. And for still wanting me around. I want to stick around. I want a lot more years together with you, Hazel, my love."

"Thank you, darling," she said.

She suddenly didn't feel so tired anymore. Amazing how much better a woman could feel when she'd been handed a nice, big helping of hope for Christmas.

Once more he reached out his hand to her, and she clasped it.

"I love you," he said.

"I love you, too," she told him. "Now, let's finish our breakfast and get back on the road. I'm anxious to see Julia."

"Me, too."

As they were heading toward the door she noticed a couple of scruffy-looking boys who looked to be in their late teens standing just outside the door. They wore sagging jeans and sweatshirts two sizes too big, and she instantly decided they were losers. They weren't smoking, so why were they standing there? Very suspicious.

Very like those crime shows she was always watching with Warren. But this wasn't a crime show, for crying out loud, and she was being silly. She told herself not to be judging those books by their covers. The boys were probably waiting for someone.

A clean-cut teen boy came up behind them as they were going out and suddenly they had a bit of a traffic jam in the doorway with the other two suddenly coming in. With the other two boys between Hazel and the door, the clean-cut youth slipped right between her and Warren, saying, "Sorry. 'Scuse me."

She gave a polite laugh and said, "No problem."

Suddenly, she felt a hard tug on her shoulder. The little weasel was yanking her purse. She stumbled back against Warren as the strap broke and little Mr. Preppie Angel yanked it free. His other two friends were already bolting out the door.

"What the hell?" Warren began as the perp started to bolt as well.

"My purse!" Hazel cried.

She had suffered a car crash with a deer and a terrible scare over Warren's heart and spent a long night in the emergency room. Enough was enough.

She grabbed the snatcher by his jacket collar. "Oh, no, you don't, mister."

The other two boys were already out the door, and he was trying to slip out of his jacket and follow them, but she screeched, "Help! Thief!"

A beefy lumberjack sort of man came in past the fleeing boys, figured out what was happening and moved in to help hold on to him. Next the manager showed up, wanting to know if everything was okay.

"It certainly is not," Hazel said, still keeping her hold on the squirming would-be thief. "This boy tried to rob me." She looked down to where her purse lay and scowled. "And he broke my purse."

"I'll call the police," said the manager.

"Hey, you still got your purse," the kid protested. "Let me go."

"And you still got your teeth," Warren said to him. "Want to keep 'em?"

The boy glared at him, but followed him, Hazel and the lumberjack, along with the manager, to a window booth, Warren and Mr. Paul Bunyan wedging him between them.

"You and your friends should be ashamed of yourselves," Hazel said. He looked puzzled. "Those other boys," she clarified. "I know you were all working together."

His brows drew down and so did his mouth. "I don't know those losers," he said in disgust.

Look who was calling whom a loser.

Their booth gave them a perfect view of the patrol car pulling up outside. Soon it was a party of six as the police took statements.

"Would you like to press charges, ma'am?" one of the officers asked.

"She's still got her purse," pointed out the would-be snatcher.

"No thanks to you," she said to him.

"It was an accident," he insisted.

"Yes, you almost *accidentally* yanked my arm out of its socket." Then, to the officer, "I won't press charges if I can talk to his mother," Hazel said.

The kid's eyes bugged out. "What?"

"I bet she doesn't know what you're up to," Hazel said to him, and he scowled at her.

She'd raised a son. His scowls didn't faze her. "You need to stop this," she scolded. The kid rolled his eyes.

"And you need to watch more *Law and Order* and see what happens to criminals," she added for emphasis.

The kid told her what she could do with her advice, and the policeman suggested he show some respect. "So what'll it be, kid?" he finished. "Do we take you in or do we call your mom?"

"Either way she'd find out. You're still a minor," said his partner.

"It was an accident," the boy muttered.

"Mom or the station?" the first officer said, running out of patience.

The bravado fell away, and the boy looked almost ready to cry. "Mom," he said.

Mother, it turned out, was a school secretary, who had been Christmas shopping and was surprised to learn that her son wasn't home watching his younger brother like he'd promised. Seeing him surrounded by a crowd of nonadmirers, two of them police, brought tears to her eyes.

"Oh, Petey, how could you?" she said after one of the officers had told her what had happened.

Petey hung his head and muttered something about being sorry.

"I think your boy needs to find something better to do with his time," Warren told her.

"I think so, too," said the mother. She looked gratefully at Hazel. "Thank you for not pressing charges."

"For all we know, the purse could have gotten caught and broken," Hazel said, taking pity on the miscreant, and was aware of the second policeman frowning in disapproval. "And we know it probably won't happen again. Don't we, Peter?"

The boy kept his gaze on the table. "Guess not."

Hazel stood up tall, channeling the scare-them-straight energy she'd seen in so many episodes of *Law and Order*. "Good. Because the next time you just happen to be around some woman whose purse strap breaks, it might not go so well for you," she continued. "The people you meet in jail will be a whole lot scarier than an unsuspecting lady like me. And I can't imagine how painful it would be to be beat up. Or knifed with a shiv."

That took the color out of his face.

"You probably know all about that," she said. "I'm sure you'd hate to find out how awful it is to be a victim. But you know what they say. *You reap what you sow. What goes around comes around.*"

Petey swallowed hard.

His mother looked ready to hug Hazel.

And she did before they followed the police out the door.

"That was impressive," Warren said to Hazel as they, too, made their way to the exit. After receiving a twenty-five-dollar gift card from the manager, along with his profuse apologies for what they'd gone through.

"It was nothing," Hazel said. "Now, how is your heart?"

He grinned. "It's fine. Maybe because I didn't even know what was happening until it had already happened."

"So no adrenaline rush? No rapid heartbeat?"

"None." He patted his coat pocket, where the pills they'd picked up sat. "I'm good to go, no matter what. And I'll be even better after I get my ticker fixed," he added, which made her smile.

They left the restaurant and hit the road.

Hazel drove.

17

After the car wouldn't start, Rand left for his garage to order the part he claimed Audrey needed. Tom had a horseshoer coming he wanted to talk to, and Shyla was ready to help Vera with preparations for the family's Christmas Day meal.

"I always wanted to make a bûche de Noël," she'd said to Vera.

It did sound like fun. But not nearly as fun as spending time with Russ. Anyway, someone had to accept his invitation to take a ride. After all, it was only polite since everyone else was busy, right? Couldn't have the man feeling neglected.

"We can go after I muck out the stalls," he'd said to her. "Meanwhile, relax and have another cup of coffee."

"Tell me more about yourselves, ladies," Vera said as she poured more coffee for the sisters.

They'd already shared about their jobs, told her where they'd grown up and a little more about their family. There wasn't much left to tell.

Except for... "I suppose you're both taken," she said.

"I am, but Audrey's not," Shyla reported.

Vera smiled. "Really. Moms are always on the look-out for good women for their sons."

"They don't come any better than Audrey," Shyla said, her sisterly sales pitch making Audrey's cheeks heat. "Even if she is a bossy big sister."

Audrey wasn't sure which was worse, being raised to sainthood or having her flaws laid out on a platter.

"Firstborns always feel responsible for the other siblings," Vera said. "Russel has always watched out for his younger brother. And now he seems to think he needs to watch out for us. He comes out a lot to make sure we're doing okay and to help Tom. He even has hopes of having some sort of family compound someday so he can take care of us in our old age. I keep telling him that's a long ways off, but age is a subjective thing."

Watch how a man treats his mother. The words of advice came back to Audrey. Russ sure passed that test. He obviously cared for both his parents and respected them.

"He's always been a little on the shy side," Vera continued. "Unlike Randal, he never had a lot of girlfriends. Of course, a man doesn't need to see a lot of gold to know when he's found treasure," she added.

Was that message for Audrey? She hoped so.

The women were still chatting when Russ appeared to take Audrey riding. "You ready?"

"I think so," she said. If this was some kind of test, she hoped she didn't flunk it.

The boots he found for her were a little loose, but an extra pair of socks solved that problem.

They made their way to the barn, Lucky the dog trotting along behind until he tried to move Audrey right along with a nip to the heel and Russ shooed him away. Once there, Russ led her past bales of hay and racks of

equestrian equipment and over to one of several stalls
with horses poking their heads over.

"Your parents have a lot of horses," she said. "One
for each of you?"

"And a couple extra. The place was a dude ranch for
several years."

He stopped at a stall that housed a chestnut with a
white blaze on its face. The horse was…big.

"This is our girl Juniper," Russ said. "Say hello to
Audrey, Juniper."

Juniper snorted and tossed her head.

"Hello, Juniper," Audrey said…from a distance.

"Don't worry. She's gentle as a lamb." He gave the
horse's neck a pat. "You can touch her, you know."

Audrey took a step closer, ran her hand down the
animal's neck like she'd seen actors do in movies.

Juniper snorted and tossed her head again, and Audrey jumped back a step. She really wanted to be with
Russ, but she wasn't so sure about Juniper, who was an
awful lot bigger than a lamb.

"She's happy to meet you," Russ explained. "I'll saddle her, then we'll get you on her."

"Take your time," Audrey said under her breath.

He chuckled. "You'll be fine."

Once Juniper was saddled, he led her out into the
corral. "We'll give you a chance to practice a little."
He stopped the horse and turned to Audrey. "Okay, put
your left foot in the stirrup, grab the saddle horn, pull
yourself up and throw a leg over."

"Just like in the movies," she said, making herself
sound confident.

"There you go."

She did manage to get up and in the saddle, and Ju-

niper shifted under her with another snort and gave her
mane a little shake. Audrey wasn't sure which was more
unnerving: the noise, or feeling the movement beneath
her. It felt like sitting on an earthquake. She swallowed
and clung to the saddle horn with both hands.

"It's kind of high up," she observed.

"No higher than being in the cab of truck," he assured her.

"Yeah, but I can't fall off the cab of a truck."

"Keep your feet in the stirrups, and you'll be fine.
Juniper's an easygoing girl. She won't throw you."

He led the horse around the corral, giving Audrey a
chance to get accustomed to the feel of swaying in the
saddle, then he showed her how to use the reins and let
her take a turn on her own.

"You look like a pro," he assured her.

"A pro in the making," she said. Maybe she could
master riding a horse.

Once Audrey felt confident, he saddled another
horse, this one a black beast even bigger than Juniper,
and they set off to explore the ranch.

"Just don't make me gallop," she said as they started
out.

"We'll take it slow," he promised. "That's the best
way to build confidence."

"I need that." Although she wasn't sure confidence
would be enough to keep her from falling. *Help me out,
Juniper. Make me look good.*

The sun was out, but the air had a bite, and she could
see her horse's breath as they ambled along. The setting was picturesque. They rode past fence-line feed-
ers and waterers for the cattle. In front of them the land
stretched on and on, with mountains in the background

lightly frosted with snow. She was aware of the animal's movement beneath her, of the creaking of the leather saddle. Mostly, though, she was aware of the man she was with. Riding next to Russ Livingston, she felt like a heroine in a novel. *The Nerd and Cowboy.*

He talked as they rode past grazing cattle, sharing how he'd loved growing up on the ranch, the satisfaction he was finding fixing up his grandparents' place.

"All this land," she said, looking around. "To someone who grew up in suburbia, it feels endless."

"We're really not a big spread. Don't need to be now, anyway, since my parents have another income stream with their stock investments. It's still hard work, but Dad loves it. He always jokes that he'll die with his boots on. He'd probably die if we made him take 'em off. I still wish he'd slow down, but at least he's got some extra hired help now, which makes it somewhat easier."

"It had to be hard work for you, growing up."

He nodded. "Oh, yeah. Rand and I worked our butts off. Baling hay, helping with calving, mending fences, taking care of the horses. I was driving a truck when I was twelve. Learned all kinds of cuss words from Dad's crusty old ranch hand. Also learned not to use 'em in front of Mom."

"Did you ever get tired of working so hard?" Audrey couldn't help asking.

"Sometimes. Between that and school and 4-H and then sports, we were busy. All good stuff, but we still loved it when we could go spend time in Tahoe with the grandparents. There's nothing like getting in that lake on a hot summer day. And at night, what a sky. The stars put on a show like nothing you've ever seen."

She couldn't help thinking that this man was too

rooted in the soil to ever be happy in a city. Could she be happy living on a ranch in the desert? Tahoe was another matter. She'd never been there, and listening to him talk made her want to see the place, especially that lake.

"Sounds like you're going to be sorry to see that place go," she observed.

"I am. Who knows? Maybe I can talk 'em into keeping it a little longer."

"Do you see yourself being a rancher someday?" she asked.

"Probably not. Ranching is my parents' thing, not mine or Rand's. I like what I'm doing. I like building stuff. Wouldn't mind having a few acres, though. I'd like to build my own house someday."

"Yeah? Where would you build it?"

"Let's see, now. If I remember, your sister said Washington has something for everyone."

"It does. Cities, beaches, dairy farms on the west side of the mountains, and ranching and orchards and vineyards on the east. But there are a lot of nice states," she added to show that she was flexible.

"Your sister's in Idaho. How do you like Idaho?"

"I'll let you know."

He nodded. "Yeah, I hear it's great. Lots of lakes and rivers. Oregon still has some open space. I could go for a small town where you get to know your neighbors."

"That sounds nice, too," she said. Actually it sounded more than nice. It sounded idyllic.

"You're easy to please," he said with a grin.

"Maybe I am. I think I could be happy almost anywhere." She'd been happy in LA when she first got there. She probably still would have been, if her love life hadn't soured. "As long as I was with someone who really cared." Someone who appreciated her for who she was.

"Home is where the heart is?"

"Something like that."

"Audrey, you are one exceptional woman."

"I know. I'm told that all the time," she said with a good seasoning of sarcasm.

"You should be. I'm sure you've had men tell you that."

She shrugged, neither confirming or denying. Before Dennis, there'd been a couple others—one who'd had a fixation on her long legs but tended to forget she had a brain, and another who had a short temper and was more likely to scream about something trivial than tell her how exceptional she was. That had been short-lived.

This probably would be, too, even if they did actually see each other after the holidays. She had to stop getting her hopes up.

Except they were already climbing so high she wasn't sure she'd ever get them down.

"How about attempting a trot?" he suggested. "Let's see if we can get you to the next level."

Getting to the next level with Juniper. She could do this. Getting to the next level with Russ. She was definitely up for that.

Vera and Shyla enjoyed a cup of coffee while the cake for their bûche de Noël baked. "This reminds me of holidays in the kitchen with my mom," Shyla said.

"She likes to bake?"

"Oh, yes, and she spent a lot of time teaching us how. Well, Audrey and me. Our sister, Julia, not so much. She wasn't all that interested." Shyla took a sip of coffee.

"We never made this, though. Mom preferred more simple recipes like cookies and pies. And she had a chocolate zucchini cake she baked every summer, always with the zucchini from the garden that got too big to do anything else with. Audrey, on the other hand, took it up a notch. Which she pretty much does with everything."

"She does?" Vera cocked an eyebrow.

Okay, that last statement had probably sounded a lot like jealousy. "Not that I'm jealous," Shyla hurried to add. Then had to amend, "Okay, maybe a little. She's such an overachiever, sometimes it was a little hard trying to get out from under her shadow."

"Did you?"

Shyla smiled over her coffee cup. "Yeah, I did. Audrey's the smart one, but I'm the creative one, and that's enough for me."

"And what about the sister you're going to see?"

"She's the fun one. Life's one big party for Julia. And being the baby, she's used to getting her way, which is why we're all going to her house for Christmas."

"And looking forward to it?"

"Oh, yeah."

"It sounds like your family is close," Vera said.

"We are."

"I can see you and your sister are."

"She's great," Shyla said simply. "I really want her to find someone as great as she is. She deserves it."

"I feel the same way about my sons."

"I can't believe neither one of them is with someone," Shyla said.

"Not yet," said Vera. "But you never know," she added, and the smile she gave Shyla felt downright conspiratorial. "I hope Russel and your sister are having a good time."

"Me, too," said Shyla.

After enjoying a late breakfast of eggs and sausage and crusty rolls, Max and Michelle gave his parents a call on speaker.

"Dad feels fine, and we're on the road," Hazel reported.

They could hear Warren saying something in the background. It sounded a little like "Your mother stopped a purse snatcher." *A purse snatcher?*

"What's Dad saying?" Max asked. "Something about a purse snatcher?"

"This little juvenile delinquent tried to take my purse. He didn't get it," Hazel reported.

"Good grief, what next?" Michelle said.

"Did you take him down, Mom?" Max asked, joking.

"Actually, I did," she said, sounding very proud of herself.

"I believe it," he said. "Look, just be careful on the road, okay?"

"We will," she promised. "Don't worry. And now, how about you two? Are you still stranded in Leavenworth?"

"Yes, but it's all good."

"We're having a wonderful time," Michelle said. "This trip is turning out to be the best thing that's happened to us in a long time," she added, smiling at Max.

"I'm glad," Hazel said, and Michelle could hear the relief in her voice. "You two enjoy yourselves."

"We already have been," Max said and winked at Michelle.

They ended the call and settled in for a second cup of coffee. Outside the dining-room window, snow glistened on the ground and the tree boughs. It looked pristine and beautiful. There was something about winter that was so soft and magical.

It felt even more so now that she had pulled down the wall she'd erected between her husband and herself. How freeing forgiveness was! And new starts—they were as promising as fresh, pure snow. There would always be an ache in their hearts for what they'd lost, but loving each other would be the balm to ease it.

"It looks like we're still stranded," Max said after checking the traffic report on his phone. "I wouldn't mind one more day here. Would you?"

"Not if I knew we could get out tomorrow," Michelle said.

A day fanning the flame they'd rekindled, strolling around town, drinking hot cider, falling onto that bed and enjoying each other. She could definitely handle another day together, just the two of them.

But she'd hate to miss Christmas with the girls.

Max was doing more research on his phone. "DOT is predicting the roads will be clear by tomorrow."

"Then, bring on today," she said and took a sip of her coffee. Morning coffee tasted so much better without the acid of bitterness that had been lurking in her heart.

"You want to call Julia and let her know we're delayed?" Max suggested.

"Oh, fine. Making me the bearer of bad news."

"You're better at that," he said.

"No, you're just a bigger chicken," Michelle teased. Max had never had a problem giving a teenage boy an intimidatingly strong handshake, but delivering disappointing news to one of his daughters was another matter. Her observation on Thanksgiving weekend had been correct. He hated being the bad guy. Funny how this fatherly flaw didn't bother her, now that she'd let go of her anger.

She made the call and put the phone on speaker so Max could hear, as well.

"First Audrey and Shyla, and now you," Julia said in disgust after Michelle had told her they were still stuck in Leavenworth. "This sucks."

"Audrey and Shyla? What's going on with them?" Max demanded. "Why aren't they with you?"

"Audrey didn't tell you? They're staying an extra day in Winnemucca with the same people who gave them a place to stay last night. She has to get her car fixed, but I think Shyla's behind it 'cause she texted me something about fixing Audrey's love life."

"What?" Michelle and Max exchanged looks.

"Last I heard from her, Audrey and one of the brothers were going horseback riding."

Horseback riding. Their girl was enjoying a nice little adventure.

Julia heaved a dramatic sigh. "We were going to have all the neighbors over."

"You can still do that," Michelle pointed out.

"I guess. But I wanted you all here. At least Gram and Grandpa are on their way. I've got fingers, toes and eyes crossed that they make it here okay."

"I'm sure they will," Michelle said. But probably later than expected. She was willing to bet that they would be driving very slowly for the rest of the trip.

"I hope you're not going to let them drive back home after Christmas," Julia said.

"No, we're not."

Michelle knew Max would insist on the folks riding with them no matter how much Warren protested. It shouldn't be too hard to convince them, though. Her father-in-law was a thrifty man, and he'd be happy to lose the cost of the rental car for a few days. And if their car was salvageable, Max and Warren could pick it up and they could caravan. They'd have time to sort things out. Max had taken time off until after the first of the year, and Michelle had cleared her calendar.

"You keep Gram and Grandpa safe. We'll be there tomorrow for sure," she said to Julia, deciding to trust that the DOT would make good on its promise.

"We need to call Audrey," Max said after she ended the call. "God only knows what these people are like."

"If they took in our girls, they're probably pretty nice," Michelle said. "And I doubt she's going horseback riding with Ted Bundy. But I'll call."

And so another call was made, the phone on speaker yet again.

Audrey had barely answered before he was asking, "What's going on? Where are you two? Are you okay?"

"Nice to hear from you, too, Dad," she replied.

He ignored the sarcasm. "We talked to Julia. She said you're staying with some people you only just met. Why didn't you tell your mother?"

"There was no need to."

"What happened to your car?" Max wanted to know.

"I'll tell you later. It's a long story. But don't worry, we're fine. The Livingstons are a great family, and they're taking good care of us."

"Why do they need to take care of you?" Max demanded.

"Like I said, it's a long story."

"We've got time."

"There was a mix-up with our reservation in Winnemucca, and we got stranded, and they helped us out. And then something weird went wrong with my car this morning, and I have to get some work done on it, but it's getting done today, and we'll be in St. Maries tomorrow. Where are you guys?"

"We're still stranded," Michelle said. "Waiting for them to clear the pass."

"Poor Julia. All her plans for a perfect Christmas are flying out the window."

"We'll all be there by tomorrow, and it will still be perfect," Michelle said. Knowing her family was all safe, seeing a new beginning for Max and herself—as far as she was concerned, it already was.

"See you then," Audrey said. "I've gotta go. I'm trying to keep from falling off a horse."

"Horseback riding," Max said after they'd said their *I love you*s and ended the call. "Somehow I never pictured Audrey on a horse."

"We never tried to put her on one."

"She'd rather have read about horses than ridden one," Max pointed out.

True. Audrey had never been their sporty daughter. Shyla had taken dance lessons, and Julia had played on the volleyball team and had gotten into rock climbing. Audrey's talents lay in a different direction.

"Anyway, it's nice to see her trying new things."

"Yeah, it is," Max agreed. "But we still don't know anything about this guy."

Michelle chuckled. "He's one of the new things she's trying out. She's not sixteen anymore, Max. You can't check out every man she dates."

"It'd be better if I did," he said, and Michelle knew he was referring to her last boyfriend, the one who had lured her off to California only to break her heart.

She and Michelle had had more than one mother-daughter talk about that, with Michelle always reminding her that it was better to find out sooner than later. Although whether it came early or late, heartbreak was still heartbreak. And her daughter had been dealing with the pain of hers for several months. Maybe this mysterious new man would be just what the doctor ordered to mend her heart.

"We'll have to trust that her sound judgment will resurface. I'm sure she'll be more cautious this time," Michelle assured him.

"I hope this guy's a good one," Max said.

"Me, too," Michelle said with a sigh. "Love's not easy." She smiled at Max and laid a hand over his. "But it always wins in the end."

He raised her hand to his lips. "Thank God," he said and kissed it. "So now we have a whole day to fill. What do you want to do?"

"What do you want to do?"

Max was still holding her hand. He ran his other hand up her arm. "I can think of something."

So could she.

Much later, they donned their coats and gloves and strolled around the town, taking in the sights. They checked out the nutcracker museum, bought an entire alphabet of wooden letters for the grandbaby at the Wood Shop, as well as books from A Book for All Seasons, the town's bookstore, then ate lunch at München Haus. Afterwards, knowing how many people were stranded in town and wanting to make sure they got a table, they made reservations for dinner at Ludwig's, another restaurant that served traditional German food.

"How about we buy you something spectacular for you to wear tonight," Max suggested. "To celebrate."

"Celebrate what?"

"Us," he said with a smile that warmed her from the inside out.

She really didn't need anything, but the idea of shopping for clothes sounded like fun, so she led him into one of the clothing boutiques where she found a powder-blue butterfly-sleeve sweater.

He gave it a thumbs-up when she modeled it for him, one side slipping off the shoulder. "Oh, yeah, that works. What about something to go with it? Although, I'd like to see you in just that," he added.

"I'll pair it with my black leggings and boots," she said.

After the clerk had rung up the sale, Michelle asked her to cut off the tag.

"I know you'll love wearing it. You looked great in it," the woman told her.

"Yes, she did," Max agreed.

It had been a long time since he'd given her a compliment. Probably for fear that it would have been a waste of breath. They had wasted a lot of time falling apart. There would be no more of that.

"And you'll look even better out of it later," he murmured as they left the store, making her giggle. No one seeing them together now would have guessed that only two days ago they'd been on the verge of breaking up.

Funny how things were turning out. What had looked like the work of gremlins had really been the work of angels.

* * *

"I still don't understand how something could have gone wrong with my car," Audrey said as she chalked her cue, waiting for her turn at the pool table.

"Cars aren't my area of expertise, that's for sure," Russ said. "But, as with people, a lot can be going on under the hood that you don't see until it manifests itself."

There was a lot going on under her hood, that was for sure. She thought she'd been smitten when she'd followed the love mistake to LA, but that was nothing compared to what she was already feeling for Russ.

Tom had gone to the feed store, and Shyla was still in the kitchen, helping Vera finish baking for the next day's festivities, leaving Audrey and Russ alone. To which Audrey had no objections beyond feeling like a mooch for not helping. But both Vera and Shyla had insisted they had it covered, all the while smiling like twin Cupid wannabes.

"You know," Russ continued, "I think sometimes things happen for a reason."

He was bent over the table getting ready for his shot, but he looked up at her and smiled, and she melted faster than a marshmallow in hot chocolate. The combination of that smile and a lean, perfectly muscled bod wrapped like so much eye candy in jeans and a Western shirt was turning up her thermostat.

How was it he could be so sexy and yet so down-to-earth and unassuming? And just plain nice? Where was the flaw? There had to be a flaw.

"Have you always been perfect?" she mused. Shit! She'd said that out loud. Oh, man. Her face was roasting.

He looked up at her, puzzled.

"I mean, you don't seem to have any flaws. That's not normal."

"I've got flaws. Ask my bro. He'll be happy to tell you about the times I beat him up when we were kids or left him to take the blame for some goofball stunt I'd suckered him into."

"I bet you don't beat him up anymore," she said.

"No way. I stopped doing that when we got to high school. He weighs more than me, and he'd beat the crap out of me."

"So, seriously."

He shrugged. "I'm a perfectionist. Irritates the hell out of my workers sometimes. And I hate to cook, which is why I like owning a share in a couple of restaurants. Great food and no mess to clean up. So I wouldn't exactly impress you in the kitchen."

I could impress you, she thought but didn't say it. It would only sound conceited.

"And I've been known to lose my temper and stomp around the house saying words my mom would wash my mouth out for saying. But I'm not mean," he added quickly. "And I haven't hit anybody since that last time I hit my bro. He socked me back so hard he almost broke my jaw."

He returned to studying his shot. "Okay, your turn. You gonna tell me you've got flaws? 'Cause I haven't found any yet."

"How hard are you looking?"

"Hard enough, but I'm not seeing any."

"They're there. I'm bossy. Just ask my sisters."

"Yeah, well, sisters are probably like brothers. They need to be bossed around sometimes."

"And I'm always right," she confessed. "Even when I'm wrong."

What an embarrassing thing to confess. But better to

be honest. If, by some wild chance, he wanted to take this further, it was only fair to warn him right then.

"The curse of being smart. I've been known to fall into that trap. Just ask my partners."

"My ex called me *Wikipedia with legs*," she blurted. *Oh, great. Let's just overshare a little.*

He looked up, studied her with a smile. "Yeah? That's pretty funny."

"I wasn't laughing."

"Okay, there's another flaw. I'm obviously insensitive."

"Maybe I'll see the humor in it someday. When I'm about a hundred."

"Guys say stuff like that when they're threatened. He was threatened by your smarts. But you know what? There's nothing wrong with knowing stuff. A man with any brains doesn't want a Barbie doll. I sure don't. I want someone I can talk with, someone who has something to say."

Audrey's thermostat got turned up higher. Except... "That's what my ex claimed when we first got together."

Russ shrugged. "Guess he was lying. To both of you."

"How do I know you're not?" Audrey instantly wished she could take back the words. "Sorry, that was..."

"Understandable," he supplied. "Look, we all get hurt. It takes a long time for bruises to heal."

"Have you been bruised?"

"Oh, yeah. Who hasn't?"

He made his shot, bouncing the cue ball off the side of the table and angling it to send his striped ball into the side pocket.

"Very impressive," she said. Like the rest of him.

He shrugged. "Simple geometry."

"And kinesthetic gifting," she added. "Of which I have none."

"Oh, I bet you do. You did pretty good on Juniper today. Riding takes some skill, and if you don't believe that, ask anyone who's done any kind of hard riding. You don't stay in a saddle with superglue."

She laughed. "I guess not. I liked it more than I thought I would. Although my butt's not very happy."

"You get used to it. As for pool, it's only a matter of practice." He pointed to a solid ball with his cue stick. "There's an easy shot."

"For you, maybe."

"And for you. Here, let me help you."

She positioned herself and her stick in front of the cue ball, and he leaned over her, his hand on hers, guiding her. His proximity turned her thermostat even higher still.

"Now," he said softly, "imagine a line running straight from your ball to that one. See it?"

All she could see was herself turning around and kissing him. "I think so," she lied.

"Nice and easy," he said. He moved her hand. The tip of the stick gave the ball a nudge, sending it clacking gently into the one they were aiming at and shoving it into the pocket. "There," he said, his breath tickling her ear. "You're a natural."

"And you are full of it."

She turned her head, and there was his face, right next to hers. His gaze dropped to her lips, and she suddenly felt like she'd just stuck her finger in an electrical outlet.

"Mom hung the mistletoe in the wrong place," he said, his voice a caress.

"Let's pretend it's right here," she said, turning in to him.

He smiled and touched her lips with his, and she got a fresh zap. He took her face in his hands and deepened the kiss, and she was a Yule log, going up in flames. Oh, yes. Merry Christmas.

"You are something. You know that?" he said softly.

"Funny, I was about to say the same thing to you," she said.

He slipped his arms around her and gave her another helping of holiday happiness.

Thank you, Santa, she thought as she threaded her fingers through his hair. This was shaping up to be the best Christmas she'd had in a long time. Maybe ever. For sure ever.

Hazel was exhausted by the time they pulled into the driveway at Julia's house. And relieved. They'd made it.

Her granddaughter's house was a blue two-story Victorian with lots of gingerbread. It definitely looked like Christmas with lights strung along the roofline and an inflatable Santa in the front yard, waving a greeting. She could see the tree through the living-room window, the lights turned on and sending out a soft glow.

Julia had been watching for her and had the door open and was hurrying down the front walk, throwing on her coat as she went before they were barely out of the car.

"I'm so glad you made it!" she cried and rushed up to Hazel to give her a hug. "Grandpa, are you okay?" she asked.

"I'm fine," he said, giving her one of his famous bear hugs.

Yes, he did look fine now, rested and happy and ready to celebrate. Thank God.

Hazel was ready to celebrate, too—not only the joys of the season but also because she still had her husband with her. And, hopefully, once he got the heart ablation, she'd have him for many more years. Modern medicine was a blessing.

So was family who cared about you, she thought later as she sat visiting with her granddaughter and holding her first great-grandchild.

"I'm so glad you and Grandpa made it here okay," Julia said. "I don't know what I'd have done if something happened to you. Well, I mean something did happen to you but...well, you know what I mean."

"I do. And I'm glad we could be here to help you celebrate Christmas in your new home," Hazel said, then sent up a silent prayer that whatever holiday guardian angels were on duty would safely bring the rest of the family to them.

Tom was back in and washing up, Russ was in the family room talking on his cell with one of his partners, and Vera was in the kitchen putting together a plate of appetizers when Rand returned home, bringing the needed part for Audrey's car. "If you give me your keys, I'll get her fixed for you and see how she starts. Then you'll be able to hit the road first thing in the morning," he said to her.

Audrey hurried to the guest room and got the keys from her purse. Rand and Shyla were in the front hallway talking like lovers with a secret. Shyla giggled. Hmm. Was her sister already forgetting about Milton?

"I really appreciate you doing this," Audrey said to Rand, handing over the keys. "What do I owe you?"

"Nothing. It's Christmas," he said, then took them and disappeared.

"Are you ready to ditch Milton?" Audrey asked her sister.

Shyla looked at her like she was nuts. "What? No. Why would you think that?"

"You and Rand are looking pretty tight."

"We're not. Milton's my lifetime man. Think you've found yours?"

Remembering that kiss? "Maybe." For sure, if it worked out.

Rand was back five minutes later. "Good as new," he said, handing the keys back to Audrey.

"Thanks so much," she said to him.

"Happy to help," he said.

And winked at Shyla.

Wait a minute. What was that about?

Shyla was grinning like those Cheshire-cat faces on Vera's slippers. Catching Audrey looking at her with narrowed eyes, she ditched the smile. "Good thing we met a car expert," she said.

"Yeah. Isn't it?" Audrey said and frowned at her.

Rand looked suddenly uncomfortable. "I need to go wash up," he said and took the stairs two at a time.

"I think I'll go see what Vera's up to," Shyla said and started for the kitchen.

Audrey grabbed her arm. "Oh, no, you don't. What's going on?"

Shyla opened her eyes wide, the picture of innocence. Which meant she was about to lie. "Nothing."

"Okay. What did you do?" Audrey demanded.

"Nothing that wasn't easily fixed."

"Which means you did something."

Shyla's chin shot up. "I bought us a little time is all."

"By sabotaging my car? Seriously?" Okay, that was it. Audrey was going to throttle her meddling little sister.

Shyla frowned at her. "Hey, will you keep it down?"

"We need to apologize to Vera and Tom."

"Did Mrs. Bennet apologize to Mr. Bingy?"

"Bingley," Audrey corrected her. "And don't tell me you're comparing yourself to a character in a book."

"I think Jane Austen would be flattered I used her idea," Shyla replied proudly. "And I'm giving you a hunk for Christmas."

"That is so inconsiderate to his family," Audrey scolded.

"Do you see anyone complaining?"

"That's beside the point. It was sneaky and...rude."

"And I apologized."

"To who?"

"To Rand. Well, sort of."

"And suckered him into helping you."

"He was happy to. Don't be such an ingrate. And when you're walking down the aisle this time next year, you can thank me."

Walking down the aisle. The romantic in her that had always dreamed of getting swept off her feet—not easy to do unless the man was tall—but she had given up on the idea. Russel Livingston was plenty tall enough, and he was doing exactly that.

"*And* I expect to be maid of honor 'cause you'll owe me," Shyla continued. "Of course, you'll probably be a complete bridezilla."

"I would never," Audrey said, and Shyla cocked an eyebrow. "Okay, maybe I would." If her sister's prediction really did come true.

"If you want, you can go ahead and thank me now," Shyla added with a smile.

"I bet Julia isn't thanking you."

Shyla shrugged. "She'll get over it." Then she switched tacks. "He is a great guy. And smart. Perfect for you."

Yes, maybe he was.

18

The snow had stopped falling by the time Max and Michelle made their way to Ludwig's Gasthaus. Colored lights lit every shop as well as every tree, including the huge one in the center of town where the town park was. Kids were sledding on the little hill above the town square, and shouts and laughter danced on the night air.

"I feel like I'm in a holiday movie," Michelle said to him.

He fingered the ring box in his coat pocket. *You ain't seen nothin' yet.*

The restaurant was packed, with waitresses in dirndls moving from table to table serving huge glass mugs of beer and plates of German specialties. The aroma of the various meats and sauces made Michelle's mouth water.

They ordered specialty cocktails to start: elderflower gin and tonic for her and a huckleberry mule for him. It felt like a date. Or an anniversary. Maybe it would become an anniversary of sorts, to celebrate Mother Nature jumping in to save their marriage.

"That sweater was a good investment," he said, admiring how well it accented her curves. "You know, you're still as beautiful as the day I met you."

Okay, was he laying on the compliments too thick? It was hard not to because she did look incredible, and it felt so good to be back to where they once were— lovers again. And friends.

"Listen to you," she scoffed. "You are so full of it."

"I am not," he insisted.

"Yes, you are. But I love it. And I love you."

"Again," he said, raising his glass to her.

"Always," she corrected him. "I never really stopped. It was just…buried."

"My fault. I threw on the first shovelful of dirt."

She shook her head, took a sip of her drink. "I did some shoveling myself. Bad things happen to everyone, but I think I found it easier to cope by blaming you. It was like that snowball you mentioned. Once I pushed it down the hill, every disappointment, every disagreement, made it bigger."

"I let you down. And I never gave you the time you needed to mourn. Not just with the baby, but with your mom, too."

Her mom had been the last parent she had left, and it had been agony for Michelle to lose her only two years after losing the baby. After the scare they'd had with his folks, he was beginning to get a glimmer of what she might have been suffering. She'd probably wanted to slap him every time he told her she needed to move on. As if she was a football player and he was her coach. *Shake it off. Get back in the game.* He'd thought he was helping, but in truth he'd wounded her even more than she'd already been. All the flare-ups, all the fights—if he'd been more patient to begin with... And even before that, if he hadn't been so selfish...

Well, no more. It was a new day.

They enjoyed sauerbraten and goulash. Then ordered coffee and German chocolate cake.

"This tops it off," Michelle said after her first bite.

That was his cue. "Actually, I have something else I hope is going to beat that."

A lot of things took guts. For him the two biggest challenges had been starting a business and asking Michelle to marry him. Those had been exciting and nerve-racking times in his life. Going down on one knee in front of a room full of strangers as a middle-aged man and making that second-chance thing official was right up there with them and he felt like a fool. But Michelle deserved the grand gesture, and he wanted to make this a night to remember, something they'd enjoy looking back on. So down he went.

Murmurs rippled out across the restaurant as he pulled the box from his coat pocket and opened it for his wife to see. He sure had everyone's attention, but in that moment all he cared about was having Michelle's. And he sure did. She was putting a hand to her mouth, a sure sign she was about to get all teary, and looking at him...the way she used to when they were young and crazy in love. Oh, man. His heart felt ready to burst right out of his chest. Yep, *king of the world.*

"Michelle Turnbull, would you do me the honor of spending the rest of your life with me?" It was a great feeling to be able to ask that question and know what the answer would be.

"Oh, Max," she said, teary-eyed, and nodded.

Her left hand still bore her engagement and wedding rings—thank God!—so he took her right hand and slipped the new ring on her ring finger. The room burst into applause, and she bent and kissed him. That beat chocolate cake, hands down.

They finished their meal, and their server brought the check and informed them that dessert was on the house. "Happy anniversary," she said.

Max didn't bother to correct her, but Michelle smiled at him and said, "Happy new beginning."

As they left, she threaded her arm through his and leaned in close. "That was so special. And undeserved," she added in a small voice. "I haven't exactly been the ideal wife."

"You were justified," he assured her.

"No, not really."

"Okay, then, *human*, and I was no saint."

"I was worse," she said sadly. "I just…hurt so badly. That's no excuse, though."

"Chelle, we each played a part in the problem. We shouldn't have let that snowball roll downhill and get bigger. And we won't in the future."

"We sure won't. That's one lesson I don't want to repeat."

Back at the room, the bed beckoned. "I can think of something worth repeating," he said.

She smiled at him, and it made his heart turn over. "Me, too," she said.

Max turned on the fireplace and then set about turning her on with slow kisses and tender touches. And words neither of them had said to each other in a long time. "I…" he kissed her shoulder "…love…" he moved to her neck "…you."

"Oh, Max, I love you, too," she said and kissed him with the same passion she'd wasted on being so angry with him.

Later that night she had a dream. She was back on that sinking ship with Max, somewhere in the Antarctic. This time they were standing side by side at the ship's rail, both in tattered finery. His tuxedo pants were shredded, and his jacket was gone and his shirt ripped and ragged. She wore a black cocktail dress that was in pieces, and she was missing her shoes. There was no one onboard but the two of them, looking at huge chunks of ice bobbing in choppy water. Marriage licenses with blurred ink floated in the water, along with a wedding veil here and there and a wilted bridal bouquet.

"We're doomed," she cried. "We're going down."

"No, we're not," Max said and pointed skyward. "Look. We can get out of here."

She looked up and saw a helicopter hovering. On its side were painted the words *Second Chance*. A rescue ladder began to lower, swinging in the air. "Grab it," called an amplified voice from above.

It was swinging wildly in the wind, and she kept reaching for it only to have it swing away.

Max reached out, and together they caught hold of the thing. "We're going to get out of this," he said. "Come on. Up you go."

He held the ladder for her and she clambered up it, the thing twirling and swinging all the way. "Max!" she cried.

"I'm right behind you," he called up to her, and she looked down and saw he was. "Keep going," he called. "We're almost there."

She woke up before they got safely on the helicopter, but that was okay. She knew they'd made it.

Max was on his side, breathing steadily, deep in sleep. She spooned up against him and put an arm around him. "We made it, Maxy," she whispered, then smiled and closed her eyes.

Audrey and Russ sat talking late into the night, long after everyone else had gone to their respective bedrooms. They covered everything from crazy childhood experiences to higher education, both in and out of the classroom. They shared classes they'd liked most in college—American literature for her, geology for him—favorite movies and what books they were reading. His reading was as all over the map, like hers. He enjoyed everything from Carl Sagan to Kurt Vonnegut.

"And I'm a big Lee Child fan," he said.

She cocked an eyebrow.

"What?" he said defensively. "Are you a reading snob?"

"Talk about fantasy," she scoffed. "Jack Reacher can outfight and outthink mortal men, plus he wears the same clothes for days but he always finds a woman willing to fall into bed with him when he rolls into town all scruffy and stinky."

"And how would you know about his hygiene habits?" countered Russ. One corner of his mouth hitched up.

Busted. "Okay, I'm not above reading an occasional bit of male fantasy," she said with a shrug, mirroring his smile. "Those books are fun. And I have to admit, they're a great lesson in self-defense. So don't mess with me, or I'll gouge out your eyeballs."

He laughed. "I guess we all enjoy some escape once in a while. So when you're not slumming, reading male fantasy, what else do you read?"

Audrey named the titles of several favorite nonfiction books, including one about the history of Uber as well as her Michio Kaku book.

"Yeah, I read that one by him," Russ said. "Fascinating stuff. But what do you read when you want to escape? Any favorite authors?"

She rattled off the names of her favorite romance authors, which ranged from Brenda Novak and Susan Wiggs to Jane Austen.

"I'm afraid I don't know any of them. Well, except for Jane Austen."

"They write romance novels." She realized she was feeling a little like someone confessing to a drug addiction. Probably because she'd just dissed his favorite escape reading.

"Ah," he said, nodding slowly.

"Don't judge. Even though I just did," she added.

"Wouldn't dream of it. We all need our fantasies, right?"

"I guess we do," she agreed. "You don't always get that happy ending in life. Maybe that's why I like to read a good romance. Everyone should have a happy ending somewhere, and if you can't get it in real life, you ought to at least be able to find it in a book."

"I think you deserve a happy ending in real life," he said.

"Yeah?"

Russ started playing with a lock of her hair, and she began to go all mushy inside. "Oh, yeah," he said, his voice a caress. "You never know where you might find a happy ending. Or with who."

"Whom," she corrected absently. Did she really just say that? "Shoot me now. I'm doing it again, being the world's biggest know-it-all."

He chuckled. "Hey, I already told you what I think about smart women, so feel free to be yourself."

Free to be herself. There were enough times growing up when she'd felt anything but. The teacher's pet, the show-off, the oddball who loved doing homework and discussing the symbolism of *Lord of the Flies* and *All Quiet on the Western Front* with the teacher.

"Being smart is a gift. You should use it. And if somebody can't deal with that, too bad," said Russ.

"My ex sure couldn't."

"He was obviously all wrong for you."

"Yes, he was," she agreed. So his rejection shouldn't have hurt. But it had.

"I, on the other hand, am a man who understands the importance of communicating properly." He moved aside the lock of hair and skated his fingers up her neck, murmuring, "How's this for a grammatically correct sentence? *You have the softest skin.*" He touched his lips to the sensitive spot behind her ear and sent tingles shooting in all directions.

Oooh. "I think that's very good."

"There you go. I'm improving already. Next time I have to write a business letter I'll have you proofread it."

That certainly sounded like they were more than simply two people whose paths were temporarily crossing. "Always happy to help," she said as those incredible lips made their way to her collarbone, spreading holiday tingles as they went.

"I think I'm going to need a lot of help," he said, planting another kiss. "What do you think?"

"I think you're doing just fine."

He smiled at her and then turned his attention to her lips, sliding a hand across her middle as he kissed her.

The kiss left her almost breathless, but she managed to say, "I can't believe this is happening."

"What?" he murmured, nuzzling her hair.

"This. You. All from having a flat tire."

"You've got to listen to all those pillows and wall hangings you see in the stores. *Believe.*"

She did. She was tingling all over when she finally made her way to the guest bedroom. Gram loved to quote Bible verses to her, and one of her faves said that everything worked together for good. Everything certainly seemed to be for Audrey. She was now very happy that they'd had that flat tire, that there'd been no rooms available in any of the town's motels. And she was especially happy she'd gotten dumped because what was developing with Russ Livingston was so superior to, so much more than what she'd had.

"Merry Christmas to you," Shyla greeted her when she slipped into the room.

"Yes, it is," she agreed.

"Do I detect whisker burn on your neck?"

"You detect nothing," Audrey said firmly.

"You lie. He really is a great guy, and a great match for you."

"Well, I'm not going to get my hopes up," Audrey said.

She sure did lie. Her hopes had climbed even higher, reaching the point where they could have joined the Hubble out there in space.

In spite of that, she still felt shy the next morning when it was time to leave. Vera served them a French toast casserole with blueberries along with high-octane

280 THE ROAD TO CHRISTMAS

coffee and promised to share the recipe, making sure she got Audrey's information in her phone.

"You girls really do have to stop by on your way back through, even if it is only for a quick visit," she said as the family walked them out. "We'll be disappointed if you don't."

"I'd like that," Audrey told her.

"Me, too," Shyla said.

Tom wished them a safe journey, then went to the barn to muck out stalls. Rand, too, said his goodbyes and went to help his dad, and Shyla moved off to warm up the car, Vera walking with her. That left just Audrey and Russ lingering on the front porch.

"You sure you want to see us back again?" she asked.

"What do you think?" he said, lowering his voice. "I'm not taking down that mistletoe anytime soon, that's for sure. I want to keep seeing you. Unless you're having second thoughts?"

"No way. I want to make sure you aren't."

"After last night? You gotta be kidding me." He slipped his arms around her waist. "Audrey, I fell for you the minute I saw you standing on the road. I'm still down for the count, and I don't want to get up."

"And he shouldn't," Shyla said after Audrey was in the car and they were on their way. "He's perfect for you, you know."

"Yes, I think he might be."

"Might?"

"Still being cautious, I guess. Everything that's happened almost seems too good to be true."

"The way he looks at you? Don't worry, it's true. Ho ho ho! Thank you, Santa and Shyla," Shyla said as they turned onto the highway. "And now, on to the next adventure."

Audrey's phone pinged with a text. "Julia's having a snort," she reported.

"Tell her to chill," said Shyla.

"On our way," Audrey dictated to her phone.

"Since when are you so nice?" Shyla teased. "Never mind, I already know. Love has mellowed you. Seriously, I'm happy for you, sissy. It's about time. I think you're going to have a happy new year."

"Not to mention a great Christmas," Audrey added.

Shyla began singing, changing the lyrics of "Deck the Halls."

"We are on the road to Christmas."

Audrey joined in, and they both sang, "Fa-la-la-la-la-la-la-la-la."

"Russ's family's gonna miss us," Shyla sang with a grin.

Audrey joined her for more *fa-la-la*s.

"Audrey finally found her mister. Fa-la-la-la-la-la-la-la-la! Merry Christmas to my sister," Shyla finished, and Audrey joined her for the last *fa-la-la*s.

What a crazy road they had been on, but what a wonderful ride.

Michelle woke up in Max's arms, and it felt so good.

"Happy?" he asked.

"Yes. And you?"

"You bet," he said. "Thanks for giving me a second chance. I promise not to waste it."

They'd both done their share of wasting. "And I promise not to hold any more grudges," she said.

He snugged her up against him. "Every time I think how close I came to losing you, it makes me sick."

"Same here," she said. "Nothing like seeing your life flash before your eyes to make you see what's important."

"That was too close for comfort, and I sure don't want a repeat of it, but I'm glad it happened. Like you said, it was a real eye-opener." He kissed the top of her head. "I love you, Chelle."

"I love you, too. I don't know how I could have lost sight of that."

"It happens, probably to thousands of people every day."

"I don't want to be one of them ever again," she said.

"We won't," he vowed and kissed her.

It was tempting to spend the morning in bed together, but Christmas was calling. "We'd better get going," she said.

"I guess you're right, but I sure hate to leave," said Max.

"We could come back," she suggested.

A slow smile grew on his face. "New Year's Eve in Leavenworth?"

"Sounds good to me. Let's make sure we include your parents," she said, which made his smile even bigger.

After reserving a room for the next few days after Christmas and through New Year's Eve, as well as a room for Hazel and Warren, they went to the dining room for breakfast.

"Oh, look, it's our romantic couple from the restaurant last night," said a woman who was seated with her husband at a nearby table. "That was so sweet," the woman said to Michelle. "You are such a lucky woman."

Michelle thought of their three lovely daughters, of the mother-in-law who was still in her life, loving her, of her father-in-law who was, thankfully, still with them.

And of the husband who had gone down on one knee to her for the second time in his life. He was a man who was simply human, flawed like any other, but a man who was also good, the man she'd given her heart to years ago and was giving it to yet again.

"Yes, I am," she said to the woman.

They would make their marriage work. Tough times either brought you together or pulled you apart. They'd almost let themselves get pulled apart. She was glad that, in the end, they'd decided to pull together. Considering her attitude before they'd started their trip, that was saying something.

Getting snowed in had looked like the worst thing that could happen to them. Instead, it had turned out to be the best.

The owner of the place stopped by their table to say hello. "I hope you're enjoying your stay."

Max and Michelle exchanged smiles. "It's been life-changing," Michelle told him.

19

"We made it!" Shyla crowed as the sisters pulled up in front of Julia's house. "I hope Julia's got the eggnog ready."

"Never mind the eggnog. I hope she and Gram have made the spritz cookies," Audrey said.

"Oh, yes. Can't have Christmas without those," Shyla agreed.

"We could be okay without those. Being without Gram or Grandpa would be another thing. I'm glad they made it here okay."

"Me, too," Shyla said. "I think I'm going to need an extra hug."

Audrey, too. She'd been relieved when Gram texted that they'd made it safely to Julia's, and the thought of how the holiday, not to mention the rest of their lives, would have looked if they'd lost their grandfather was a sobering one. Grandpa had given them piggyback rides when they were little and was their biggest fan when they were older. Even though they hadn't lived close by, he and Gram had never missed a school concert or play or a dance recital. He'd tried his best to turn Audrey into a basketball player, and when it became evident to both of them that, in spite of her height, she wasn't going to be a jock, he had focused on what he called her super smarts. She still remembered the birthday she'd gotten a T-shirt from Gram and him with the Superman emblem on it. The card had been signed from both of them, but she knew who'd been behind it.

What would life be like without him?

Or Gram, for that matter. Gram, the queen of the cookies and hugs, knitting coach and baking buddy.

Happily, they weren't going to find out this Christmas.

The moment Julia opened the door, the fragrance of Christmas greeted them: the mouth-watering aroma of baking ham, the aroma from Julia's favorite balsam-cedar-scented candle.

Julia was looking festive in jeans and a red sweater and Santa hat. "It's about time," she said, hugging them both.

Beyond her, in the living room, Audrey could see Grandpa relaxing on the couch, watching the sports channel on TV. Next to him sat Gram, holding baby Caroline, who was dolled up in a little red velvet dress.

"Hello, darlings," she called. "Come give us a kiss."

The luggage was left in the hallway as the sisters hurried to kiss their grandparents.

And to ooh and aah over the baby. Someday, Audrey promised her biological clock.

"How was the drive?" Gramps wanted to know.

"No problem," Audrey said, neglecting to mention their flat tire.

Once their luggage was stowed and their presents were under the tree, their sister hauled them into the kitchen, where her mother-in-law, a petite woman with long salt-and-pepper hair, was busy hovering over several pots on the stove.

"Gino's outside, deep-frying the turkey," Julia said. "You guys are gonna love it. Mama, my sisters are here," she announced.

"So nice to meet you," said Gino's mom, Lina.

"What can we do to help?" Audrey asked her.

"Oh, we have everything under control. Your grandma, she made cupcakes and the red velvet cake yesterday, and I've made buñuelos. My mother brought the recipe with her when she immigrated to this country from Mexico as a young woman. You must try some."

"Good idea," said Julia. "Can you spare me for a few moments, Mama?"

"Of course, I can, querida."

"Come on and check out the dining room," Julia said. "We've got hot cider out there and a plate of buñuelos and Gram's fruitcake cupcakes on the buffet. I made the spritz cookies And the red velvet cake."

"You? Wow, you are developing hidden talents," said Shyla.

"Well, Gram supervised," Julia admitted. "Closely."

The table had been extended and set for ten. It was covered with one of Gram's vintage tablecloths, an old white cotton number with candy canes and ribbons, and Julia had set it with white plates and red napkins and a mix of Christmas-themed goblets that she bragged she'd found at her local thrift store. She'd set a poinsettia in the middle of the table to serve as a centerpiece.

A trio of ceramic angels watched over the array of plates of goodies on the buffet. In addition to the buñuelos, the cookies, and their grandmother's cupcakes, there was a cut glass stand with the requisite red velvet cake. Next to the treats was a thermal pot, which contained the hot cider as well as a punch bowl, waiting to be filled later with eggnog punch, another family holiday requisite.

"It all looks great," Audrey told her.

"I had so much fun getting the house fixed up," Julia said as they all helped themselves to goodies. "Thanks, guys, for coming all this way. It really means a lot."

"You owe us big-time," Shyla teased as she put a cookie on her plate.

"From what I hear, one of you owes *me* big-time," Julia said, cocking an eyebrow at Audrey. "What happened in Winnemucca?"

"Stays in Winnemucca," Shyla cracked.

Audrey rolled her eyes. Her sister, the comic. "I did meet someone amazing."

"I want every juicy detail," Julia said, seating herself at one corner of the table.

"He's smart," Shyla said. "I think he might actually be as smart as Miss Brainiac here."

"That's good," Julia said encouragingly.

"He's really sweet," Audrey added.

"And hot. Don't forget that," put in Shyla.

"Is he real, or did you guys make him up?" scoffed Julia.

"Oh, no, he's real," Audrey said. Those kisses they'd shared had been very real.

"I hope it turns into something great," Julia told her.

"I think it will," Audrey said, her hope turning into something more solid.

"We're supposed to stop by there on our way back," Shyla told Julia. "The whole family loves us."

"They love you, too?" Julia teased.

"They love me more, but they'll have to settle for Audrey since I'm already taken."

That made Julia giggle and Audrey shake her head and do another eye roll.

Julia turned serious. "I'm happy for you, though, really. Here's to a great new year."

"For all of us," Shyla added. "I'm sure glad we've still got Gramps."

"Same here," said Julia. "Poor Gram, having to drive in the snow and get him to the emergency room. I was majorly relieved when they finally got here."

"Now all we need is Mom and Dad," said Audrey.

"Mom just texted me before you guys arrived. They'll be here in time for dinner. With all the stuff that's happened, I'll sure feel better once they're here, too."

Talk of their parents was followed by silence. "I hope they don't break up," Shyla said at last.

"Me, too," said Julia. "But they're not very happy together."

"They haven't been for a long time," said Audrey.

"So how long can you hold out when you're not happy together?" Julia wondered. She chewed on one side of her lip. "Do you guys ever worry that we might end up like them? I mean, I can't imagine ever falling out of love with Gino, but you never know."

"You are not going to fall out of love with Gino," Audrey said sternly. As if she knew. When she was a girl, she'd never thought her parents would fall out of love. "Anyway, after seeing Mom's text, I think things might be changing for the better with them."

"What did it say?" Julia asked.

"That they were having a great time in Leavenworth. They must have been 'cause it took forever for her to reply."

"I hope you're right," Julia said.

"If Santa could find someone for our bossy big sister, he can probably patch things up between Mom and Dad," Shyla cracked.

"We'll know when they get here," Audrey said.

Evening was throwing its black blanket over dusk when Max and Michelle pulled up in front of their daughter's house. The lights were on, both inside and out, and the inflatable Santa in the yard was waving his welcome.

"We made it," Michelle said.

"Yes, we did," Max said and reached for her hand.

All three daughters were at the door to greet them when they came up the walk, smiles on their faces. "Finally," Julia said.

"I'm sorry I didn't get here in time to make the red velvet cake," Michelle said as she hugged her.

"No worries," Julia replied. "I'm just glad you're here."

"Me, too," said Shyla.

"Both of you," added Audrey.

Yes, both of them. What kind of unhappy future Christmases would they have offered their daughters if they'd split? Of course, couples split for all kinds of reasons, and often it was inevitable, but Michelle was happy they'd found another road to take.

Max hauled in the presents and set them under the tree, and Michelle got a chance to hold her granddaughter, who gave her a drooly smile and showed off her first tooth.

Christmas dinner was a festive affair, with both families seated at the table, the two sets of parents getting a chance to become better acquainted. Warren and Hazel and Max and Michelle and the girls all shared their travel adventures, and everyone was horrified to hear of Max and Michelle's near collision with the semi. When the sisters joked about their misadventure in Winnemucca, Michelle found herself feeling immensely grateful to the family who had taken in Audrey and Shyla.

She enjoyed talking about Pinterest finds with Lina, and when Lina said, "You must come back in the summer so we can go garage-saling," Michelle knew she hadn't lost a daughter, she'd gained a buddy. And buddies shared.

Lina had insisted on helping host the travelers and wanted to get a breakfast casserole made to serve their houseguests the next morning, so she and her husband, Elijah, departed after dessert, leaving the immediate family to settle in the living room and open presents. The girls all loved the quilts Hazel had made. Michelle got teary-eyed, looking at a framed picture Audrey gave her of the three girls. They'd all gone in together and gotten her a mother's ring bearing their birthstones. Shyla and Julia gave Audrey a T-shirt with a stack of books, announcing to the world that she read books and she knew things.

"It's true. We admit it. You're the smart one," Julia said.

"And that's a good thing," added Shyla, who handed over another package. This one contained ankle socks. The words on the bottom of the first one read *Do Not Disturb* while the second sock explained *I'm Reading*. Perfect gifts.

As the opening of presents continued, there was much squealing and laughter and many *thank you*s. Warren and Max both got mugs—*World's Best Dad* and *World's Best Grandpa*. Even though those had become a tradition, both men teared up.

"Now I got enough for all my pals to use when they come by," Warren said.

After the presents were opened it was time to serve the red velvet cake. Hazel offered to cut and serve it as Julia went to put the baby to bed, and Shyla went to help her while the two men got busy cleaning up the usual postpresent mess.

Audrey was about to go help her sisters, but Michelle summoned her to come sit with her for a moment. Of all her daughters, Michelle knew Audrey worried the most.

"I'm sorry you missed so much of Christmas," Audrey said.

"The important thing is that we're all together now."

Audrey bit her lip, then asked, "Are we? Are you and Dad okay?"

"Never better," Michelle said.

"We were kind of worried about you guys."

"There's no need to be now."

"Really?"

"Really. You know, people do go through rough patches."

"No offense or anything, but I think you guys set a record for the longest one."

Michelle smiled. "We did. I tried not to let you girls see."

"We'd have been blind not to."

Michelle laid a hand on her daughter's. "You can stop worrying. We're all right."

And maybe they were proof that forgiveness and humility were tools powerful enough to knock down some of the tallest walls.

Audrey beamed. "That's the best Christmas present ever."

Yes, it was. Christmas was not about the presents

but about the presence of those you loved, of forgiveness and grace from on high and sharing that forgiveness and grace with each other.

Julia's cake was delicious, but feasting on it was not half as enjoyable for Michelle as watching her three girls settled together on the living-room couch with hot chocolate to talk before Audrey and Shyla made their way down the block to the in-laws' guest quarters. Where she knew they would be talking late into the night for, like so many sisters, even though they squabbled, they were still each other's best friend.

Hazel and Warren departed for one of the guest rooms, her claiming a need for beauty sleep and him insisting she didn't need it. Michelle saw Max smiling at her and decided to follow suit. Audrey would eventually fill her in on her budding romance, and meanwhile she had a romance of her own going and was ready to snuggle up to her husband.

She couldn't help feeling grateful that they'd all made it safely to their destination. They'd come from different places, human animals with a homing instinct, determined to be with each other.

Maybe that instinct played a part in her reuniting emotionally with her husband. Maybe, deep down, in spite of the chasm between them, they'd known they needed to cross it, known that theirs was a lifetime commitment. Or had some Christmas angel opened their eyes and given them a nudge? She'd probably never figure out how it was that two people had started out on a journey apart from each other and yet wound up together again.

Maybe she didn't need to.

On the Road Again

You guys on the road yet? Rand texted Shyla.

Almost, she texted back.

"Don't tell me, let me guess. It's your new best friend," said Milton as he loaded her suitcase in the car.

She snickered. "Still jealous?"

"Maybe."

She held up her left hand and wriggled her fingers, making the diamond in the ring on her finger twinkle. "This girl's heart is already taken."

"He better remember that," Milton said.

"When he sees you he'll know he can't compete," she said, making Milton smile. Gorgeous and fun as Rand was, Milton would always have her heart. "Anyway, marrying my brother-in-law's brother, that's just too, I don't know, weird."

"It's been done."

"Oh, stop," she said with a laugh.

In came the next text from Rand. *Tell Milton I just got tickets for us guys to the Automobile Museum.*

She turned her phone so Milton could see. "All right," he said, forgetting his jealous moment. Yep, a bromance in the making.

The next text came through as they got in the car. *"The climbing wall is waiting,"* she read aloud.

Milton didn't look quite so excited about that. He wasn't fond of heights. But if everyone else was climbing (except Audrey, who said they were all crazy), he was determined to keep up.

They got their lattes and then gunned it for Reno and prewedding fun. The girls would have their bachelorette party there, doing spa treatments and a girls' night out, and the boys would be doing manly things like checking out the car museum and gambling at Eldorado...with only the play money their women had allowed them. No shirts would be lost. "And I sure don't want to have to pawn my ring," Shyla had joked.

Hitting the open road brought back memories of the road trip she had taken only a year earlier. It had turned out to be a great adventure.

Now it was Road Trip, Take Two. She and Rand had planned the prewedding activities, and she'd booked rooms for everyone. And had texted the confirmation to Audrey, along with, Got rooms for sure this time, unable to resist getting in a little jab. Hehe. Then she'd added, Good thing we didn't have 1 last time. She received a smiley-face emoji in return.

Yep, boo-boos and mishaps sometimes turned into golden opportunities. She was so happy for her sister that theirs had.

She checked in with her mom. You guys at the Livingstons' yet?

Almost, Mom texted back. Where are you?

Halfway to Reno.

Tell Milton to drive carefully, texted Mom, always the worrywart. Love you.

Shyla sent a string of hearts back to her. "This is going to be so fun," she said to Milton.

"Anything with you always is," he said.

All that happy anticipation, of course, inspired a song. The melody for "Deck the Halls" was once more employed as she began to sing. "We are on the way to Reno. Fa-la-la-la-la-la-la-la-la-la."

Milton supplied the next line. "I am going to win at Keno," followed by the *fa-la-la*s.

"Even if you lose we're winners," she sang and they *fa-la-la*ed together.

"What rhymes with *winner*?" Milton asked.

"Hope that we can afford dinner," she sang, and they laughed.

Yep, road trips were the best.

"Come on, Chelle, we've got to get going," Max called from the doorway of their motel room on the day of Audrey's wedding. "We're supposed to be there by three for pictures."

"I'm coming," Michelle called back from the bathroom as she put in her second earring. She smiled. Her husband was almost more excited than her about their daughter's wedding and had hardly slept the night before once they were in their room after the rehearsal dinner.

Vera had offered them a room at their house, but she and Tom already had out-of-town relatives coming and certainly didn't have room for Michelle's clan, which included Warren and Hazel as well as her brother and his family. So they'd taken over a motel in Winnemucca. Ironically, the very one that had lost Audrey's reservation.

"We don't want to be late," Max said.

It wasn't that far from the motel to the Livingstons'

ranch, where the wedding was being held. "They can't start without the father of the bride," she said to him as she came out.

"Still, we don't want to keep everyone waiting," he said. He looked at her and smiled. "But you were worth waiting for. You look great, babe."

Warren appeared at the door. "We're ready to go. How about you two?"

"We're ready," Michelle said and grabbed her coat.

"You look like a bride yourself, kiddo," Warren said to her.

Sometimes she felt like a bride. The last year had been one of healing: dinners for two in quiet corners of small restaurants, shared laughter and a road trip or two to visit the Livingstons, with whom they'd hit it off instantly. And, of course, the big move to Northern California, where they'd found a large property not far from Michelle's brother with two houses on it. A three-bedroom for Max and Michelle, and a smaller two-bedroom guest house that was perfect for Hazel and Warren. Michelle was no longer managing a Hallmark store, but she was happily living a Hallmark life, working at the local food bank three days a week and hitting garage sales with Hazel.

The four of them had driven together to Winnemucca, arriving early to help with wedding preparation. Soon the whole family would be enjoying an intimate wedding at the Livingstons', followed by Christmas together at their ranch later in the month.

"I better call Jay and see if they're ready," Michelle said.

"No need. Your brother's already got everyone loaded in his car and is wanting to know what's taking his sister so long," Max said.

"I'm ready," she said, picking up her purse.

And then they all were off, hustling down the highway to watch Audrey get her happy ending.

Vera greeted both Michelle and Hazel with hugs once they arrived. "Isn't this exciting?"

"It is," Michelle agreed.

She'd enjoyed watching the relationship develop between her daughter and her future son-in-law and had been delighted when Audrey, who was always so competent and in control, asked her to help plan the wedding.

Helping Vera decorate had also been special, and the ranch was decked out for the holidays with wreaths and red ribbons everywhere. The ceremony would take place in the large family room, and at the end of each row of seats they'd hung small Christmas wreaths decked out with red and white roses. The fireplace was festooned with greenery and red ribbons, and a small table in front of it held a red unity candle for the bride and groom to light during the ceremony.

Michelle and Max had hired a caterer recommended by Vera, and all manner of enticing aromas drifted out to them from the kitchen. Added to that was the scent of peppermint and Douglas fir coming from votive candles nestled in greens on the pool table, which had been covered with plywood and a long linen tablecloth, turning it into a perfect buffet table.

Russ beamed as he shook hands with his future father-in-law.

"No cold feet?" teased Max.

"No way," Russ said. "She's the best."

"She is," Max agreed.

"So is the man she's marrying," Michelle said and hugged him.

"Come on upstairs, ladies," Vera said to Michelle

and Hazel. "Tom, can you help our guests settle in? And make sure our father of the bride gets something to drink to calm his nerves," she called over her shoulder as she led the way to the large master bedroom where the bride was getting ready.

Michelle had seen the designs for the wedding gown, which Shyla had made for her sister, but that wasn't the same as seeing her daughter in it on her wedding day. Audrey looked radiant, tall and willowy in a gown of red velvet, off the shoulder with white faux-fur trim.

Both Shyla and Julia were with her, clad in shorter versions of the same dress. Julia was standing ready with the pearl earrings Hazel had once given Michelle— the same ones Hazel had worn on her wedding day—to signify something old and Shyla was settling the crystal tiara on her sister's head. The diamond in the engagement ring on Shyla's hand winked a hello. Her wedding would take place right before Valentine's Day. The photographer Michelle had hired stood nearby, recording the moment.

Audrey saw her and Hazel and smiled. "Hi, Mom. Hi, Gram."

Michelle hurried over to kiss her daughter, followed by Hazel. "You look beautiful," she told Audrey.

Audrey's smile grew. "I feel beautiful."

"You all look so lovely," added Hazel before taking her turn to kiss Audrey. "The gowns are a work of art."

"That's because they were made by an artist," said Audrey, giving kudos to Shyla.

Shyla grinned. "Yes, they were."

"Everything looks perfect," Hazel said.

And so it should be on a woman's wedding day. There would be enough imperfect moments ahead. But maybe Max and Michelle were now proof that you could get through them.

"I'd better get back downstairs and start welcoming our guests," Vera said and slipped away.

"How about a picture of all of you?" the photographer suggested.

"Oh, yes," said Audrey, holding out her arms.

Michelle and Hazel each took one side, and Audrey slipped her arms around them. Shyla and Julia moved in for a group hug.

"On three," said the photographer.

"Say *sex*," quipped Julia, making her sisters giggle.

And on three all women chorused, "Sex."

"And more grandbabies," added Hazel.

"Don't wait forever," Julia said to Audrey. "Caroline wants cousins."

"Okay, now, how about one with the bridesmaids?" suggested the photographer.

Seeing her three girls standing arm in arm, beaming, brought the tears to Michelle's eyes. Her daughters, all grown. How had they gotten here so fast?

Two local musicians, a cellist and a pianist who had brought along her keyboard, played Christmas carols as the guests arrived—a small gathering of family with only a few old friends added to the mix—and were duly seated. Russ's brother Rand then escorted the mothers and grandmothers to their seats.

The pianist and cellist began Pachelbel's "Canon in D," and Hazel reached for Michelle's hand as first Julia came down the short aisle between the seats, followed by Shyla. Then came the bride, walking next to her father, and Michelle felt a fresh arrival of happy tears. Was there anything more wondrous than a wedding?

Her heart clutched when Max let go of his daughter

and she turned to the new most important man in her life, who was looking at her with adoration. And so the cycle continued. Love passed on, from generation to generation.

Max joined Michelle, and together they sat, hand in hand, watching another daughter step into her new life with the love of her life.

After the ceremony the party began in earnest: the rows of chairs were cleared away, and the food was served. It was a buffet feast, offering chocolate-covered strawberries dressed up to look like mini bridal gowns and tuxedos for starters, and moving on to an enormous charcuterie board loaded with cheeses, olives, grapes, salami slices and crackers. After that came salads, sliders, grilled chicken, salmon and an elaborate pasta dish.

A pyramid of champagne glasses waited on a separate table for toasts later, and on the dessert table, surrounded by a bevy of pink rose-frosted cupcakes sat the cake, a gorgeous tiered red-velvet creation.

"Looks like something out of a magazine," Max said and grinned like the proud papa he was.

The groom's brother gave a toast that was sweet and succinct. "What can I say? My brother found his perfect woman. No need to wish them a great life together. We all know they're going to have one. Here's to you, Russ and Audrey. And, Audrey, welcome to the family."

Welcome to the family. Michelle teared up. Yet again. They were a family, an expanding one, all together and happy. She sent up a silent prayer of thanks that she and Max had found their way back to what they'd once had.

Warren's toast said it all. "Congratulations on finding your other half. There's nothing better than living your life with the person you were meant to be with."

The couple cut their cake, and there was no cake

smearing on faces. "Audrey can do it to me if she wants," Russ had told Michelle, looking lovingly at Audrey as he said it, "but no way am I messing her makeup."

"I'm not shoving it in your face, either," she said. "I think it's rude." Yep, that was Audrey, always a woman of strong opinions.

And a kind heart, Michelle thought as the two exchanged a quick kiss. And her daughter had found the right man for her, one who really appreciated and respected her. Michelle had seen enough of both Russ and his family to know that respect and kindness were a way of life for them.

After the meal, a DJ was put to work. Warren, feeling chipper and invincible since his successful heart-ablation procedure, demonstrated his dance moves with Hazel until he put his back out, and Max tried to impress the younger generation by doing the Sprinkler and the Robot, which merely made them laugh.

Before the bride and groom left for Tahoe, fireworks were set off, writing the event on the night sky. Max put an arm around Michelle, snugging her up close against him, and she wrapped an arm around his waist.

Later that night, in their hotel room, she lay in her husband's arms, basking in the day's memories. And the next morning, after a breakfast with the Livingstons, she and Max held hands as they followed Hazel and Warren and her brother Jay and his family to their respective SUVs.

Two weeks at home, and then she and Max and Hazel and Warren would be back again for Christmas. Another road trip.

She could hardly wait. Road trips were a wonderful thing.

Road Trip Tips
from Michelle and
Her Family

From Audrey:
  Pack plenty of snacks and water. If you're traveling with someone like my sister, you'll need them.
  Make sure your spare tire is in good condition and that you know how to change a tire. (A Russ Livingston type may not show up to help you.)
  Confirm any hotel or motel reservations before you leave, both online and with the front desk.

From Shyla:
  Allow plenty of time for stopping to see the sights. And for shopping. I highly recommend pawnshops for great bargains.
  Have a plan B. (Like I did. LOL.)
  Have a blanket in the car in case you get stranded.
  Make sure you're traveling with someone you like so you don't kill each other.

From Hazel:
  Always double-check to be sure that you've packed all necessary medications. Make sure your other half has also!

From Michelle:

Leave a day early if possible so you're prepared for delays.

Always remember: sometimes the trip itself is as important as the destination.

And Now, for Dessert

BUÑUELOS

Ingredients:

2 cups flour
1 ½ tsp baking powder
½ tsp salt
½ tsp orange extract
¾ cup warm water
4 tbsp oil for dough, plus more for frying
Cinnamon sugar for topping
(⅓ cup granulated sugar and ¾ tbsp cinnamon)

Directions:

Mix dry ingredients, then add oil, orange extract and water and mix until it forms a ball. Transfer the dough to a clean, floured surface, and knead several times until it's smooth. Return to the bowl, cover with a towel and let it rest.

While the dough is resting, mix up your cinnamon sugar in a small bowl and fill a large frying pan with one to two inches of oil. Set out a large plate with two

paper towels and have extras on hand to drain your buñuelos. Once the dough has rested, divide it into eight
balls. Roll them out into eight-inch disks and set on a
clean towel to wait their turn in the pan. (Don't stack
them or they'll stick together.) When the oil is hot, fry
the flour disks, one at a time until golden brown. With
tongs, press the disk under the oil to avoid it getting
bubbles. Once each disk is cooked, drain on the paper
towel and sprinkle with powdered sugar. Once cooled,
stack on a large plate. Don't cover them or they'll lose
their crispness.

FRUITCAKE CUPCAKES

Ingredients for cake:

2 ¼ cups cake flour
2 ½ tsp baking powder
1 tsp salt
1 ½ cups sugar
½ cup butter, room temperature
2 whole eggs
1 cup milk
1 tsp rum
½ tsp cinnamon
½ tsp nutmeg
1 cup chopped candied fruit

Ingredients for frosting:

1 ¾ cup powdered sugar
¼ cup butter, room temperature
1 ½ tsp rum
2 tbsp cream or whole milk

Directions:

Sift the dry ingredients together in a large mixing bowl.
Combine the sugar, butter, rum and two-thirds of the

milk, mixing at low speed until combined. Then add eggs and remaining milk. Beat two minutes longer, then add candied fruit and blend in by hand. Pour into muffin tins lined with paper baking cups. Bake at 350 degrees farenheit for 20 minutes or until a toothpick inserted comes out clean. Cool on a rack.

Directions for frosting:

Cream the butter and the powdered sugar. Add rum and cream or milk, and mix until smooth. Top cooled cupcakes with frosting and, if you like, decorate with sprinkles. You can also add green food coloring to your frosting if desired.

* * * * *

Acknowledgments

I do believe that friends are one of life's greatest gifts. The ones in my life certainly are, and I want to thank a couple of them here. First, a big thank-you to my lifelong bestie, Jan Kragen, who is always great to brainstorm with. I owe you chocolate for life, not only for helping me create Trevor March, the chocolate king, one of my favorite characters in *One Charmed Christmas*, but for always being a sounding board for ideas. Thank you, also, to my good friend and librarian extraordinaire, Ruth Ross Saucier, who was kind enough to be a first reader for this book (and many in the past, as well) and who caught a lot of mistakes. With my lack of attention to detail, Ruth would not want me in charge of planning any road trip!

I also want to thank my editor, April Osborn, who is so insightful and brilliant. And patient! And my fabulous agent, my sister from another mister, Paige Wheeler. Both these women have been such gifts.

As has the whole MIRA/Harlequin team. Thank you for continuing to work so hard on sculpting my stories, on giving me beautiful cover art and then getting the books on the shelves, making it possible that I can keep writing. This holiday season, as I count my blessings, I will be counting all of you.

HARLEQUIN
PLUS

Try the best multimedia subscription service for romance readers like you!

Read, Watch and Play.

Experience the easiest way to get the romance content you crave.

Start your **FREE TRIAL** at
www.harlequinplus.com/freetrial.

Get 3 FREE REWARDS!

We'll send you 2 FREE Books plus a FREE Mystery Gift.